A Mountain Worth

Moving

I

A Mountain Worth Moving

A Christian Fiction Novel

Amanda Mason

III

Dedication

To my husband, Jeff, who always believed even when I did not and encouraged me to pursue my dreams.

To my Lord and Savior, Jesus Christ, here I am Lord, send me.

Table of Contents

Chapter 1 Broken

If I have the gift of prophecy and can fathom all mysteries and all knowledge, and if I have a faith that can move mountains, but do not have love, I am nothing. 1 Corinthians 13:2

John Mitchell didn't particularly dislike guns. He owned several himself. Nor did he have anything against hunting; in fact, he'd gone hunting himself. So his reaction to the report of a rifle being fired just over the ridge from his morning trail ride had more to do with emotions triggered by the sound and less to do with the hunting. He ducked his head as his horse galloped under a low-hanging tree limb. His heart was beating as fast as his horses' hooves were pounding up the steep hillside to reach the top of the ridge.

He reined his horse in sharply as they crested the steep incline and scanned the field ahead of him. He squinted against the morning sun. The meadow was wide, one of the many fields hidden away in the mountains of his family's ranch, the Triple M. He was reaching for the binoculars he kept in his saddle bag, when something gleaming in the southern corner of the meadow caught his eye. He slowly brought the binoculars into focus.

A young boy, maybe ten, and a man John assumed was his father were walking across the mountain meadow. Both grinned from ear to ear, the older man patting the boy on the back. John watched them through the binoculars. Everyone in the county knew John did not allow strangers on his property. The father and son must not be locals, which was all the more reason John should run them off his property. He lowered the binoculars for a few seconds, then raised them and looked at the duo again. Something about the proud look in the father's eyes and the grin on the boy's face caused John to second-guess his no-hunting policy, if only just this once. Memories of his own hunting adventures with his father floated through his mind. He remembered how happy he had been sharing those times with his father, much like the young boy across the meadow. John didn't want to ruin the happy moment. If life had taught John anything, it was that happiness was fleeting at best, and life had a cruel way of making sure happy moments were few and far between. Who was John to destroy this moment for the pair?

He reined his horse back down the steep ridge, mentally planning the day ahead while still thinking of the hunting pair back on the ridge. He made a mental list of the hunting guides in town he was familiar with. He would need to contact them to reiterate there was no hunting on Mitchell land; at least there hadn't been for the last four years. Years of managing his family's two-thousand-acre ranch had taught him to compartmentalize his thoughts. While the report of the rifle had triggered memories he would rather keep buried, he had developed coping skills. He could be overcome with anger and emotion and yet still manage to make decisions about the day-to-day operations of his ranch. It was a skill he had developed out of necessity. Everyone counted on him, and he couldn't let them down. Not again.

He glanced at his watch. The detour had disturbed his morning ritual, which had been the same for nearly the last four years. A morning ride on his favorite horse into the mountains to plead with God. And each morning he returned to his daily tasks disappointed. Not that anyone would have noticed his disappointment. He was reticent and businesslike no matter how bad his heart ached. No one knew the burden he carried, nor would he share it. Brokenness brought destruction and destruction had wreaked enough havoc on the Mitchells' lives. He wouldn't allow destruction any more of a foothold.

The ranch was buzzing with activity as he descended from the mountains and headed into the valley where the heart of his family's ranch had been for more than one hundred years. He felt a warmth come over him when the ranch house came into view. At one time, his life had been far removed from this place, but he could now admit that he loved this land, that house, and all that it stood for. He had given his life to this ranch and his family. Thirty years old and running one of largest working cattle ranches in northern Montana was not an easy task, nor one he had taken lightly. While others his age were marrying and starting families he only had time for one thing: making sure his family's ranch was prosperous. That was the least he could do for them.

He reined his horse in at the largest of the four barns. He knew his foreman, Buck, would be inside getting ready for the work day. He briefly discussed the things they needed to do today while unsaddling his horse. He went into the ranch office located in the back of the barn, checked his email, and rifled through the mail piled up on the corner of his desk. None of these tasks were pertinent, but it allowed him to avoid the main house. When the office phone rang, John had a sinking suspicion that he knew who it was before glancing at the caller ID.

"He didn't come home last night." His sister-in-law's frantic voice echoed throughout the office before John could mutter a greeting.

John sat down heavily and sighed. He ground his back molars and silently wondered why Amber had ever married his wild younger brother, Jamie. He had hoped their whirlwind marriage would have been just the thing Jamie needed to get his life together. But after months of fights and phone calls like this one, John was beginning to lose hope.

"John!?" The frantic voice in the phone brought him back to reality.

"Calm down, tell me what happened." John hated that he had gotten used to these calls. His pulse didn't even pump harder at the frightened tone in his sister-in-law Amber's voice. While he had spent the last four years taking care of the family ranch, his younger brother had spent most of that time trying to see how much alcohol his body could withstand. When their small hometown of Pine Bluff, Montana, couldn't keep him entertained, he would take off for days, sometimes weeks, at a time. Several months ago he had returned from an extended bender with a young lady John had never met before and claimed proudly that they were married. John hadn't asked a lot of questions. Instead, he had settled them into a small cabin on the ranch that had been built for use by ranch hands, hoping marriage would be just the thing to settle Jamie down. So far, marriage had done nothing to hinder Jamie's lifestyle. John quietly listened as Amber related a very familiar story, a fight which led to Jamie storming out the door and not returning.

3

The weight of responsibility hung like iron chains around John's neck. "I'll find him, don't worry, Amber." John knew where to start the search, and after a few more comforting words to Amber and instructing her not to share this news with his mother, he hung up the phone.

John had driven the road to town so many times in his life, he probably could do it blindfolded. At the least he could drive it distracted, which he was this morning. He released a heavy sigh; the weight of his family's situation pressed on him. He felt tired and glanced at the clock. Eight a.m. No physical reason to be exhausted, but he had been on a mentally draining roller coaster for too long and this morning it was taking its toll. Normally he never thought about what-ifs. He lived the life he had been dealt, knowing that it was his responsibility, his lot in life, to deal with his family, to protect them, and to make sure they had everything they needed.

His mind drifted to what it would be like, what his life, his family, would be like if things had gone differently that early fall morning four years ago? What if he hadn't picked up that gun? What if he hadn't pulled the trigger? What if he could live his own life, not constantly trying to put the pieces of his shattered family back together? What if he had stayed in Billings instead of coming home that weekend? John forced his thoughts back to the task at hand of finding his brother. "What-if" thinking did nothing but make an already tough situation tougher.

He slowed the truck and pulled into a gravel parking lot, eyeing Jamie's truck parked next to the building. His long legs ate the distance across the empty lot in moments. John paused at the door to let his eyes adjust as he stepped inside the County Line Tavern. The establishment, named because it sat on the border of Glacier and Flathead counties, was located right on the edge of a remote piece of highway and was a favorite watering hole for his brother and other serious drinkers. John and the owner, Tim, had attended high school together. Tim tipped his chin up in recognition as John approached the bar.

"Morning, John. What'll it be?" the bartender asked as he wiped down glasses and placed them under the bar. John briefly wondered if anyone would be drinking this early in the morning, but quickly realized his brother probably would and decided to keep his mouth shut on the topic.

"Just looking for Jamie." He scanned the empty bar room to locate him.

"He's in the back booth sleeping it off. Got a little out of control last night." The barkeep placed a coffee cup in front of John and filled with steaming hot liquid.

"Thanks." John nodded as he sipped the coffee.

"For the coffee or for letting Jamie sleep it off?" Tim raised his eyebrows and grinned. John appreciated the effort to lighten the mood.

"Both."

"Well, don't thank me yet. Like I said, Jamie was a little out of control last night. Got into a fight with some of the Flying K's crew."

John's head snapped to attention at the name of the ranch that was their neighbor on the southern border. Ranchers helped each other out; it was a way of life, he didn't need to have a dependable neighbor angry with him over a drunken bar fight. "What happened?"

"Oh, you know Jamie, somebody looked at him wrong, or said the wrong thing or just was purely breathing and it aggravated him."

"Yeah, I know Jamie." John sighed heavily, briefly thinking of the Jamie he used to know. The Jamie before the accident. John's heart ached, missing the relationship he had once had with his younger brother.

"He got some pretty good licks in before my guys broke it up; being neighbors and all, you might want to check on them and make sure no hard feelings. I know Red always got along well with the Flying K, would hate to see that change because of Jamie's hot head."

John flinched at the nickname many in the community had used for his father. Gut-wrenching pain seared through him but his face remained unchanged. It had been four years, but grief had a funny way of sneaking up on you when you least expected it. Not for the first time, John wished his father were here to give him advice.

"I'll go over there this afternoon." John folded his arms on the bar and leaned forward, releasing a pent-up breath he didn't realize he had been holding.

"Hey, how's Ben?" Tim asked after a few minutes.

John studied his coffee intently before answering. "'Bout the same." He avoided Tim's face as he sipped his coffee.

"Your momma?"

"It takes its toll, you know, it's a full-time job taking care of Ben." John stared into his coffee cup, hoping the conversation was over.

"You know everybody in town really admires what you've done and all. I mean after Ben's accident and then Red dying…the way you came back and took over the ranch, made sure Ben's taken care of. Well, it could have went a lot different. What you did…well, people noticed and think it's a good thing."

"I didn't do anything. We've had some tough times, but so has everybody. Nothing special about us." John stood up and threw a couple of dollars on the bar for the coffee. The conversation was not an unfamiliar one. He had had similar discussions with people who knew about his family and their heartaches, but he would never be comfortable talking about his family's problems. Not when he had caused them. It was time to get Jamie and leave.

Tim waved his hands at the money. "Nope, put that up. I ain't charging you for a measly cup of coffee."

A loud snort from the back booth drew their attention. "NO, because the great and wonderful John Mitchell should never have to pay like regular folks!" John recognized his younger brother's loud, slurred voice. He exchanged looks with the bartender and walked to the back booth. His younger brother lay on his back on the bench, his booted feet resting on the floor, eyes closed and a grin on his face.

"Come on, Jamie, Amber is worried about you. Let's go home." He nudged Jamie's boot with his own.

"Good! She should worry after the way she talked to me." Jamie never moved or opened his eyes.

"Come on, let's go. Got a lot to do today." He nudged his boot harder this time.

"What's on the agenda today for the great and mighty John Mitchell?" Jamie suddenly sat up. "Saving damsels in distress? Or maybe brokering Middle East peace? Solving world hunger? Wait, I know, single-handedly refreezing the polar ice caps!"

"Let's go," John repeated with an edge in his voice. He reached for his brother's arm to lift him out of the booth.

"I can do it." Jamie jerked his arm away. He rose and stumbled toward the bar. "Give me my keys, Tim."

"You can't drive, you still smell like beer," John said, making eye contact with Tim, and his look alone let the bartender know that he would not be giving the keys to Jamie.

"Naw, you better ride on home with your brother." The bartender nodded in acknowledgment of John's silent command.

Jamie stared at the bartender for few moments, his back stiff, arms akimbo. To his credit the bartender never blinked but returned Jamie's glare. And while Jamie had about an inch in height on his oldest brother, he knew the twenty-five pounds that John had on him was muscle developed from years of hard labor on the ranch. Even still half drunk, he knew he was no match for his brother. He grumbled under his breath and headed for the door.

"See ya later, John." Tim continued to wipe down glasses. John nodded and quietly thanked the barkeep. But Jamie just couldn't resist having the last word and yelled over his shoulder as he shoved open the front door, "You won't see Saint John in a bar. He's too good for a bar. He's too good to drink like the rest of us."

Chapter 2 Burdens

Fools give full vent to their rage, but the wise bring calm in the end. Proverbs 29:11

P   *lease, Lord, keep me from punching him,* John silently prayed. Anger boiled in him and he was afraid if he hit his brother once, he wouldn't be able to stop. He wasn't sure why he continued to pray; obviously the God of the universe had stopped listening to him years ago. He was confident his prayers fell on deaf ears, but something in him kept sending them up.

Lord, heal Ben.

Lord, please take this from Ben.

Lord, please heal Daddy.

Lord, please forgive me.

All his prayers seemed to be met with silence, but he couldn't quit. That part of the Bible that told believers to keep asking and they would receive was indelibly stamped on his brain. He had to keep asking, not for himself, but for his family.

"Drop me at the barn." Jamie's voice broke into his thoughts.

John let a few moments pass before answering him. "I'm not dropping you at the barn. You've got a wife at home worried about you. She deserves an explanation. I'm takin' you home." And because he let anger get the best of him, he added, "You do remember you have a wife, right?"

"Oh, I remember." Jamie chuckled bitterly as he gazed out the passenger's window. "I was there. I remember."

John's usual cool, detached demeanor slipped away as he snapped, "You remember it? You weren't too drunk?"

"Sober as a judge, big brother." Jamie continued to gaze out the window. "I'm just not too sure about her sobriety on that particular day."

After a few moments of silence John began an all too familiar speech. "You got a wife now and responsibilities—"

"Don't preach to me about responsibilities!" Jamie interrupted angrily.

John gripped the steering wheel to keep from reaching out with a right hook and clocking his brother.

"Don't you ever get tired of being so self-righteous?" Jamie swung his gaze from the window to stare at his older brother's profile. He could see the tick in John's jaw; saw the tension in his brother's arm as it gripped the steering wheel. He was in this far, might as well go all the way. "Do you know how hard it is to be your little brother? Everybody in this town worships you! *That John*," he mimicked, "*sure is a standup guy the way he stepped up after Ben's accident, how he took over after Red died. Gave up that good job down in Billings to single-handedly save that ranch from near bankruptcy.* Everywhere I go it's all I hear."

He paused for just a moment before he continued, "I'm sick of this town. They can't do anything but sing your praises and I'm sick of you looking down on the rest of us."

"Just because I'm trying to help you save your marriage, doesn't mean I'm looking down on you."

"Don't even start with me about marriage. What would you know about being married? You don't even have time for a girlfriend, you're too busy saving the day." Jamie rubbed his hand over his face. "Lord, no wonder I drink, if you ain't raggin' on me, she is."

John slammed on the brakes as he pulled the truck roughly into the front yard of Jamie's house. He turned to face his brother. "Is that why you drink? Because you hate me so much?"

Jamie looked deeply into his brother's eyes. He could see the hurt there, the concern. It had been that way for so long, sometimes it was hard to remember what John used to be like. But if he tried hard enough he could remember the way his older brother had been before Ben's accident, before everything changed. John had been funny and carefree; indeed, they had all been different before that morning. Jamie felt guilty about his tirade against his brother. He knew John meant well and he also knew that the reasons he drank had nothing to do with John, not really. It had everything to do with trying to forget that chilly fall morning four years ago when everything in their lives had been flipped upside down. He slowly got out of the truck and as he did Amber stepped out the front door, pausing at the top of the porch steps waiting on him. He caught her gaze and saw the hurt and worry on her face. His gut twisted knowing he had put it there. He slowly shut the truck door and spoke to his brother through the open window, never taking his eyes off his wife.

"No, big brother, I don't drink because I hate you. I drink because I hate me."

Chapter 3 Memories

Who remembered us in our low estate, For His lovingkindness is everlasting." Psalm 136:23

John worked straight through lunch. They were well into the spring thaw and summer was the busiest time of year for the ranch. Fences had to be mended, cattle moved, hay baled and put up in the barn; the list was never ending and John welcomed it. Working at a pace that would exhaust his body, slipping into a deep sleep at night that allowed him to escape his thoughts, was a reprieve for him. The sun had long ago set when he sat down at his desk in the barn to go through the mail. His phone buzzed under a pile of *Cattleman* magazines.

You going to eat with us? The text from his mom flashed on his screen.

He considered telling her that he wasn't hungry but knowing better than to tell her no, he finished a few chores in the barn, shut down his computer, and headed for the main house.

His stomach betrayed him with a loud growl as he opened the back door and was assaulted with the aroma of dinner. He knocked the dirt off his boots and headed for the kitchen. Ben was seated in his wheelchair at the table. John wondered for the millionth time if he could ever look at him and not feel his heart break. His once strong, athletic younger brother now sentenced to life trapped in a body that didn't work. Ben was strapped into his custom-made wheelchair at the waist and his chest. The chair was motorized and had been reclined to a small degree to keep Ben from tipping forward. His head bobbed between the headrest and a mounted rest to the right of his head. One arm rested on a pillow, curled inward. His "good hand," as his mother called it, waved in the air as if he was greeting John.

"Well, look who decided to join us, Ben." His momma turned from the stove and set a platter of roast, carrots, and potatoes on the table. She motioned for John to take a seat and settled herself in beside Ben's wheelchair. In front of Ben sat a bowl of runny mashed potatoes, which had become a staple at every meal for the last few years. Ben received most of his meals through a tube in his stomach, but his mother insisted that he enjoyed the mashed potatoes and made them at every meal. Every meal John watched as his mother spooned the runny goop into his brother's mouth, as most of it ran back out and dribbled down his shirt.

"Let's say the blessing." His mother nodded at him and John complied.

"Lord, bless this food to the nourishment of our bodies and our bodies to your kingdom. Amen." It was a prayer he had heard his father pray his whole life.

"And please heal Ben," his mother added as she did every night. She immediately began telling John about a trip to town that morning. John nodded and grunted enough to keep her from realizing he was lost in his own thoughts. She rattled on as she alternated between feeding herself and trying to spoon mashed potatoes into Ben's mouth. John kept his head down and ate. Watching his once athletic, funny, capable brother being spoon fed never got easier.

It had been a horrible accident. A chilly fall morning four years ago, John had come home from his job in Billings for the weekend to hunt with his brothers. He had made a good life for himself in the city working as a veterinarian pharmaceutical representative. And much to his and his family's surprise he enjoyed living in the city. He liked the busyness and availability that city life had to offer. He dated casually and his life was carefree and fun.

That fateful morning, all three Mitchell boys had headed out into the mountains to the south of the main house to hunt. John would never forget that morning. He could recall their conversation word for word. The two younger brothers had been pumping him for details about a girl he had been seeing in the city. He had brushed them off and Ben had told them in detail about scoring two touchdowns in the football game the week before. They had split up, John directing his two younger brothers to go to a familiar hunting blind quite a distance from the spot he had chosen. Of course he had picked the prime location for himself. They had argued briefly about that fact and finally had agreed to let John have the best location. Ben and Jamie had ridden off still grumbling. John had scouted this spot all summer, knowing a buck had taken up residence in the mountain meadow. He sat down in the edge of the meadow and waited. It didn't take long until the buck had inched its way into the open field. A trophy winner for sure—John could already see it hanging in the main house above the fireplace. He quietly brought the rifle up to his shoulder, found the deer in his sights, and gently squeezed the trigger. The deer staggered and fell. John made his way over to the deer and fist pumped when he saw that its rack was bigger than he had originally estimated. He had begun to prepare to get the deer back to the house when Jamie had come galloping through the meadow screaming his name. He would never as long as he lived be able to forget the look of terror in Jamie's eyes. At twenty-four years of age, he had looked so young and scared in that moment. He had practically jumped off his galloping horse into John's arms. Jamie's words ran together, his eyes wide with fear. Ben had fallen off his horse; that was what John was able to decipher from Jamie. He remembered telling him to calm down, that everything would be okay. He remembered thinking a broken arm or leg shouldn't cause Jamie to panic so much.

Jamie led him across a familiar meadow that ended with a steep ravine; at the bottom of the ravine was the creek that wound through the middle of the Triple M ranch that they called home. When John reined his horse and peered over the side of the ravine at Ben's limp body, he realized why Jamie had panicked. Ben's body lay crumpled about thirty feet down the ravine. John abandoned his horse and began running down the steep incline toward his brother. He remembered falling, the loose dirt and rock that made up the steep banks of the ravine giving way under his weight. He stumbled and rolled to his brother's body, frantically repeating Ben's name. Immediately realizing Ben was seriously injured, he shouted for Jamie to get back to the main house and call for an ambulance. He had stayed with Ben, begging and praying for him to wake up, for God to take care of him. John didn't know how long it was until Jamie came back with their parents. An ambulance couldn't reach Ben; instead, they waited in agony for a medical transport to fly him out of the ravine and take him to the hospital in Billings. John could still see his mother collapsing to the floor when the doctor had announced his initial diagnosis, which had proved correct. Traumatic brain injury.

A sickening feeling had settled in the pit of John's stomach that day and had never subsided. Carrying around that feeling was a small price to pay, he thought, since he had been the cause of Ben's injury. Ben had been an excellent horseman and his horse that morning had been a familiar one. The doctors, nurses, therapist, even his family said it was a terrible accident. John knew different. In his excitement to kill the record buck, he had not given his brothers enough time to get to their hunting spots. The sound of his rifle had spooked Ben's horse that morning, causing the fall. He had caused his brother's injury just as sure as if he had pushed him off that horse himself.

"Did you hear me, John?"

He glanced up at his mother. At fifty-two, she was still beautiful. The stress of taking care of Ben had taken its toll, but for the most part, his mother's faith had kept her optimistic and hopeful. Ben had been in a coma for months following the injury. They had wondered if he would ever wake up. But wake up he finally did and that was when they discovered the extent of the injury. Ben had no control of lower extremities, movement of his left hand was minimal, and he had lost all ability to communicate. For months they took turns keeping a vigil at his bedside. He fought infections and blood clots, and all manner of other illnesses that came with being bedridden.

About a year after the accident, the insurance company had called and told them Ben would be sent home, they would no longer pay for his care in the hospital rehabilitation center. Around the time Ben came home, John began to notice how old his father looked. Maybe the accident had taken its toll on him, or maybe he was just growing older, but he didn't have the same spring in his step. Three months after Ben came home, his father was diagnosed with stage four liver cancer. They buried him in late summer up on the hill overlooking the ranch. John had quit his job and sold his house in Billings to move home. He had taken over the ranch and thrown himself into making it successful. That was the least he could do for his family.

"John! Did you hear me?" his mother repeated.

"What? Sorry, I was thinking about the hay mowers that needed fixing."

"I said…" She turned to spoon more watery mashed potatoes into Ben's mouth just to have most of it run back out of his mouth… "we've got an appointment over in Brisbane on Friday with a new therapist. Can you go with us?"

"New therapist? For what?" John leaned back in his chair, dropping his fork on his plate.

"For Ben." She motioned toward his brother with another spoonful of white mush. "I told you Mary had recommended her, remember? She took Daniel and he has made some real improvements."

John nodded absently. He recognized the name Mary from the support group for family members of traumatic brain injury patients that his mother had recently joined. The group, with its testimonies of improvement for brain injury patients, had renewed a fire in Pattie that more could be done for Ben.

"So can you go?" she repeated and stared at him pointedly.

"We'll see." John had no intention of going. He didn't want his mother to go either for that matter. He didn't need some therapist with a god complex getting his mom's hopes up that Ben could be helped. No matter how many times she had her hopes dashed about Ben's healing, she continued to search for help for her son. Her faith in God was unwavering. When one therapy or doctor didn't work out, she had faith that eventually her son would be healed, even if they had to wait until Heaven to see that healing. John always worried that the next let-down would be the one that finally broke her. She had been through so much, he owed it to her to try to protect her from any more pain. As she continued to discuss what she had learned about the therapist through her support group, John could tell that talking her out of this trip would be almost impossible.

"So what do you think?" The hope shined in his mother's eyes.

"Sounds great, Momma." What could one more lie hurt?

Chapter 4 Guilt

*"I, I am the one who blots out your transgression
for my own sake, and I'll remember your sins no
more. Isaiah 43:25*

John rose before the rest of the house and made his way to the barn. He took his normal morning ride, his heartache weighing heavy this morning. He crested the hill leading down into the valley that held his home and the barns and he immediately noticed Jamie's truck parked in front of the barn. John reined his favorite horse, Sysco, to a stop and shifted in the saddle. He wasn't sure he had it in him this morning to go another round with his little brother. After dinner last night he had helped his mother clean up and then put Ben to bed. His brother had become agitated when John had lifted him out of his chair and placed him in the hospital bed that had been placed in the den. John remembered his mother saying the bed was temporary when they had moved it in four years ago. Every night was the same—his mother would ready Ben for bed and someone would help lift him into the hospital bed. John had made a point to avoid the den at that time of night. But with Jamie now married, he had no choice but to help his mother. And as had been their routine for the past few months, when John began to pick him up, Ben would become agitated. His mother could not figure it out and had chastised Ben on several occasions. She believed that Ben understood when she spoke to him. John wasn't sure if Ben understood their words or not, but he was sure that Ben understood John was to blame for his situation. He couldn't blame his brother for not wanting him around. So every night it was the same. Ben would swing his arm wildly and moan when John began to pick him up. Once John had him in the bed, he would bend and whisper in his ear, "I'm so sorry." John could only assume, since the behavior was the same every night, his apology was not accepted.

When he reached the barn, he dismounted and led Sysco into the barn. Not seeing Jamie, he began to unsaddle his horse.

"Amber says I owe you an apology."

John glanced up to see his brother behind him. He turned his attention back to the care of his horse. "You don't owe me anything, Jamie."

Jamie stood up from the hay bale he had been sitting on and made his way over to John. He picked up a brush and began to help curry Sysco. The silence stretched between them. Regret ate at John as he realized the sullen stranger that stood across from him had once been his best friend in the world.

"She says I should thank you for bringing me home."

"Is that what you're doing...thanking me?" John rested his arms on the horse's back. "Don't worry about it. I gave you ride home when you needed it. I would like to think you'd do the same for me if I needed it."

Jamie hung the brush back on its peg and took a step back. "Well now, you and I both know that Saint John would never get himself in a situation to need a ride home."

John studied his brother and the regret he had felt only moments before turned to anger.

"I guess you've done what she told you to do. You can go now; I have work to do." John gritted his teeth and turned on his heel before he gave his brother the fight he was obviously looking for. He reached the ranch office and began absently rifling through a stack of papers. Out of the corner of his eye, he caught a glimpse of Jamie's frame in the door. He pretended to ignore him.

"Sorry," Jamie mumbled.

John stilled and studied his brother, who refused to meet his gaze. He wanted to rail at him, wanted to lecture him about his irresponsible behavior, wanted to tell Jamie what a living hell it was being "Saint John," but in the end he knew that it would all fall on deaf ears so he shrugged and replied, "Forget it."

17

John assumed that the conversation was over. He sat down and turned on his computer to check his email. After a few minutes he glanced over his shoulder to see Jamie still leaning on the door frame.

"Jamie, I said forget about it. You can go and do whatever it is that you do all day long." He watched and waited for anger to take over his brother, but instead Jamie just stood there, a distant look in his eyes. "Jamie," John called out, "are you okay?"

"No…no, I'm not okay." Jamie looked up at the ceiling and John could tell he was struggling. A small ray of hope sprang inside John's heart. Had Jamie finally realized he had a drinking problem and would agree to get help? John knew Jamie's drinking habits weighed heavily on all the family, but no one more than their mother. John waited for him to continue.

Jamie tapped his tightly held fist against the door frame, struggling to find the words. John leaned back in his chair, waiting for Jamie to speak. After several long moments, Jamie cleared his throat and spoke. "I…we…well, Amber and I…we need money."

John tepeed his fingers and tapped them against his mouth. "I see." He cleared his throat and added, "How much?"

"They are going to cut our electricity off on Friday…and I'm behind on some other bills…"

"How much?" John repeated.

"Three hundred should cover it." Jamie's voice was low and John could tell that his pride had taken a beating asking for the money.

John leaned his arms on the desk and studied Jamie. He glanced around the room and counted to ten, trying to avoid another fight with his brother. He took a deep breath and offered the same solution he had offered to Jamie a hundred times before. "Jamie, why don't you work here at the ranch. I can put you on the payroll. You don't even have to answer to me; you can work for Buck."

Jamie immediately began shaking his head. "You know ranch work isn't for me. It's not in my blood the way it is yours." He paused for a moment and then added, "I don't love this place the way you do."

"You think I love this place?" John could hear the anger rising in his voice even as he tried to keep it in check. He stood suddenly, the desk chair scooting across the office from the force. "I don't love this place, and maybe ranch work isn't for me either. I had a job...I had a life...remember?" He didn't give Jamie an opportunity to respond. "I didn't have a choice. Ben was sick. Dad was sick and somebody had to take care of things. God knows we couldn't depend on you." John immediately regretted the last words and he could tell they had hit a deep spot in Jamie.

"Are you going to give me the money or not?" Jamie crossed his arms over his chest.

John studied him intently and waited for several moments before he responded, "No, I'm not going to give you the money, but I will give you a chance to earn it."

"I've already told you that I won't do ranch work." Jamie pushed off the door face, arms akimbo, eyeing him suspiciously.

"Ben has an appointment over in Brisbane on Friday. Momma needs someone to drive them over."

"Brisbane?" Jamie asked incredulously. "That is a three-hour drive!"

"Then you're getting paid fifty dollars an hour for a six-hour round trip, that's a great deal. Take it or leave it." John crossed his arms and stood his ground.

"John..." Jamie started.

"Jamie, this is the only deal I'm offering."

Jamie hesitated for a moment and then he softened his stance. "I hate doctors' offices, John."

"We all do." And then John couldn't stop himself from adding, "You also hate ranch work so this is all I have for you because I am not just going to give you this money."

"Okay," Jamie growled and clenched his teeth.

. "Okay, I'll do it. Can I get the money now?"

"I'll go by the electric company and pay your bill. You get me the rest of the bills that need paying and I'll take care of them," John replied as he retrieved his

19

chair and settled in to do work. He could tell Jamie was angry over not receiving the actual cash in hand.

"Whatever," Jamie mumbled and then he challenged, "It's been four years, John, you know as well as I do that Ben is as good as he is going to get, this trip is a complete waste of time."

John paused for a moment. He knew his brother was right, but he also knew his mother lived on hope. "You're getting what you want, and all you have to do is drive for a few hours. Besides, she's given up way too much for us to ask her to give up her hope too. Take her. Do whatever she says. We owe her that."

Chapter 5 Changes

*And immediately the Spirit drove Him into the
wilderness. Mark 1:12*

Jill Morgan stood in the corner of the gym at the Brisbane Therapy Clinic and surveyed the patients who had arrived. It was an open gym with multiple therapists milling about taking information from clients and their loved ones. Jill sipped her coffee and thought about her bittersweet job. The clinic at Brisbane was one of many that St. Patrick's Brain Injury Institute, a large hospital located in Billings, Montana, conducted several times a year. The Brain Injury Institute was one of the most cutting edge in the country, relying on current technology and therapy techniques to try to rehabilitate brain injury patients.

Unfortunately, they had limited space in their program due to their intense therapy techniques. The process to be admitted to the clinic was rigorous. Patients had to be referred by their doctors after meeting certain criteria and then be evaluated by St. Patrick's team of top-notch therapists. Jill was the lead therapist at the clinic today, which meant she would see every patient today. She would be the determining factor on whether or not they made it into the program. With limited number of spaces available at St. Patrick's, Dr. Olivia Bryan, the neurosurgeon over the program, was adamant that they chose their patients wisely, and that they always had a backup therapy option for those not selected for the intense in-house program.

As Jill glanced through the appointment list she knew it would be a busy day. She began making her way through the gym, weaving through patients' wheelchairs. Immediately Jill could tell which patients would benefit most from the in-house program. She picked up the evaluation forms and began to complete the appropriate paperwork. Each patient would spend time in the open gym with their team of therapists, then one by one, all twenty patients with appointments today would have one-on-one evaluations with Jill.

As she headed for the examination room she would use for the day, Jill couldn't help but notice the patient entering the gym for the first time. He appeared to only have limited control of his left hand. Little head control and the slack in his jaw indicated to Jill that his trauma was severe. Her gaze shifted to his family members. The older attractive lady who followed him, Jill assumed his mother, looked around hopefully. She was followed by a handsome young man; Jill immediately dismissed the thought of how handsome he was. There was no way she could be attracted to a patient's family member; that would cause too many complications. A cowboy for sure in his button-down shirt, neatly tucked in Levi's, scuffed cowboy boots. He turned his hat over nervously in his hands. As she watched his hands work his beaten ball cap, she saw a slender hand reach over and take his…girlfriend or wife for sure. No way would someone look at a sister like that.

She focused back on the patient and watched as a therapist from the team began taking their information. She noticed the cowboy now had his arm around the slender young lady. A slight stab of jealousy clouded her mind for a moment. She watched the cowboy slightly squeeze the younger woman to his side and she wondered how she could miss something so much that she had never had. She had begun to accept that God had given her this life's work with these patients and maybe it wasn't in His plan for her to have a family of her own. She quickly prayed that God would give her discernment today and that she would address these patients wisely. She watched the cowboy grab the handles of the wheelchair and move the patient over to an assessment area.

Help him.

She stopped quickly as the thought flitted through her heart and mind. She brushed it off; of course she wanted to help him. She wanted to help them all. She glanced at her watch. She should begin her evaluations soon. She headed to the private room, but she couldn't stop thinking about the patient with the cowboy pushing his chair. She would spend the day evaluating each of the twenty patients; reading their charts, mulling over their backgrounds, the reports of their initial accident. There were eight beds open for the intensive in-house therapy located at St. Patrick's. Jill would pick twelve of the most promising patients, and then she and Dr. Bryan would sit down and select the final eight. Jill's heart always broke when they had to make those final decisions. She wanted to help them all, but budget limits and bureaucracy kept that from happening. All patients not selected for the program would then become patients in St. Patrick's outpatient rehabilitation center.

She turned her computer on, organized her paperwork, and found the name of her first patient. She looked over his paperwork before calling him back.

Ben Mitchell.

Twenty-two years old.

Horse riding accident.

Jill read the accident and diagnosis summaries. Her initial thoughts were that his injury was too traumatic for the program to help him. Her second thought was to wonder why his doctor had recommended him to the program. There was no way that he would have met the criteria for an appointment.

"Help him."

There it was, the thought presented itself again. She brushed it off and went to the door to call him back. She saw the fatigue in his mother's eyes, but there was something else there. Hope, maybe? Jill's heart contracted as she was almost certain that she would have to dash that hope. They exchanged pleasantries as they maneuvered the wheelchair into the exam room. She soon learned that Pattie, Ben's mother, was his full-time caregiver. Ben's brother Jamie and his wife, Amber, had helped Pattie bring Ben to the clinic today. She sat and listened to Pattie describe Ben's limited daily activities. Jill flipped through the evaluation paperwork that had been completed by the therapist team again. Finally she began her own physical exam of Ben Mitchell.

As she approached the wheelchair, Ben seemed to be looking at her eye to eye. She reached for his left hand, his "good hand" as his mother had referred to it. He gripped her hand firmly, refusing to release it. She caught his eye again.

"*Help him.*"

She pushed the thought aside and continued her examination. His trauma was severe. The program included physical, occupational, and speech therapy to try to help patients regain some quality of life. For those who were nonverbal, but had cognitive ability, the therapist taught them basic sign language to aid in communication with caregivers. Honestly, she didn't see that Ben would be able to benefit from any of the therapy.

At the end of her assessment, she turned to face the family. She hated the hopeful way they watched her.

"As you may or may not know, St. Patrick's facility has a limited number of beds. It's our job to ensure that we pick the patients that will benefit the most from our program." She pulled her stool closer to them and looked them in the eye. "I just don't feel that Ben is a good fit for our program. The therapy techniques we use to try and improve quality of life are just not suited to Ben's injury, but I can recommend him—"

"I…I thought there was a selection process?" Tears welled and threatened to spill down Pattie Mitchell's cheeks as she interrupted. "My friend's son, he went through your program and she said it took several trips before they found out if he was admitted or not."

"Yes, Ms. Mitchell." Jill hated this part of her job. "When we feel like a candidate has potential, we sometimes ask them to return for additional evaluations."

Jill paused, hoping her words would resonate with Ms. Mitchell.

"But not my Ben?" Pattie bit her bottom lip.

Jill pushed her stool closer so that she could touch the other woman's hand. "Ms. Mitchell, I am so sorry." She hated the way hope quickly left the mother's face and then just as quickly as her face crumbled, she wiped the tears and composed herself. "I have a list of several therapy programs that might benefit Ben. I'll help you contact them, if you would like?"

"Well, we had to try, right?" Pattie began to nervously gather up Ben's things. "Thank you for your time…"

"Momma." Jamie stepped up and grasped his mother's shaking hand. Pattie looked into his eyes and collapsed in his arms sobbing. Jamie looked over his mother's head in, to Jill's eyes pleading for her to help.

"Mrs. Mitchell, I'm so sorry. I know how hard this must be for you," she repeated, patting the woman's back.

"Lady, you don't have a clue how hard this is," Jamie snapped.

Taken aback, Jill gathered her paperwork. "I am truly sorry. I hate turning patients away from our program, but we do have some options for Ben. I'd be happy to get a list together for you."

"Um, well, yes, that would be fine," Pattie stammered as more tears filled her eyes. She gathered Ben's things and began pushing his chair toward the door.

Jamie stood between her and his mother, his hands on his hips. "Lady, we've been through therapy program after therapy program, I'm not sure what good going to one more will do, but we'll take your list if that's all you can do for us." He glanced over his shoulder as Amber helped his mother guide Ben's chair from the room.

"There will be a list of available therapy programs for you at the registration table."

Jamie pulled on the brim of his hat and turned to follow his family. Jill fell back on her stool and wiped the tears that refused not to fall.

For days after the clinic at Brisbane, Jill could not get Ben Mitchell and his family off her mind. She awoke in the morning and her first thought was of Ben.

"*Lord, what do you want me to do?*" she began praying. And she was always answered with, *"Help him."*

"How can I help him? He's beyond help!" she cried out angrily after a week of waking up to thoughts of Ben Mitchell.

"*Nothing is impossible with God.*" The verse from Luke flashed through her mind and stayed on repeat in her heart and mind for the rest of the day. She went through the rest of her clinic evaluations that day and by the time she reached her apartment in Billings she was convinced that not only did Ben Mitchell need to be at St. Patrick's for the therapy program but that God was specifically calling her to help him. She fell into her bed knowing she would need a good night's sleep if she were to convince Olivia Bryan to admit Ben to her therapy program, but then again, she thought, nothing is impossible with God.

The next day she sat across a conference room table from Dr. Bryan going through each patient's file that had been selected for treatment. Dr. Bryan was a no-nonsense, passionate individual. She attacked her work with such a fervor that some days just being around her wore Jill out physically and mentally. But she was a renowned neurosurgeon who had helped countless patients regain some aspect of their previous life and Jill felt blessed to be a part of that.

For hours they had been reviewing the files and mapping out individual care plans for each patient that would be invited to join them. Jill knew Ben Mitchell's file was at the bottom of her tote bag.

"Okay." Dr. Bryan shuffled some papers. "I think we've got a good solid eight patients here that we can help. What do you think?"

Jill rifled through her bag and grabbed Ben's folder. She said a quick prayer and slid it across the table. "I have one more that I would like for you to consider."

"We already have our eight." Dr. Bryan looked over the top of her glasses as she took the file from Jill.

"I know that, but just consider this one." Jill prayed Dr. Bryan would approve Ben's admission to the program without an argument.

"Jill…" Dr. Bryan closed Ben's file after reviewing it quickly. She pulled her glasses off. "This patient does not meet the basic ability requirements for our program."

"I know that," Jill responded, leveling her gaze.

"So let me get this straight." Dr. Bryan leaned back in her chair. "You are presenting me with a patient that you know is not a good fit for our program, and yet you are asking me to appropriate funds to admit this patient to our program?

Do you want me to place him ahead of one of the eight we all agreed we could help?"

"Yes and no. Yes, I want you to admit him, and not ahead of any of the others." Jill returned the doctor's intense gaze. "I'm asking for a ninth spot during this rotation."

"Jill…" Dr. Bryan flipped the file folder closed and stared at her. "What's going on here? Have you lost your mind? We've worked together for several years and we've always been very clear on what our mission is here."

"Dr….I…" Jill sputtered, "I, uh, I just think we can help him."

"There is no indication in his medical history that our program could help him." Dr. Bryan tapped Ben's medical file.

"I know that." Jill nodded.

"So you agree that medically there is no indication that he can be helped by our program, and yet you want to admit him?" Dr. Bryan leaned toward Jill and looked at her as if she had suddenly sprouted two heads.

"Yes."

"Okay, Jill, what is going on with you?" Dr. Bryan scoffed. "Listen, I remember him from the clinic. I also remember that the family got to you. You have to understand that they are coming from a place of deep hurt and emotion. Don't take it personally." And then the doctor added, "I shouldn't have to have this conversation with you. This is something I should have to explain to a new therapist. Now for the last time, what is going in here?"

Dr. Olivia Bryan was nothing if not direct and to the point. She had no time for anyone who was not likeminded.

Jill gazed at the doctor and tried to choose her words carefully. After some thought she decided to just go for the truth. "I think God is telling me to help him."

The room was silent as the doctor absorbed what Jill had said. Jill thought she would jump out of her skin waiting for the woman to respond. Seconds ticked off into minutes and still the doctor studied Jill in silence. Finally, after what seemed like an eternity, the doctor opened her mouth, just to shut it, press her fingertips to her lips, and wait several more agonizing minutes before answering.

"Jill." Dr. Bryan finally crossed her arms, rested them on the table, and leaned toward her. "You really feel that way? That God is telling you to help this man?"

"Yes, I do. I know it may sound crazy, but ever since I saw him and his family at the clinic. I cannot quit thinking about him and I keep getting this crazy thought over and over that we need to help him and I know it's crazy and I've studied his medical records over and over." Jill felt as though a dam had broken inside her and if she didn't explain this to someone she would surely burst.

Dr. Bryan held up her hand and interrupted, "Jill, you are not the only Christian in this program. You don't do this work…see the miracles that happen in these patients…and not believe that there is something or someone greater at work here. But you are asking me to go to the board of directors of a major medical institution and tell them we are over budget because God is telling us to help this man."

"I know what I'm asking is…unusual to say the least, but…I feel like I have to try." Jill clasped her hands in her lap. Pattie Mitchell's broken face came to mind as she used her words.

Dr. Bryan tapped her fingers on the stack of approved files in front of her and gazed at Jill. After contemplating Jill for several moments, she picked up Ben's file and added it to the stack.

"Okay, you win." Dr. Bryan gathered the files and stood up.

Jill collapsed into the back of her chair, shocked that it had been that easy to convince Dr. Bryan to admit Ben. "Thank you, Doctor."

"Don't thank me yet." Dr. Bryan pointed her finger at her. "He's yours. You are responsible for all of his care. I'm taking a big enough risk adding a patient to the program without board approval, I can't add that burden to the nursing staff as well. I'll extend an invitation to his family for two weeks. Two weeks only. If he hasn't shown improvement in that time, he will have to leave. I can't give you more than that."

Jill sat back in her chair, feeling confident. God had created the world and all its inhabitants in six days, no telling what he could with fourteen. She almost shared that thought with Dr. Bryan, but the serious look on the doctor's face changed her mind.

Chapter 6 Suspicion

By this all people will know that you are my disciples, if you have love for one another." John 13:35

The back door slammed as John ran through the kitchen to answer the phone. "Hello," he answered breathlessly. Anger bubbled in him. He had no time to waste talking on the phone to anybody. He normally ignored the disturbance and would have let it just keep ringing, but John had been waiting for Mitch Winters, owner of the Flying K spread, to call about the dust-up between his hands and Jamie. The last thing John needed was for Mitch to be angry and refuse to share some of his summer hands with John. John needed all the help he could get to prepare for the winter.

Jill had been expecting Ben's mother to answer the phone. She remembered from meeting the family at the clinic that his mother was his main caregiver. She had dialed the first number on Ben's application and had been directed to a voicemail box that had not been set up. She tapped in the second number listed and waited to hear a woman's voice. When the deep gravelly voice answered, she was taken aback and double-checked her cell phone screen to make sure she had dialed the number correctly.

"Hello?!" John barked into the phone and brought Jill back to the present.

"Um, I'm calling for Pattie Mitchell, please." Jill cleared her throat.

29

"She isn't here right now." John leaned a hip against the kitchen counter, trying to place the honey-smooth voice coming through the phone. This voice sure didn't sound like any of his mother's friends who usually called for her. "This is her son John. Can I take a message?" His mother was forever trying to set him up with different young women. If this was the beginning of another set-up, John wanted to nip it in the bud quickly. Tall, dark, handsome, the iconic picture of what a cowboy should look like, John had no trouble attracting women. The problem was he didn't have time for them.

"My name is Jill Morgan. I'm with St. Patrick's Brain Injury Institute. I was calling to let your family know that Ben has been selected to participate in our advanced therapy program." It took so long for the voice on the other end to respond that Jill thought she had been disconnected.

"My brother, Ben Mitchell?" John finally responded.

"Yes, I was hoping—"

"Lady, you have got to have your wires crossed," John interrupted. "My brother has a severe brain injury, he's in a wheelchair, he can't walk or talk, and it's been four years since his accident. There is no way he's a candidate for your program."

"I'm aware of Ben's condition. Mr. Mitchell, I've studied your brother's medical file extensively. I assure you that my wires aren't crossed and that your brother indeed has been selected as a candidate for our program." Jill hoped her voice didn't sound as shaky to him as it did to her.

Silence answered Jill for several moments. "Hello?" She looked at her phone screen to make sure she was still connected.

"My mother was told at the clinic that Ben wasn't a candidate. What's going on here?" John asked. His mother had been distraught when she had gotten home from the appointment and he was not about to let that happen again.

"We have reevaluated Ben's records and believe that he could benefit from our program." Jill wished fervently that she had just waited and called the first number back.

"Changed your mind just like that, huh? And just what's the purpose of this program?" John questioned.

"To try and improve the patient's way of life, to regain some of the fine motor skills, to regain some independence." Jill cringed as she heard herself. She sounded like a brochure.

"And you think Ben is a good candidate for this program?" She could hear the skepticism in his voice.

"Yes, we feel like we can help Ben." It wasn't a lie; she felt like God needed her to help Ben in some way.

"Are you a doctor, Ms....uh, I'm sorry, what's your name was again?" The contempt in his voice could not be concealed.

"My name is Jill...Jill Morgan, and no, I'm not a doctor. I'm a therapist; I'll be working with Ben." She hated how shaky she sounded, caught off guard with his questions.

"A therapist, huh? And you think you can help Ben?" He wasn't even trying to keep the bitter tone out of his voice.

"Yes, Mr. Mitchell. If we didn't believe that, we would not be extending this offer to your family," she replied, using the most professional voice she could muster.

"We? Just exactly who is 'we'?" John crossed his arms, using his shoulder to hold the phone to his ear.

"Well, myself and the doctor in charge of the program, along with a team of therapists that evaluated Ben at the clinic in Brisbane," she replied, wondering if Ben had been as angry and bitter before the accident as his two brothers appeared to be.

Again silence for several moments, and then, "Ms. Morgan, we have seen countless doctors, specialists, and therapists over the past four years and all of them said the same things. Ben is about as good as he is going to get. You think you know more than all these doctors?"

Jill thought for a moment before she responded, "I don't pretend to know more than the doctors your family has seen. I...my team...thinks we can help Ben. If we can improve his quality of life, even just a little bit, isn't it worth trying? Why would you not want to at least try that?"

"This is our life, do you get that?" he replied angrily. "You see them a few hours and they are just a file, a number to you. We live this every hour of every day. My mother has been through hell the last four years. She was devastated when she got home from your clinic and now just like that, you call up and say you changed your mind. Are you going to call again next week and say you changed it again? The last thing I need is for you to give her false hope that Ben can improve or be helped just to see those hopes crushed when it doesn't happen or when you change your mind again. This is not some case to us, this is our life."

"Mr. Mitchell—"

"No! You don't get it." He was shouting into the phone at this point. "This doesn't work out and you move on to the next patient and forget about Ben. You go find someone else that you can help that will make you feel good about yourself. You don't have to see Ben every day and be reminded that you didn't or couldn't help him. You don't realize what this does to our family. I won't let you do this."

She sat stunned at this response. She had thought the hard part would be convincing Dr. Bryan to admit Ben to the program. She had never imagined that his family would be an obstacle.

"Mr. Mitchell"—she cleared her throat—"Ben's records state that your mother is his legal guardian. It will be up to her to decide whether or not Ben attends our program. Please let her know that I called."

Jill hung up the phone before he could respond, her hands shaking after the encounter.

"Lord, please help me. I didn't think the family would be the problem. I thought they would be thrilled. Did I hear you wrong?"

John slammed the phone into the receiver. Just one more situation he had to handle that he didn't have time to handle.

"Whoa, whoa, whoa." Jamie let the door slam loudly behind him. "What's got you all upset?"

"Nothing that I can't handle," John grumbled, turning around to face his brother. The smell of alcohol slapped him in the face. "Have you been drinking?" he questioned incredulously.

"I had a beer, relax." Jamie crossed his arms and leaned on the kitchen counter. "I'm not drunk. Amber was just bitching this morning and I needed something to take the edge off."

John stared at his brother, clenching his jaw shut to keep from blasting his brother and his fist clinched to keep from punching him. Jamie's behavior never ceased to amaze him. Just when John thought his brother couldn't disappoint him anymore, he always seemed to find a way. The entire weight of the family, the ranch, and their survival seemed to fall anew on John's shoulders.

"So who was on the phone?" Jamie questioned.

"Don't worry about it," John bit out angrily and pushed past his brother to head outside.

"Hey." Jamie grabbed his arm. "What is your problem?"

"Why are you drunk in the middle of the day?" John planted his hands on his hips.

"Is that your problem? I'm not drunk, I had one beer over lunch. Chill out, dude. I've drunk a whole lot more than that and still functioned. What's got you so angry?" Jamie demanded.

"You can't drink during the day, you're a grown man with responsibilities." John pushed past him and headed for his truck.

"John!" Jamie barked loudly as he followed him outside.

Something brought John up short, and he turned on his brother. "Nothing you can say is a good excuse for being drunk during the middle of the day!" He took a step toward Jamie and continued, "Who do you think you are? You need a job so that you can take care of the wife you have and all you want to do is climb in the bottom of a bottle!"

"That's right! That's exactly what I want to do!" Jamie screamed back at him. "I do." Jamie threw his hands up in the air. "I would love nothing more than to get rip-roaring drunk right now, so drunk that I don't even know my name, but I'm not! I had one beer!"

John was shocked by his brother's outrage. Normally Jamie blew everything off. Laughter and sarcasm were his best weapons, so the anger and outrage were not something John was used to seeing from him.

John softened. "I just don't understand you, Jamie. Don't understand why you want to do this to yourself, to Amber."

Jamie leaned his forearms on the bed of John's pickup truck. He studied John momentarily before he began speaking.

"I don't understand you either, brother. We all changed after Ben's accident. I may drink to cope with it all, but I'm trying. I'm trying to do better. Yes, I had a beer, one beer. I wanted a hundred, but I stopped, I didn't do it. I'm trying. But you…you shut everybody out. You try to do everything for everybody but you don't do anything for yourself. You're like a robot…no emotions. I remember you. You used to laugh, you used to be the funniest guy I knew. God, I wanted to be just like you. But all you are now is work, that's all you do. I'm trying here, John. God help me, I'm trying. I wish…I just wish…it's like I lost both brothers that day."

John could hardly stand the desperate look in Jamie's eyes coupled with the desperate tone of his voice. He knew he had changed. The burden he carried wouldn't let him be that fun, easygoing person he was four years ago. But he had never thought about how his burden affected the rest of the family. That his emotional detachment might have encouraged Jamie's drinking. Jamie's words found a deep place inside John and they hurt.

"John, I couldn't tell you the last time I saw you let loose, smile, I mean really smile…and laugh. Your laugh was just like Dad's…I miss it. I can't remember the last time you showed any emotion whatsoever. That's why I was shocked to see you lose your temper over whatever that phone call was about." Jamie stood straight now, facing his brother. "I ain't going to lie, it was good to see." Jamie grinned.

John took off his hat and turned it in his hands, looking down at his boots. He knew Jamie was right, but it was another thing entirely to admit that to his little brother. Better to let his brother in on the phone conversation than to have to delve into the changes in the family since Ben's accident. He had never broached the subject with his family that it was his fault that Ben had been injured. For the first few months after the accident, John couldn't look at Jamie or be in the same room with him. He felt as though every time Jamie looked at him, there was hate in his eyes. Why would his brother not hate him after what he had done? His family had to know, they had to have figured it out. Everyone went around acting as if it were some freak accident, but John knew that deep down they all knew that he was at fault.

John looked up to meet his brother's steady gaze. "That phone call? Looks like Ben made it into the therapy program at St. Patrick's after all."

Jamie let out a loud whoop and threw his ball cap in the air. John settled his hands on his hips. So much for his brother helping him protect his family from this disaster.

Chapter 7 Distrust

*Do not trust in princes, in mortal man, in whom
there is no salvation." Psalm 146:3*

Jill almost jumped out of her skin as a fellow therapist let the gym door slam behind them as they came in to start their day.

"Jumpy this morning?" Dr. Bryan raised an eyebrow at Jill as she bent to help her gather up the paperwork she had dropped when startled.

"Just a little. Too much coffee." Jill smiled. She didn't want to give Dr. Bryan any reason to think she was second-guessing her demand that Ben Mitchell be admitted to the program.

She was just that, though, second-guessing her push to admit Ben Mitchell. The phone conversation with his mother had been strikingly different from the conversation she had had with his brother. She had spent the two weeks since the conversation praying about her decision. Had she heard God correctly? No matter how much time she spent in prayer, she could not shake the notion that she was meant to be in Ben Mitchell's life for some reason. Over the weekend, she had found herself selfishly praying that Ben's brother would not be the one to bring him to the program's first session.

As she turned to return her paperwork to the therapy office, she realized that God did not answer all prayers in the way that she hoped. There, coming through the gym doors, were Ben Mitchell's mother, her face blazing with a hopeful smile, followed by Ben and what had to be Ben's other brother. He could be described as the quintessential tall, dark, handsome cowboy and Jill could immediately see the resemblance between this brother and the one from the clinci. Jill couldn't help but think how handsome he would be if he didn't have his faced configured in an angry scowl. She watched them enter the gym and be directed by a fellow therapist to a table to complete the necessary paperwork. She had to forcibly take her gaze from Ben's brother to look upon her patient, the one she had fought for to be admitted. As she watched him being wheeled around the gym, she began to second-guess herself yet again. She had practically memorized his medical records and now a list of his diagnoses followed by doctor's notes on his condition began to play in her head. Maybe she had been wrong; maybe she wasn't intended to help Ben after all. As she studied him and his family, his head swung in her direction, as if he were looking for her, and their eyes met.

"Help him, beloved."

The words were so clear to her she looked around to see if someone else had actually heard them. Everyone seemed to be going about their business. No one was looking around as if trying to discover where the mysterious voice had come from. Jill looked back at Ben Mitchell's family with joy in her heart. She would help him, whether his family liked it or not. She squared her shoulders and headed in their direction. Now was as good a time as any to meet his angry brother face to face.

John saw her coming out of the corner of his eye as he stood by Ben's chair, watching his mother fill out paperwork and produce insurance cards and papers. He had eyed the blonde when he had first entered the gym. She has dressed in blue scrubs and tennis shoes. Nothing in her dress would make her stand out from anybody else in the room, but when John had first seen her, she had been smiling at a doctor. Her face lit up with so much life and hope he was immediately intrigued by her. By society's standards she was beautiful, but he had long since become immune to a pretty face. No, it was something else; something in her smile, in her eyes, that drew him to her. Her long blonde hair was pulled back into a smooth ponytail, her hair softly curling down her back. Long layered bangs slipped from the hair band and she had absently tucked them behind her ear. He watched her long legs eat away at the distance between them as she seemed to head right for him.

"Mrs. Mitchell?" She approached his mother and extended her hand. Her gentle voice dove inside him, a soothing balm to places so long laid bare and desolate he had forgotten they existed. An unusual tension curled through his belly. It shocked him when he realized it was nervousness. He could single-handedly run a ranch, contain his drunk brother, and support his family. He had watched his father die and his brother be rendered a fate worse than death in his opinion. But here he was still standing, still putting one foot in front of the other. He did not get nervous, he berated himself.

"John?" His mother was looking up at him expectantly. "This is Jill, the therapist that I was telling you about. She's going to be working with Bennie."

He met her eyes then and their telephone conversation replayed in his mind. He reminded himself that behind those eyes that were as green as the mountains behind his home in the spring, lay a woman who was going to wreak havoc on his family. This woman was playing god with his family and he would not allow her to do that.

"I believe we spoke on the phone." Jill smiled at him and extended her hand.

"Yes, I believe we did." He had every intention to look her in the eye and firmly shake her hand. To send her a silent message that he would not back down from his original opinion of her and this program. But the moment his hand touched hers, the nervous sliver slicing through his belly erupted into a full-blown sensory overload. Her hands were soft, and his grip softened as he touched her. He felt something pulse from his hand, up his arm, and through his body as he touched her. Their eyes met and the noise of the gym around them faded into oblivion.

His mother cleared her throat and he broke the trance he was under by looking down at Pattie's smiling face. "Well," she said to no one in particular, "must have been some phone call."

John quickly released Jill's hand, shoving both of his own into his front pockets. His eyes darted around the gym, avoiding making eye contact with anyone. Noticing the other patients, he quickly attempted to summarize their conditions and compare them to Ben. He was a master of putting aside his emotions, and he would not let one pretty face distract him. Especially when that one pretty face was potentially going to break his family all over again. John was no doctor, but he quickly summarized that Ben's disabilities were by far the most severe. Some of the other patients were mobile and verbal, two things that seemed out of the realm of possibility with Ben. Anger, fueled by suspicion, threatened to take control over John's outwardly calm demeanor.

"Let's get Ben into his first evaluation and then we can discuss our goals for the program." Jill's voice broke into his thoughts. Her voice was smooth, confident, even calming. He hated how his insides reacted to it. He looked at his mother as she stood beside Ben's chair, her eyes alight with hope. That's what he needed to focus on; protecting his mother from this woman's false hope. He had agreed to come so that he could be the voice of reason.

Jill directed them to a therapist waiting to give Ben his initial evaluation. She then gave them a tour of the gym, pointing out different machines and techniques that would be used during the program.

"Would you like to see Ben's room? You can leave his bag there." She gestured to the bag that John had been carrying.

"That would be great," his mom gushed. John cringed at the excitement he heard in her voice. He was going to have to work overtime to curb his mother's optimism.

Jill escorted them down a hallway from the gym. She held a door for them and gestured for them to enter the room. "This will be Ben's room." The room was small, a single bed centered against the wall. It looked like the dozen other hospital rooms that Ben had called home over the last four years. A single cot had been placed in the corner. Jill noticed John's gaze lingering on the cot.

"We normally don't have family members stay in the room. But we thought that you might not want to leave Ben, so I had the cot moved in for you for tonight." Jill's eyes searched Pattie's face, but she could feel the daggers being thrown her way from the tall, taciturn man in the corner.

"Yes, thank you. I would feel better about things if I could stay with Ben." Pattie smiled her thanks. "It's all so exciting. This is going to be so good for Ben."

"Let's discuss our goals for Ben while he's here." Jill gestured for Pattie to sit in the only chair in the room, while she perched on the edge of the bed, completely ignoring John.

"Some of the goals my team and I came up with for Ben was more use and coordination of his hands. I also want to try and get Ben to control his head more."

"Yes, that would be wonderful if he could do those things. He seems to become very agitated at times. I wish there was some way we could figure out what is getting him so upset." Pattie glanced nervously from Jill to John.

Jill thought for a moment and then asked, "Tell me about when he becomes agitated. What time during the day?"

"Well… at night mostly…when we are trying to put him to bed."

"I'll make a note of it and we will try to determine if there is a certain pattern to it." Jill jotted a note in the file she held. They discussed other things for Ben to work on for the next few minutes, nothing that John felt was anything to get real excited about. "Let's head back and see how Ben is doing," Jill finally suggested.

As they headed back to the gym, Jill could feel John's eyes burning into her back. All she wanted was to avoid the cowboy for the rest of the day. She had hoped he would leave when they returned to the gym, but he hung around for several hours, quietly observing.

By the end of the day she had become so engaged with the new group of patients, she had temporarily forgotten that John was there, lurking in the corner, watching the entire gym and mentally taking notes. Jill refused to be intimidated by his behavior. She squared her shoulders and headed straight for Pattie Mitchell.

"Ben did well today, Ms. Mitchell." Jill smiled, hoping to be able to relieve some of the worry in the woman's eyes.

"Oh, do you think so?" Pattie clasped and unclasped her hands nervously.

"Well, it's the first day, but he was responsive to the small things we tried today, and that's the biggest hurdle with a brain injury, being able to determine whether or not they will be responsive to our therapy techniques." She reached out to cover the woman's fidgeting hands and squeezed.

"Oh, good. I'm glad you thought so." Pattie looked past Jill to the gym door. Jill couldn't help but notice she seemed distracted.

"Why don't you go check on Ben? Make sure he's getting settled in," Jill suggested.

"Really? That would be okay?" Pattie's eyes brightened.

"Of course." Jill motioned for a therapy technician to come over and instructed him to take Pattie to Ben's room, leaving her alone with Mr. Personality.

She turned her eyes to John and met his level gaze. Before she could ask him what he thought of the gym, he took a step toward her.

"Look, Ms. Morgan," he said in a low, gravelly voice, "I still for the life of me cannot figure out why you would want Ben in this program—"

"I've told you, I think we can help him," she interrupted.

"He's by far the worst case here!" John raised his voice as his arms gestured toward the other patients still in the gym.

"Yes, I'll give you that. Ben's case is by far the most traumatic in the gym, maybe that we've ever allowed in the program. But I know we can help him." Jill hoped the confidence in her voice was convincing.

He studied her a moment. She held his steady gaze. She couldn't help but realize how blue his eyes were. They reminded her of the spring sky over her mother's house in Tennessee, blue and clear enough to lose yourself in. What was this sliver of warmth that speared though her body, betraying her? He took one step closer and her eyes shifted to his lips. She screamed internally at herself when she briefly wondered what would his lips feel like on hers. She quickly averted her eyes.

"I don't know what game you're playing, Ms. Morgan. Do you get some kind of sick pleasure in messing with people's lives?" He spat the words at her in a low voice filled with contempt.

"Excuse me?" She was shocked at his accusation, her kissing fantasy quickly forgotten.

"Or maybe you like playing God? Having power over people? Maybe you can help them, maybe you can't. What about the ones you can't help? You just move on to the next case, the next poor patient that you will use to stroke your own ego. Do you ever think about the fall-out? Do you ever think about what impact you have on these families?" He stood mere inches from her, legs apart and hands splayed on his hips, accusing her.

Tears threatened to spill down her cheeks but she refused to give him the satisfaction. "Mr. Mitchell, I am trying to help your brother. Period. I have never tried to lead your family on. I have been very upfront about the amount of progress I expect Ben to make."

"Have you?" he demanded angrily. "Have you really been upfront?! Because I don't see any way Ben is ever going to improve and you are giving my family false hope…leading them on."

Jill stood there, mouth agape, shocked out his outburst. He didn't give her a chance to respond.

"I'm watching you, Ms. Morgan. Don't think for one minute I'm going to let you hurt my family. They have been hurt enough, I won't let you add to their pain." And with that he turned on his heel and quickly strode away.

Jill stood in the gym, mouth open. What had she done to deserve such anger from this man? She was trying to help his family. She had gone out of her way to get his brother in this program and he repaid her with contempt and anger? Was she wrong to think she could help Ben? She hadn't even considered the emotions of Ben's family. She had assumed they would be thrilled to have Ben in such a great program. Had she heard God wrong? She didn't know the answers to those questions, but one thing she did know was that she was going to avoid John Mitchell at all costs from this point forward.

Chapter 8 Confrontation

*My brothers, if anyone among you wanders from
the truth and someone brings him back let him know
that whoever brings back a sinner from his wandering
will save his soul from death and will cover a
multitude of sins.," James 5:19-20*

By Wednesday, John sat down at this desk and was confident the family was not going to make it to Saturday and the scheduled visit with Ben without having some type of meltdown. They had dropped Ben off just five days before, even spending the first night in the hospital with Ben, unlike the other patients' families, who had all left on drop-off day. His mother had been a bundle of nerves, her usually sunny disposition taken by worry about Ben being so far away from her. She had been his primary caregiver for four years, and now someone else had taken that job. She wandered the house and barns trying to find something to keep her busy.

John was more taciturn than normal. He had replayed the encounter with Jill Morgan over and over in his mind. Maybe he had been too hard on her, maybe he should apologize when he saw her again. The questions kept eating at him, but the thing that kept him up nights was the memory of how his body had betrayed him when he had first caught a glimpse of her across the room. He had been shocked to feel the zing of nervousness cut through his belly at the sight of her. When he could close his eyes the sight of her deep green eyes fighting back tears over his tirade haunted him. Yep, that was that, he would definitely apologize.

And Jamie, sensing all the tension in the family, had taken off late yesterday evening to run an errand, and based on the frantic voicemail John had just listened to, he had not returned. Of course Amber wanted John to come to the rescue, and John wanted to leave Jamie flapping in the wind. It was early summer. John had too many things to do to get prepared for winter to spend the day chasing down his brother. In the high country winter came early and harshly. If a rancher didn't prepare, he along with his livestock could find themselves in for the fight of their lives. He closed his eyes and the first image that appeared was Jill Morgan's green eyes. He rubbed his eyes as if that would remove the image and let out a breath.

"Worried about Ben?" His mother's voice interrupted his thoughts.

She stepped through the office door and took the seat across from him. "Um…yeah, I am." John had long ago rationalized that a few lies to his mother here and there would not condemn him to hell. He was quite sure he was already living in it.

"Me too. I'm so lonely I've been talking to the house plants. Ben doesn't talk back, but he's sure a good listener." She laughed nervously.

"I'm sure he's missing you too," he tried to reassure her. She nodded her head in agreement and glanced out the window as if gathering her thoughts.

"You think we did the right thing? Taking him there and leaving him?" She looked at John and he could tell she needed his reassurance. John squared his shoulders. He wanted to tell her that he thought it was a waste of time, that he didn't trust Jill Morgan, and that Ben was about as good as he would ever be, but he didn't. He couldn't. He had taken enough from her, he wouldn't take her hope too.

"Yeah, I think we did the right thing. I think Ben's in good hands."

Some days he wondered if God would ever get so tired of all his lies that he would just strike him dead. No matter how many he told, it never got easier. The biggest lie, the biggest secret that he buried deep down inside, ate at him every moment of every day. When he looked at Ben, when he looked at his mother and Jamie, he knew he had caused all of their problems. The least he could do was work himself relentlessly to provide for them. No, John decided, God would not strike him dead. He deserved to be punished for what he had put his family through and the anguish he felt was his punishment. John was confident he would live to a ripe old age, regretting that one morning every day for the rest of his life with no reprieve.

****

By Thursday, Jill was questioning if she had completely misunderstood God's direction when it came to Ben Mitchell. She worked tirelessly with him, staying every night to give him extra therapy. She had two weeks to show improvement in Ben's condition or he would be removed from the program. She had two main goals to achieve with Ben. She wanted him to be able to have more control over his head and more flexibility in his left arm. Both were simple tasks that she had helped hundreds of patients achieve over the past few years. But Ben seemed, if not incapable, at least unwilling to attempt the exercises.

She watched as Ben was wheeled into the gym that morning. All of the accusations from John came rushing back to her mind. Was he right? Had she done more harm than good by bringing him into the program? Fear and panic gripped her. *"God, what have I done? Did I hear you wrong?"*

"My thoughts are not your thoughts, my plans are not your plans."

The verse popped into her mind. She mulled it for a moment and made up her mind that she would continue to work as hard as she could and throw every therapy technique she had ever read about at Ben until something happened.

****

When John returned from his early morning ride on Saturday, he found his mother seated at the kitchen table, nervously gripping her coffee cup, overnight bag at her feet.

45

"Momma, its six o'clock in the morning, what are you doing?" John gently closed the door behind him.

"I thought we might get a head start this morning." She glanced at him hopefully. He let out a sigh. He wanted to give her a list of all the things he had to get done today before they left. He wanted to remind her that winter would be here before they knew it and horses and cows didn't really care if she was missing her son. They had to be fed no matter what. But the hopeful look in her eyes was more than he could crush.

"Sure, Momma, let me take care of a few things around here and we will hit the road." He tried to reassure her with his best smile as he turned and headed back to the barn. He hoped she didn't see that the smile never got beyond his lips.

When John finished up at his office over an hour later, the ranch had begun to buzz with activity. The few hired hands who lived on the ranch were around the barns preparing for the day. John loved this time of day. The ranch was waking up and everything seemed fresh, peaceful. He thought about the day ahead as he drove back to the house to pick up his mother. He was determined to make this a good day. He would apologize to Ms. Morgan as soon as he got the opportunity. He would be positive and support his mother in this endeavor even if he felt like it was a waste of time. The peace and confidence he felt as he slipped out of the truck fled when he caught the dust of a pickup truck speeding up the road past the barns headed straight for the main house. The truck came careening to a halt and Jamie jumped out, bag in hand.

"We about ready to go?" Jamie asked as he opened the back hatch of the ranch's SUV and threw his bag inside, glancing nervously over his shoulder.

"*We?*" John crossed his arms. "Momma and I are about ready to go. I'm not sure what you think you're doing."

"Well, I'm going too, big brother." The way he called John brother sounded more like a curse word than a term of endearment.

They stared at each other for a moment, each contemplating their next move.

John stepped toward him and sniffed. "Have you even been home?" John asked as he studied his brother's disheveled appearance.

"Don't worry about my home life, big brother," Jamie spat.

"Maybe if you worried about it a little more, then I wouldn't have to." John leveled his gaze on his younger brother.

Jamie looked down and let out a bitter laugh. "I'm going, John; he's my brother too. I'm going and there is nothing you can do to stop me."

John watched his brother for a moment before responding, "You just make sure you're going for Ben and not just running from Amber." He stepped forward to slap Jamie's shoulder and pointed to the plume of smoke billowing up from the car speeding up the driveway. "Looks like Amber decided to go too."

John stepped inside the kitchen to find his mother watching from the window. "Lord, John, what are those two into it about now?"

"Looks like it's a whole family road trip." John tried to make light of the situation. His mother didn't need any extra stress. He laid his hand on his mother's shoulder and guided her from the window. "Let's give them a few minutes to work this out."

After twenty minutes watching his mother pacing around the kitchen, nervously glancing toward the window, John knew she couldn't take much more of the waiting. He grabbed their bags and held the door for Pattie, who practically ran to the SUV. As he opened the back hatch to add their bags, he glanced up at the back seat. Both Amber and Jamie were stubbornly seated at each window, arms crossed, refusing to look at or acknowledge the other. John shook his head, dreading the weekend ahead in Billings for more than one reason now.

Between his mother's nervous fidgeting and the icy silent treatment going on the back seat, John couldn't wait to get out of the car when they arrived at the hospital. He rolled his shoulders, trying to relieve some of the tension in his neck. Maybe once they saw Ben, things would be better.

Ben was in the gym working on using a modified spoon to feed himself. Pattie hugged him and talked a mile a minute to Ben and a therapist whose name tag read *Sam*. Jamie patted Ben on the back and asked him how he was, as if Ben could respond. John stood back and observed the reunion, not joining in on the family moment. He knew Ben wouldn't care if he was there or not. Ben moved his head and raised his arm as if trying to greet them.

"Well," the therapist said, sitting back in his chair, "that's the most activity I've seen out of Ben in days. He must be glad to see you all."

Pattie bent to put her arms around Ben and hug him again. "Well, I know we sure are glad to see him."

The buzz of conversation filled the room, but John could only focus on one thing. After a few minutes he stepped forward. "What did you mean by that's the most activity you've seen out of Ben in days?"

The therapist leaned back in his chair and dropped his hands in his lap. He studied each family member's face as if trying to determine if he should speak openly with them. "Honestly, Ben hasn't been very responsive to therapy this week."

The look of determination Pattie gave John was meant to silence him he felt sure, but he ignored it and pushed on. "What do you mean not very responsive?" John stepped between his family and the therapist.

"Well, Jill—you all have met Jill Morgan, right, Ben's lead therapist?"

"Yeah, we've met," John replied curtly. The tension of the morning had done nothing for his patience.

"Well, Jill had set some very basic goals for Ben. One of which was to help him learn to use this utensil"—he held up the modified spoon—"to learn to feed himself. Ben just doesn't seem very interested in doing it."

"Not interested?" John couldn't keep the anger out of his voice and at this point he wasn't sure he even wanted to. "So what are you saying? He can do it but he won't? Or maybe he isn't capable of doing it at all. Maybe this is all just a waste of time!"

"John!" Pattie whispered harshly, tears threatening her eyes.

He ignored his mother, determined to get an answer to his question. He glanced at the therapist's name tag. "So which is it, Sam, he can't or he won't?"

"Listen," Sam replied, "I didn't mean to upset you. I'm not sure why he isn't responding to the therapy. Jill wouldn't have insisted he be in the program if she didn't think he could improve. She's a brilliant therapist. One of the best I've ever seen. If she thinks he can, then I think he can too."

"Ms. Morgan, she's a brilliant therapist?" John's voiced dripped with contempt.

The therapist stood slowly and reached out to touch John's shoulder. John stepped out of his reach.

"Mr. Mitchell, I know how frustrating it can be not to see the improvement we had hoped for. I promise you that we are doing everything possible to make sure Ben shows improvement in these first two weeks."

"Two weeks? Why two weeks? It's been four years, I think it might take longer than two weeks to show improvement." By now the stress of the morning plus the frustration he had been feeling over Ben's situation came to a boil. He could feel his temper rising.

Sam glanced at Pattie and the other family members as if looking for help.

"John—" his mother began.

"No." He glanced toward his mother and then pointed to the therapist. "I asked him a question."

"Are you not aware of the two-week period?" Sam glanced around at each family member.

Pattie looked nervously from Sam to John. John turned to see Jamie looking down, pretending to study the toe of his boot.

"Well, I'm not aware of a two-week period, but apparently everyone else here is," John spat between gritted teeth.

Sam squared his shoulders and sighed. "Ben has been admitted to our program on a temporary two-week time frame. He must show improvement in the first two weeks or he will be dismissed from our program."

John stood with his hands on his hips, staring out the window directly behind Sam for a few moments before he spoke. "Is this two-week trial period for every patient?"

Sam fidgeted and glanced behind John as if looking for someone to come along and save him. Realizing that he would not be able to avoid the tall cowboy standing in front of him, he finally looked John in the eye and responded, "No. No, it's not for every patient. Ben's the only patient that's ever been admitted on a trial period that I know of."

Roaring filled John's ears. He could see his mother's mouth moving, speaking to him, but he couldn't hear her words. His focus was singular: Find Jill Morgan and let her know exactly what he thought of her. He turned on his heels and with long, confident strides ate up the distance of the gym. He had no idea where Ms. Morgan might be, but he wouldn't stop until he found her.

Jill sat in the hospital chapel unsure of what to pray for. For the past week she had worked tirelessly with Ben Mitchell. She had delegated every other patient in the program to other very capable therapist and assistant and focused on Ben herself. She had worked late, and come in early every day since he had arrived at the hospital. And for all of her efforts, Ben had shown no improvement. She had begun to question herself, to question if she had misinterpreted God's direction. Had she really heard God telling her to help Ben? The self-doubt was debilitating this morning. She had left Ben with Sam, one of her best therapists, and sought refuge in the chapel.

"Lord, did I hear you wrong? Have I totally messed up everything with this family?" Jill dropped her head into her hands.

"For my thoughts are not your thoughts, neither are your ways my ways."

Pieces of the verse from Isaiah kept coming to her.

"So are my ways higher than your ways and my thoughts than your thoughts."

"Lord, please let him show some improvement. Enough to keep him in the program. Please, Lord," Jill pleaded.

Jill sat in the quiet chapel for a few more minutes, collecting her thoughts and planning her day. With a new resolve and determination, she stood, ready to head back to the gym and work with Ben. The hustle and bustle of the busy hospital was a stark contrast compared to the stillness of the chapel. She slipped from the chapel doors and immediately missed its calmness, but, determined to focus on Ben Mitchell's improvement, she was ready to face the day. She headed for the gym, mulling over the techniques that had not worked with Ben and trying to formulate a plan to reach him. She felt rejuvenated and her hope for helping Ben was renewed.

"Ms. Morgan." She heard her name being called from the hallway behind her. She turned to see John Mitchell, quickly shortening the distance between them with his long, determined strides.

Her entire body reacted at the sight of him. Her pulse quickened and palms sweated as she watched his handsome frame approach her. She smoothed the front of her scrubs, determined to have a pleasant interaction with him this time.

"Good morning, Mr. Mitch—"

"Two weeks?!" he roared at her. "You upset our whole lives for two weeks?!"

"Mr. Mitchell, what in the world is going on?" Jill nervously glanced around at bystanders who had stopped to witness the exchange.

"Two weeks? Ben's only here for two weeks?" he demanded loudly.

"Mr. Mitchell." She reached for his arm to try and lead him into a more private area. "Please keep your voice down."

"No." He jerked his arm away from her. "I will not keep my voice down. You've got some explaining to do."

She paused and gathered her thoughts before she began. "Yes. Ben was admitted to the program on a two-week trial basis. When he shows improvement then he will stay for the duration of the program or as long as he needs to so that he can continue to improve."

John turned his back to her and began to walk away. He turned on a dime and quickly walked back to her, quickly standing toe to toe with her. "Who do you think you are?" Anger emanated from his body as he gritted his teeth, his voice low and wrought with emotion. "This is my family. This is our life! And you think you can just play around with that? You are the most heartless, selfish—"

"John!" Pattie's voice interrupted his tirade.

"Stay out of this." He lifted his hand palm up, as if to stop his mother, but his eyes never left Jill's.

"John Mitchell, you will not treat Ms. Morgan this way," his mother demanded as she stepped closer.

"Go back to Ben, Momma." His eyes bored into Jill's, never wavering.

"It was my decision, John. When Ms. Morgan called me she was upfront about the two week trial period. I didn't care. I would do anything to give Ben a chance." Pattie placed her hand on John's shoulder and gently pulled him away from Jill.

51

"And I told everyone not to mention it to you. I knew you would use it to keep Ben at home."

As his mother's words registered in his thoughts, Jill watched his face change from anger to hurt. He turned his gaze on his mother. "Why would you agree to this? Why would you not tell me?" he said incredulously.

"Look at how you're acting. THIS is why I didn't tell you!" His mother turned him away from Jill and steered him toward the chapel doors. "Come on, let's talk."

Pattie quietly opened the chapel doors and stepped inside, thankful that it was empty.

"Why would you agree to this? Upset our whole lives…" John asked before she could begin explaining herself.

Pattie sat down on the back pew and released a breath. If she were honest with herself she was glad the secret was out in the open. "Sit down, John." She patted the seat beside her.

"No," he replied, hands on hips. "I don't want to sit; I want answers."

"I'm still your mother and I said to sit." She summoned as much motherly tone to her voice as she could.

John studied his mother for several long moments before sitting down beside her, leaning forward, his forearms resting on his knees.

"When Ben got hurt, I leaned so heavily on your father. Some days I would be about at the end of myself and he could just give me a look or tell me everything was going to be okay and I believed him. He was my rock." She sighed and briefly closed her eyes. John knew she was back there. Back in those horrible days right after the accident.

"He was a rock to all of us," John added quietly.

"It was all such a roller coaster, you know? I mean Ben finally gets stable enough for us to feel confident we weren't going to lose him and your dad gets sick."

"I know it was a rough time, Momma." John sat up and turned slightly to face her, reached over and grabbed her hand. "But… I don't understand…why go back to it? Why make times rough for ourselves again?"

Pattie sighed. "I knew….we knew something was wrong with Red while Ben was still in the hospital."

"You knew Dad had cancer and didn't tell us?" John reeled at the admission and the sudden change in the direction of the conversation.

"No, not that it was cancer, but something. Red always had the energy of a teenager, and suddenly it was just gone. At first I—we thought it was the stress of Ben's situation. But it just kept getting worse. I was scared. I couldn't lose Red too, we'd already lost Ben in a way and I …well, the thought of losing Red scared the life out of me." His mother suddenly looked older to him as tears threatened to spill over.

"Momma, of course, we were all scared. None of us wanted to lose Dad." He leaned back and put his arm around her shoulders.

"Ben got a little better, at least stable, and I shifted—my focus shifted to Red, I think. I needed to make sure he was okay, and then when the cancer diagnosis came, I focused on keeping him alive. Whatever it took, I needed Red to live. Red had to live and then I would focus on Ben, I would do whatever it took to get Ben better, but Red had to live! I couldn't do this without him!" She emphasized the last words by clenching her fist.

John nodded for her to continue.

"In the whirlwind of it all… I look back and I think…." She paused as if searching for the right words. Her fingers shook, and she pressed them to her lips. "Did I miss something? In all the turmoil of chemotherapy and doctor's visits for them both, did I miss something?"

"What do you mean did you miss something?" John questioned.

"I read all these stories of people with brain injuries. And they come back…maybe months, sometimes years later, but they come back at least a little bit. They can communicate or they can learn to walk and talk…and I think…could that have been Ben? If we hadn't had so much going on, just one storm after another, could that have been Ben? Could we have found him a program like this one, or something else that could have helped him? But instead, we accepted it and went home and he never got the opportunity to improve?" She looked at John with pleading in her eyes, as if begging him to understand.

"Momma," John began.

"So I accepted the two-week trial period for Ben to be in this program," she interrupted, brushing tears off her cheeks and straightening her spine. "Because he deserves that. He deserves every opportunity that we can give him."

John sat for a moment, thinking about everything his mother had just told him. "Yes. Yes, he does deserve every opportunity, but you should have told me."

"I didn't because you wouldn't have agreed to it," she answered quickly. "And not that I need your approval, young man, because I do not, but I wanted it."

"I might have agreed to it." He raised his eyebrows and tried to sound light.

"No, you wouldn't have," she chuckled. "I've leaned on you too much since all this happened. I let you take responsibility for too many things. After Red, I was lost, for a long time I was just lost. I was always the weak one. Red was my strength, my rock, and when he was gone, I turned to you to be those things. I let you take over so many things that I shouldn't have."

"Momma, I wanted to help our family. It was my job. I'm the oldest."

"No, just because of what happened to Ben and your father, you shouldn't have had to give up your life, your job, your house…your future, for us." She wiped a tear that slipped down her cheek.

"Hey," he said softly, reaching to reassure her by squeezing her hand. "Don't cry. That's what families do. They take care of each other. I wanted to do it."

"You were happy when you lived here in Billings. You had a future; a good job…you smiled. I don't see you smile much anymore." She dropped her hands in her lap, biting her lower lip to keep more tears from falling.

"I'm right where I'm supposed to be. I wouldn't be anywhere else," he tried to reassure her.

"If you want to leave the ranch and go back to your old job, we can make it, we can do it."

"And who's going to run the ranch? Jamie?" He gave a short, bitter laugh. "He'd lose the whole thing in a poker game within a week."

"You aren't responsible for Jamie. He's grown. You've got to stop cleaning up his messes or he'll never quit making them," she advised. "I know why you do it; it's why you do everything to try to keep the family together and from any more heartache. But you can't protect us forever. You can't fix everything, John. You've got to accept what is and go on. And if that means going back to your old life, if that is what will make you happy, then you need to go."

"Who says I'm not happy?" he questioned.

She studied him before she answered, "The perpetual scowl on your face says a lot."

"I don't always scowl," he tried to defend himself.

"You need to apologize to Ms. Morgan." She turned to face him. "She's a good person… a good Christian. She sees something in Ben, she told me that. She fought hard to get Ben in this program. She put herself on the line for him because she thinks she can really help him. She's only trying to help us and you have been downright rude to her."

He studied his mother for a moment. He could see a new strength emerging from her, a new determination, and for a moment he felt hope springing forth in his heart. "I'll make it right, Momma."

"You better." She pointed her finger at him. "I raised you better than to treat a lady like that."

****

Jill was completely shaken up after her encounter with John Mitchell. Convinced she had completely misunderstood God's directions she slipped into her office and quietly sat down in the chair beside the door. Lights off; only the glow from her computer screen illuminated the room. She sat in the chair and stared at her desk. She wondered how many family members had sat in this very chair waiting, hoping for her to deliver good news. To some she had and to some she had not. They left either elated or heartbroken. Her job was not one for the faint of heart. She had always been able to handle the emotions from family members. She understood better than most what it meant to sit in that chair and have all the hope in the world resting on what a doctor or therapist was about to say. How many people had she helped? How many people had she crushed with news that a loved one would not walk again, would not talk again, and would never be the person that they were before again?

HOPE.

The word screamed into her thoughts. HOPE. She grasped the thought and held on tightly. Yes, hope! No matter what the situation she might be facing, she always tried to leave the family with hope. Hope that they could deal with the situation. Hope that while their family member might never be the same again, life could and would go on and that life could and would be beautiful again. A beautiful life took many forms. And at times she gave them hope that their family member would recover, would walk and talk again.

She glanced at a picture on her desk. Two young teenagers smiled back at her. For a moment she drifted back, and a tear slipped from her eye. She read the scripture from Romans written on the frame.

"Rejoice in hope, be patient in tribulation, be constant in prayer."

Rejoice in hope. Hope. Hope. Hope that a spiritual walk with Jesus here on this earth was better than any physical walking a patient could do. She thought of John. In the two brief meetings she had had with him she could surmise two things: he was not rejoicing and he had very little hope for his brother.

Maybe she had two brothers to help.

She headed for the gym. She would work with Ben all day today. After her meetings with John, she was beginning to think that maybe Ben would be the easier brother to help.

Jill used a variety of different machines to test the strength of Ben's left hand. She attached various utensils to his hand and helped guide the spoons with various shapes and sizes to his mouth. Repetition was key, along with muscle memory. She talked to Ben as they worked, and she realized she knew very little about him. She noticed that he had on a high school football T-shirt from a school she had never heard of.

"Pine Bluff High School," she read. "Is that where you went to school?"

She watched his face carefully for any hint of recognition. She caught his eyes and for a moment he held her gaze.

"I've never heard of that school. Is that the high school in your hometown? Ben, was your high school called Pine Bluff?"

"Yes ma'am. Pine Bluff High School. Home of the Bears."

She jumped and turned toward the voice behind her and her stomach fell at the sight of John Mitchell standing behind her with all his cowboy good looks, hat in hand, sheepish look on his face.

"Mr. Mitchell." She turned quickly back to the exercises she had been directing Ben through. "Didn't anyone ever tell you not to sneak up on someone like that? You've scared the life out of me." She tried to keep her voice light, not wanting to let the anger that still simmered from this morning's meeting to surface.

He stepped up to the opposite side of Ben's chair. He stood there facing her for several moments, waiting for her to look up at him. Finally she met his gaze.

"I've been told a lot in my life, including the proper way to treat a lady. But it would seem that I momentarily forgot a lot of what I have been told."

Jill hated the way her anger melted at the sight of him standing in front of her, slowly turning his hat over in his hands, glancing down at the toes of his boots.

"I'm real sorry, Ms. Morgan." He looked up to meet her gaze and Jill felt like the world around them fell away. His eyes were the bluest she had ever seen and the way he looked at her, so sincere and apologetic, she couldn't hold a grudge against him. Besides, the pounding of her heart and the chaotic yet intoxicating energy that soared through her body at the mere sight of the man made it near impossible to think straight at the moment, much less muster up her anger.

"It's fine, Mr. Mitchell," she said on a breath.

He looked at her skeptically and she willed her heart to stop its pounding, knowing that if there was too much silence he would surely hear it. "Really it is," she continued. "I understand that emotions run high in these situations."

"Emotions or not, I had no right to speak to you that way and I am truly sorry."

Jill heard the words, but her mind wandered. As he stood there in his hip-hugging blue jeans, boots, and a white-button down shirt, holding his hat in his hands, she couldn't help but think that he looked like he had just walked off a western movie set, complete with good looks and all.

"Mr. Mitchell, I accept your apology and I truly don't want you to give it another thought." She glanced down at Ben as she continued guiding him in the exercises.

57

John studied the scene in front of him thoughtfully. "Why don't we drop the formalities. My name is John."

"Okay, John." She tested his name on her lips and a sliver of nerves sliced through her stomach. "Please call me Jill."

"Fair enough." He smiled and Jill couldn't help but wonder how many hearts those dimples had broken.

In an effort to get her mind off of how good-looking the cowboy in front of her was, she gestured to Ben's shirt. "So did Ben play football at Pine Bluff High School?"

She watched John's face. She knew in his mind, he was reliving a past memory. He finally responded.

"Yeah… yeah, he did." He looked away and shifted uncomfortably.

"What position did he play?" she asked, getting the impression that John was not going to just offer up a lot of information. He was guarded, which wasn't uncommon among caretakers of disabled individuals.

"Uh, he was a fullback." He glanced at his brother and watched his hand move along with Jill's.

"Ben, were you a good fullback?" She directed her question to the patient. Even if the patient couldn't respond she made a point to include them in the conversation.

John waited a few minutes before responding, "Yeah, he was….he really was."

"So what does a fullback do, Ben?" She again addressed her patient while continuing with the exercises.

"He can't respond," John said flatly, seemingly agitated at her inclusion of Ben in the conversation.

Jill studied Ben while she answered, "No, not verbally, but we don't know what Ben is capable of understanding. If there is some level of understanding, we can expect a response in some nonverbal way."

"And you think he understands what you are asking him?" John asked, and Jill could not detect what emotion was simmering underneath his taciturn exterior. Was this the beginning of hope?

She tilted her head thoughtfully. "Do you think he understands when you talk to him? You've spent much more time with him than I have."

His body stiffened at her words and Jill knew immediately that she had hit a nerve. He stood there looking from her to his brother. "No. No, I don't think he understands."

And with those words he turned and with long strides quickly exited the gym.

"Hope is a hard thing to get back when you lose it," Jill whispered as the gym door shut.

Ben's hand slipped from the spoon and grasped her ring and pinky fingers.

"Oops! Did you lose your grip?" Jill went to move his hand back to the spoon.

He gripped her fingers tightly. She would have to note how strong his grip was in his chart. Had it been this strong on his initial evaluation? She moved the spoon to her other hand and let him continue holding her fingers. She gazed at him intently and he returned her gaze without wavering. Jill could feel her insides churning. Something was happening here, but she wasn't sure what.

"Ben, did you lose your grip?" She glanced at his fingers holding on to hers. No change. No movement.

Again, "Ben did you lose your grip?" No change. No movement.

She studied Ben. His gaze was unwavering. His grip still strong. She couldn't help but think that he was trying to communicate something.

"Ben…" She thought about the conversation with John. "Have you lost your hope?" No change, no movement.

Again she studied him. "Ben, has your brother lost his hope?"

Jill could chalk it up to hopeful thinking and it wasn't a concrete milestone that she could add to his chart. But she wanted to shout for joy and cry tears of happiness all at once because slightly, ever so slightly, Ben Mitchell had squeezed her hand. Later she would question herself. Was it coincidence? Was it an accident? Did she imagine it? But for right now in that moment it was the hope she needed to keep moving forward.

Chapter 9 Truce

"The LORD gives strength to his people; the LORD blesses his people with peace." Psalm 29:11

J ohn sat in the courtyard of the hospital alone. Mentally he was not ready to go back to the hotel room and deal with his brother and sister-in-law. He sat mulling over Jill's question.

"Do you think he understands when you talk to him? You've spent much more time with him than I have."

What would she think or what would she have said if he had told her the truth? What if he had told her that he had not spoken directly to Ben since he had first woken up in the hospital? He was pretty sure she would have looked at him in disgust, just the way he looked at himself. She probably would have kicked him out of the gym and told security that he couldn't return, and who would blame her? Jamie and his mom, and now even Amber, spoke to Ben as if they expected him to respond, but not John. John dealt in absolutes, in realities; anything else was a waste of time.

The other nagging thought that wouldn't quite let go was why did he care about what Jill Morgan thought of him? In a few weeks she would be out of their lives for good and what she thought of him wouldn't matter anymore. He shoved his hand through his hair and let out a sigh. And why did it seem to cause a sickening knot in his stomach to think about her being out of his life in a matter of weeks?

****

The following week brought an unnerving quietness to the ranch, but just under the surface bubbled a jumble of emotions that threatened to explode. Everyone went about their business as if nothing unusual was afoot, never mentioning that this week would be the end of the two-week trial for Ben. The family would again travel to Billings for the weekend to find out what the future held for them. John went about ranch business as if a major snowstorm was about to dump two feet of snow on them in the middle of summer, stopping long enough to fall in bed at night only to get up and begin the rigorous work detail again in the morning. Jamie and his ranch hands secretly wondered what had gotten into John to drive him so. Hard work was nothing new to the ranch, but John had stepped it up this week, accomplishing tasks that had long been pushed to the "someday" list. By Friday, stress and fatigue had frayed everyone's nerves to the breaking point.

John sat at his computer screen. A spreadsheet showed the ranch inventory on the screen, but inventory was the furthest thing from his mind. He rubbed his hands down his face and suddenly shoved his chair away from his desk. All week he had battled to forget his conversation with Jill Morgan.

"Do you think he understands when you talk to him? You've spent much more time with him than I have."

Why did her question bother him so? Why every single night when he fell in bed did he see her face when he closed his eyes? Those hypnotizing green eyes searching him for an answer to her question? And why did he care what she thought of him? He had worked like a madman for the last week. He had probably driven away some of his hired help for the summer because of this week's work load alone. The lie he told to everyone else, that they were just getting prepared for a hard winter, was not one he could swallow himself. Deep down, in a place where he bared his soul, he had to admit he was trying to work her and her question out of his mind.

"Do you think he understands when you talk to him?"

Throughout the day her image would appear, unwanted, in his mind, repeating the same question. He would see the tree limbs blowing in the summer breeze and it would remind him of her eyes, eyes that seemed to see to the very depths of his soul. His next thought was that he was going to have his men cut down every tree on the ranch. Despite his mind's best efforts to banish her image, she was never far from his thoughts.

In a few hours, he would take his mother and begin the several-hour drive to Billings. In a few hours they would know Ben's fate. Was he to stay with the program or come back home, with no improvements to show for having been gone? John tried to focus on Ben, on the turmoil this two-week program had caused in their lives. He tried to channel anger by focusing on all his family had been through. He wanted to be angry at Jill Morgan. He wanted to hate her, so she would quit haunting his every waking thought. But no matter how hard he tried, he couldn't muster up any anger, not a smidge of bitterness, and not a drop of rage. And in that same place, where he bared his soul, if he wanted to get real honest with himself, he could admit that right now all he felt was a nervous excitement. And while he was being honest he could say that the excitement wasn't over just seeing his brother, but might include seeing his brother's pretty therapist.

John leaned back in his chair, gazing out the window but seeing nothing. How had this happened? John had always guarded his emotions. He didn't have the luxury of exploring them. He had a commitment to his family; he did not have time to be acting like a teenage boy. A fleeting thought crossed his mind of backing out of the trip, using the excuse that he was just too busy and Jamie would have to drive his mother down.

"Hey, John." Jamie's quick knock on the door startled John out of his deep thoughts.

"Jumpy, huh?" Jamie sat across from him.

"No," John answered and moved the mouse around as if he was actually working on the spreadsheet.

"Well, you almost jumped out of your chair when I knocked. Must be a guilty conscience for working these poor ol' boys to the bone." Jamie grinned.

Jamie wanted something; that much John could tell. His little brother didn't just stop by for idle chitchat. John just grunted his reply and continue pretending to work on the spreadsheet.

"Listen"—Jamie leaned forward—"I don't think I'm going to be able to make this trip down to Billings today."

John leaned back in this chair, crossed his arms, and leveled his gaze on his brother, waiting for him to continue.

Jamie averted his eyes as John's bored into him. Jamie smiled, trying to keep the conversation light. "I think I'm going to hang around here and spend some time with Amber this weekend, just the two of us."

John studied Jamie thoughtfully, trying to determine whether there was a grain of truth to anything he had said. So much for him being able to dump this trip off on Jamie.

"Just the two of you?" John raised his eyebrows skeptically.

"Yep, I think we need it, I've barely seen her this week."

"And this has nothing to do with the fact that we will find out if Ben stays in the program or comes home?" John questioned, sure that at least some part of Jamie was attempting to avoid a potentially uncomfortable situation.

"John, aren't you the one always telling me that I need to be a better husband? I thought you'd be happy that I was trying." Jamie's incredulous act just wasn't quite believable for John.

John put his hands palm up toward Jamie. "Its fine. I can handle it." And he was not sure why, but he just couldn't keep himself from adding, "Like I always do."

Jamie stood and met his brother's gaze. "I'm sure you will…Saint John, you always do the right thing." He spat the words over his shoulder as he left the office.

John slammed the computer screen shut and fought the urge to throw it out the door after his brother. He couldn't decide who he was more upset with; Jamie for backing out and avoiding a potentially uncomfortable situation or himself for being a little bit excited about the trip and seeing Jill.

The ride to Billings was deafeningly quiet, each traveler lost in their own thoughts. But once parked and heading into the hospital, John's long strides barely kept up with his mother's frantic pace. He suppressed a grin as his petite mother practically ran to the open gym where they expected to find Ben. John followed her through the gym doors, chastising himself as he scanned the gym looking for a certain blonde therapist and not his brother.

"I don't see him." His mother chewed her bottom lip nervously. He knew her mind had already conjured up at least fifty worst-case scenarios.

"I'm sure he's fine." He squeezed her shoulder. "Let's see if he's in his room."

John fought the dread trying to build in his stomach has he hoped that the worst-case scenario was not playing out.

Sure enough, they found Ben in his room. He was seated in his wheelchair, his few possessions they had brought stacked neatly on the end of the bed. As John looked at his mother's crestfallen impression, rage boiled inside him. He determined at that moment to crush any attraction he might have felt for the conniving Jill Morgan. Just as he was plotting her demise, the object of his rage surged into Ben's room.

Jill stopped abruptly when she saw them, a look of surprise on her face.

"Wow, you all are early today!" She smiled.

The audacity of this woman to grin while their son and brother sat with his bags packed apparently ready to be wheeled out. Did she have no heart at all?

"Were you just going to wheel him to the curb for us to pick up?" John spat bitterly, hands framing his hips.

Jill stepped back at his biting remark, mouth agape.

"No, I was going to have him moved into his new room before you got here." She gathered herself up as tall as she could and met the cowboy's angry eyes.

"He's staying?" Pattie interrupted the exchange excitedly.

Jill held John's gaze for a moment before she turned to face Pattie. "Yes, Ms. Mitchell, he is definitely staying! He's made some real improvement this week with his head control."

Jill continued to explain to an increasingly excited Pattie about Ben's improvements for the week. John halfway listened. Nothing seemed too earth-shattering to him, but apparently it was enough to buy Ben a few more weeks in the program. Mentally John berated himself for immediately assuming the worst. He hated the look of hurt he had caused on Jill's face. He stepped aside as several nurses and assistants entered the room.

"Looks like it's time to move, Ben." Jill patted Ben's shoulder as she talked to him. John watched from the edge of the scene, not taking part as nurses and staff began moving Ben's personal belongings out the door. In a matter of moments he found himself alone with Jill.

"It seems that every time I'm around you I end up apologizing for something." He smiled, trying to sound light.

Jill jumped at the voice behind her, unaware that she was not alone in the room. She turned to look at John. He held his hat in his hands, turning it over nervously, looking down. He glanced up at her sheepishly.

"Well, maybe if you weren't so quick to think the worst of me, Mr. Mitchell." She turned to gather Ben's final personal effects and had every intention of brushing past John without another look.

He stepped in front of her to block her exit. It was instinct more than anything else; he didn't want her to leave the room, much less leave while mad at him. He was as shocked by the move as the look on her face said she was.

He searched her eyes for a moment before saying softly, "I'm sorry."

Jill nodded; the emotion in his voice had caught her off guard.

"I truly am," he continued. He shuffled his weight from one leg to the other and glanced at the ceiling. "My family has been through hell. I guess I think I have to protect them from anything else bad happening to them."

Jill wanted to remain angry. She wanted to be able to come back with a really witty retort, but the emotion in his voice and the pain in his eyes were more than she could handle. She quickly felt her anger subside and replied gently, "I understand the emotions that a family goes through when something like this happens to them. But I'm not the enemy and I'm not trying to hurt your family. I truly want to help Ben."

He met her steady gaze and suddenly he wanted to tell her everything; wanted to unload every burden he had carried for the past four years at her feet and let her comfort him. He quickly reined his emotions in and replied, "I promise not to jump to conclusions again or to be rude to you."

"Well, based on your track record, we shall see about that." She laughed, hoping to lighten the mood. "Honestly, it's nice to see a family stick together in a crisis. So many fall apart when something like this happens."

John nodded and in his mind he fought an unexplainable urge to tell her how close his family was to imploding.

"Well, I better get Ben to the gym. We have a lot of work to do." She brushed past him, and he watched her glide to the door. She abruptly stopped and turned to face him, cocking her head to the side. "He's doing really well. You should be proud of him."

He wasn't sure how long he stood in that room, staring at the door she had left through. He finally made himself walk to the gym. His mother was there, never far from Ben's side. He went in and watched Ben's therapy. If he were honest, he didn't see improvements, but his mother was happier than he had seen her in a long time, and if these unseen improvements bought Ben more time and his mother more happiness, then he would take them.

He made a few phone calls to set up an appointment to look at some livestock just outside of Billings he was thinking of purchasing. He walked around the hospital and sometime that afternoon he found himself in his truck driving past his old town house. He sat in front of the place he had once called home and studied the front door. If he were honest he would admit that this place had never felt like home. It was a diversion for a while, but it had never been a place where he envisioned raising a family and growing old.

He let out a bitter laugh. Thinking about a family and growing old hadn't been something he had let himself think about for a long time. He let his mind wander, a luxury he usually did not afford himself. He conjured up a long-ago dream of having a family, raising them on the ranch; little boys in cowboy hats following his every move; little girls in pigtails that he twirled high above his head and made them squeal; and someday building a big sprawling house on the hill that overlooked the valley that had held his family's ranch for years. A blaring horn from a car zipping past him jerked him back to reality. With one glance at his old home, he pulled out onto the street and headed back toward the hospital. He grumbled at himself for wasting time daydreaming.

It was later than he intended when he returned to the hospital. A nurse in the gym informed him that his mother had taken a shuttle over to the hotel a half hour ago. His phone buzzed in his back pocket.

Terrible headache. Lying down.

As he closed the text from his mother his stomach rumbled. In all of his daydreaming and life pondering today he had forgotten to eat lunch. The thought of sitting alone in a crowded restaurant was more than he wanted to deal with. He followed the hallway signs to the hospital cafeteria. He would pick up a sandwich, maybe grab his mom one too.

He had eaten more meals than he cared to remember in a hospital cafeteria. This one was no different from the many others he had been in. Tired faces sat huddled over coffee cups, blankly staring out windows or into a family member's eyes trying to find some shred of hope. John tried to ignore the people sitting like that. It reminded him of his own family and their own hurt. They had searched each other for hope and found none. Trying not to make eye contact or study any one person for too long almost caused him to miss the flash of a blonde ponytail across the food court from him. He quickly grabbed a sandwich and made his way over to the cash register just in time to slide in line behind her. When she tried to hand the cashier a bill to pay for her dinner, he quickly reached out and touched her arm, handing the cashier enough money to pay for both of their meals.

"The least you can do is let me pay for your dinner after the way I acted today." He grinned as she turned a surprised expression on him.

"It's fine, you don't have to do that." She shook her head. He nodded to the cashier to take his extended bill. Jill picked up her salad and waited for him to receive his change.

"Thank you. You didn't have to do that," she said with a smile.

"It's nothing. Consider it a peace offering. I've acted pretty rude toward you since the first time we spoke on the phone. A salad is the very least I can do." He nodded toward the plate in her hands.

"John, I've dealt with lots of patients and their families. You aren't the first family member to be"—she paused as if searching for the best word and then emphasized her next word—"overprotective of their family member. I'm used to it. Please don't waste another minute thinking about it."

He shifted from one foot to the other and cocked one eyebrow. "Other people may have treated you that way, but that is no excuse for me doing it. I'm usually not such a jerk. I promise."

"I'll take your word on that," she tossed over her shoulder as she turned to exit the cafeteria.

John stood watching her leave and couldn't quite explain the feeling of loneliness that seemed to seep into his bones. He glanced around the cafeteria and decided to take this food to the bench he had spotted outside the hospital. He had hoped to find the courtyard deserted, but much to his chagrin, he found several people occupying various benches scattered throughout. In the corner of the yard an old oak tree twisted its way over the courtyard wall. In long strides, John covered the distance to the tree and sat under its massive shade. He bit into his sandwich without tasting it and thought about the day. He leaned his head against the tree trunk and began to wonder if his life would ever resemble anything close to normal again. When he had lived in Billings he had never had a shortage of women to date or friends to hang out with. Now he had neither and after today, he wondered if he even knew how to relate to people anymore. He replayed his conversation with Jill Morgan and once again decided to double down on his efforts to make amends with her.

His thoughts were interrupted when a foam football landed at his foot. He glanced up to see a dark-headed boy looking at him shyly. John glanced from the boy to the football before picking it up and extending it to him. The boy quickly grabbed the ball and headed back to a nearby picnic table. John noticed what appeared to be a younger boy waiting for his return. John watched them play with the ball for several minutes, before the ball inevitably landed near his tree once again. He picked the ball up and watched as both boys approached him. He could see a young couple, whom he assumed were their parents, sitting at the nearby picnic table. John had spent too many days in hospital waiting rooms not to recognize the look of fear and desperation on their faces. He glanced at the two young boys that approached. He guessed that the oldest might be eight years old. He thought briefly of his own brothers and his heart broke for this family, whatever their reason for being at the hospital.

He handed the ball back to the oldest boy, who immediately gripped it to throw to his younger brother.

"Hey, wait a minute, kid." John reached his hand out to stop the throw. "Anybody ever teach you how to throw a spiral?"

The boy silently shook his head no.

"Well, I just happen to know how....I could show you," John offered.

The young boy looked from John to his parents. John followed his gaze and found the parents studying him. He must have met with their approval, as they nodded for the young boy to give him the football.

The young boy handed him the football. He showed the boy how to throw, giving him encouragement and showing him adjustments when needed. After several minutes the younger boy came forward and John began showing him how to throw as well. It didn't take long before John was out from under his tree and jogging across the courtyard to catch the wobbly balls being tossed by the two boys. The parents watched and smiled gratefully at him. After almost an hour of constant ball tossing, the kids dropped to the ground beside their parents' spots at the picnic table. John remembered a vending machine he had passed on his way to the courtyard. He ventured inside and deposited enough money in the machine to purchase enough ice cream sandwiches for the entire family. He returned to the courtyard and sat down beside the boys. He passed each of them an ice cream sandwich, while eyeing their parents to make sure his gift was acceptable. Then he and his football protégés sat on the ground eating ice cream and discussing their favorite sports team. John couldn't help thinking this might have been the best night he had had in a long time. Maybe he could still relate to people after all.

****

Jill let the shade to her office window drop and glanced at the clock on her computer. She had just spent the last hour watching John Mitchell play backyard football with two boys in the courtyard. Maybe she wouldn't just have to take his word on not being a jerk after all.

Chapter 10 Revelation

*"He reveals mysteries from the darkness and
brings the deep darkness into light." Job 12:22*

Jill was back at work early the next morning. She began working with Ben as
soon as a therapist brought him into the gym. She couldn't help but recall
the football game she had witnessed. She studied Ben and wondered if
similar games had taken place between Ben and his brothers. She worked with him
for about an hour before she decided to give him a break and head down to the
cafeteria for some coffee. As she passed a small alcove, she stopped short at the
sight of John Mitchell sitting slouched in one of the two vinyl-covered chairs, a
ball cap pulled over his eyes. She glanced around to make sure no one was around
before she studied him. Long legs encased in blue jeans stretched for what seemed
like miles; narrow hips and a flat stomach gave way to broad shoulders and strong
arms. A fleeting thought of how nice those strong arms would feel around her
flitted through her head. There was no doubt that John Mitchell was an attractive
man, but he was also the brother of her patient and she would do well to remember
that, she reminded herself. As she started to leave, he stirred and tipped his hat
back on his head, just in time to catch her staring at him.

"Good morning, Mr. Mitchell." She stepped toward him, deciding the worst thing she could do now would be to run.

"Uh, good morning." He seemed embarrassed that she had caught him sleeping.

"You're up early this morning." She took a step into the alcove, biting her tongue not to mention the football game she had witnessed last night.

"Couldn't sleep….I can't get used to all this blowing air…being inside…I, well our family, runs a cattle ranch. I spend most of my days outdoors, or at least in a barn." He grinned and she silently chided herself for the way her stomach flip-flopped at the sight.

"A cattle ranch? That's interesting. Is it up in Brisbane? That's where we first saw Ben, right?" She knew exactly when she had first laid eyes on Ben and had every minute of every encounter since then memorized.

"No, we are about three hours west of Brisbane." He nodded.

She mentally calculated what a long distance they had traveled to visit Ben this weekend.

"That's quite a distance away," she ventured.

"Yep, quite a distance."

"Well, I'm headed to the cafeteria for some coffee, can I get you something, Mr. Mitchell?" She turned to leave the alcove.

"No thank you. I'm fine." He rubbed the side of his jaw and she could see something in his face; fatigue or worry, she wasn't sure.

Help him.

The thought flitted through her mind and shook her to her core. She abruptly walked to the elevator and pushed the down button over and over in hopes of making the machine move quicker. She tried to reason herself out of the thought, but a nagging feeling kept telling her to help John Mitchell.

"Lord, I thought I was supposed to help Ben," she whispered as she glanced at the ceiling of the elevator car as if she would see God there.

"Rejoice in hope, be patient in tribulation, be constant in prayer." The verse from her office picture frame came to mind. John Mitchell appeared to be carrying the weight of the world on his shoulders. Jill chewed her bottom lip trying to decide what to do. She quickly grabbed her cell phone out of her pocket and texted Sam, her most trusted therapist, a list of exercises to put Ben through. A cup of coffee might not fix all of John's problems, but it might be a start.

She returned to the alcove with two steaming cups of coffee in her hands, praying he would still be there. As she rounded the corner she saw him, still in the same chair, leaning forward, forearms resting on his knees, staring out into space.

"I know you said you didn't need any, but you looked like you could really use a cup." She extended a cup to him.

"You read my mind. I sure could; thank you." He grinned and her stomach did that funny flip-flop again.

"Straight black? No creamer, right? You struck me as a black coffee, no creamer kind of guy," she said as she took the seat beside him.

"Wow, I didn't realize I was so easy to read…that's exactly right." He removed the plastic lid and took a gulp of the steaming liquid. He turned to her and winked. "Perfect, thank you."

She grinned and looked down so he wouldn't detect the heat rising on her face. Inwardly she chastised herself for the giddy feeling she had experienced when he winked.

"So where's your mom?" she asked, trying to regain her composure.

"Sleeping," he replied, holding the coffee cup between two large, work-hardened hands. "She doesn't get a chance to sleep in much at home, so I figured I'd let her sleep."

"She's very dedicated to Ben." Jill sipped her steaming coffee, its heat burning her mouth.

"That she is." John paused before he continued. "It's been a hard four years for her." He paused for a few more moments before he added, "My dad died about a year after Ben's accident."

"Oh, I'm so sorry." Without thinking she reached out and laid her hand on his forearm. He glanced down at her hand and then back up to her face, holding her gaze for a brief moment.

She removed her hand, wrapping it around her coffee cup. She couldn't help but think the heat from the cup paled in comparison to the warmth radiating from his skin. She stared into the cup and said softly, "That's a lot for a family to endure."

He straightened in his chair. "Well, it was the hand we were dealt; we had to play it."

She turned in her chair to face him. "I've seen a lot of families that fall apart when something like this happens to them. That fact that your family has stuck together, well, that's a blessing."

"A blessing?" He snapped his head up and furrowed his brow.

"Well, yes." His reaction caught her off guard and she tried to formulate her thought. "That you still have each other and are still together, even after everything that has happened. Lots of families would have fallen apart. It's a blessing that you still have your family intact."

He studied her for a long moment before he looked away and said softly, "We'll just have to agree to disagree on the definition of a 'blessing.'"

"What I mean is your family is probably closer, you've been through things together that have brought you closer. Many families would have fallen apart, would have crumbled." She felt as if she were sinking quickly so she threw out the first verse that came to mind: "All things work together for the good of those who love Him."

"Romans 8:28," John replied and Jill couldn't help but be shocked. She hadn't expected him to know the verse. "That's a good one, but I think Man who is born of a woman is few of days and full of trouble is a more fitting quote for our lives." He quoted his own verse and turned to study her expression. "That's from Job."

"Umm, yeah." She gulped her coffee, burning her mouth, totally taken off guard by his response.

"You're surprised I can quote the Bible?" he asked without looking at her, making more of a statement than asking a question.

"N-No…" she stammered and quickly gulped coffee.

"It's fine. I can see where you might be surprised. I've not exactly acted very Christian as far as you are concerned."

"Jill!" Sam stuck his head around the corner. She had never felt so relieved. "Dr. Bryan is on the phone for you."

She glanced at John and caught him studying her. "Thanks for the coffee," he said.

"No problem," she mumbled as she hurried into the gym and away from the man who surprised her at every turn.

For the remainder of the day, she couldn't get John Mitchell out of her mind. She had thought God had been leading her to help Ben—but maybe John too. After the final patients had been returned to their room for the evening, Jill slipped into the courtyard of the hospital. It was calm tonight, but in her mind's eye she could replay the football game that had taken place there the night before. John Mitchell was causing her confusion. She hated the way her stomach flipped when he smiled at her and she hated even more the way that she looked for him when she knew he was around the hospital. He had been nothing less than rude to her so why were her emotions betraying her? She had thought God had sent both brothers into her life for a reason.

She sat down on a bench and leaned her head back, gazing into the evening sky. "God, he knows you. He can quote your words. He doesn't need me. Show me how to help Ben."

Again she thought of the verse from Isaiah…My thoughts are not your thoughts…

She slipped her phone from her pocket and opened the Bible app, tapping icons until she reached Isaiah. She wasn't sure how long she had been sitting on the bench when she heard someone clearing their throat behind her. She jumped and turned to see John Mitchell standing there.

"Sorry." He scuffed his boot on the ground. "I didn't want to scare you, but you seemed pretty involved with your phone there."

"It's fine. I was reading." She scooted over and gestured for him to take a seat.

"Ben do well today?' he asked as he sat down beside her.

"Yes, he did." She smiled at him, hoping the awkwardness from this morning would be gone.

"Just for the record, I don't know why you are doing this, but if it helps Ben at all…thank you."

She bit her lower lip. Should she tell him? Should she tell him she had been told by God to help his brother? He obviously was a believer. Wouldn't he understand? Before she could answer, her stomach rumbled loudly, reminding her that she hadn't eaten since breakfast that morning.

She could feel the heat rising on her cheeks. "Sorry, I forgot to eat lunch," she mumbled.

"Too busy?" He raised his eyebrows.

"I guess. Your brother kept me pretty busy today."

"I was going to the cafeteria, why don't you join me?"

"You sure you want to have dinner with me? It wasn't so long ago you thought I was heartless and selfish." She smiled to try and soften her comment, but couldn't resist giving his words back to him.

"Well, I owe you for the coffee, plus I've not completely forgiven myself for being rude to you. I guess I'm trying to buy my forgiveness."

She cocked her head to the side and grinned. "Lucky for you, I'm easily bought by free food, especially if you throw in dessert."

He returned her grin. It felt as though it had been ages since he flirted with an attractive woman and the exchange felt good; it made him feel alive. "I could throw in some ice cream."

"Tempting…," She screamed at herself internally for flirting with him. As much as the tall, taciturn cowboy intrigued her, it hadn't been that long ago that he had accused her of horrible things and been extremely rude to her.

"Come on, let me do buy you dinner so I can ease my guilty conscience." He raised an eyebrow skeptically.

She nodded and answered before she could think about it further. "Sure."

"Well, by all means, lead the way." He gestured to the door behind them.

They walked to the cafeteria together making small talk about nothing of great importance. Jill couldn't help but think how nice it was just to talk to someone about nothing in particular. She felt stress leave her body. She made her selections and followed him to the cash register. When they had their food he nodded for her to lead the way.

She led them to a table tucked away in the corner of the cafeteria, away from the main walkway. Without thinking, he reached out and pulled her chair out for her, falling back on his manners lessons from his mother. He took the seat across from her.

Her tender conscience won out as she thought of their banter in the courtyard and she leaned forward slightly. "You know, you've really not been that bad. I've heard a lot worse from patients and families before."

"Well, that may be, but my mother reminded me that I had been raised better than to talk to a lady like that." He took a drink from his soda.

"I can see her doing that. She's a very special woman, John." She laughed. She thought for a moment before she continued, "Ben's illness has been hard on her."

John relaxed in his chair. "Yeah, it really has. He's the baby of the family and truth be told probably her favorite." He winked.

"I can see that." Jill tried to conceal her grin. "Does it bother you that you aren't the favorite?"

"Well, Ben's more outgoing than me." He winked and laughed and thought how good it felt to feel the rumble of laughter rolling through his chest.

"So Ben's the youngest…and you have one other brother?" she questioned as she stirred the lettuce around on her plate.

"Yeah." He hated the bitterness that crept into his voice. "Jamie… he's between me and Ben."

Jill could see the tension mount in John's shoulders at the mention of Jamie and she quickly tried to change the subject. "So tell me what Ben was like before the accident."

John let out a pent-up breath, relieved that she hadn't asked him to talk about Jamie. He relaxed and let his mind wander back four years. He hadn't allowed himself to do that in a long time.

"He was athletic."

She nodded. "Yes, I remember you told me he played football."

He rested his elbow on the table and swiped his hand down his jaw, trying to absorb all the memories. "He was—well, he's eight years younger than me. There are six years between him and Jamie, so he was the baby." John chuckled. "He was a momma's boy. Man, we used to terrorize him. When he was little we would put him up in the hayloft and take the ladder so he couldn't get down. We would leave him up there until Momma found him. She would be ready to kill us by the time she got him down and stopped his crying."

She nodded and it was all the encouragement he needed to continue. "But he got a little older, and a little bigger, and learned how to fight back. When it got to the point that I wasn't one hundred percent certain I would win those scuffles, I quit trying to fight him. We use to catch each other off of our mounts during a round up and take off with each other's horses. I've had to walk some pretty long distances to make it home, just to find Ben and Jamie waiting on me so they could laugh at me."

"Oh wow, that's kind of mean!" She laughed.

"He was a good kid…stubborn, good lord he was the most stubborn person I ever met…a good athlete, but I already told you that…he would come stay with me some on the weekends when I lived here." Memories he hadn't allowed to surface for a long time came flooding back.

Jill stopped her fork in midair. "You lived here? In Billings?"

"Yes." He grinned. "I lived here in Billings." He mocked her incredulous tone.

"Really? When?" She set her fork down and leaned back, crossing her arms.

"Before Ben's accident," he replied.

Her expression told him she wanted him to elaborate.

"I got a job and moved here after college." He shrugged his shoulders, a little uncomfortable that he was now the subject of the conversation.

"I'm sorry, you just don't strike me as a city boy." She giggled.

"Believe it. I was." He leaned back in his chair, resting one palm on his thigh and the other on the table, and Jill briefly thought he probably could have been a model.

"What made you leave?" Her question wasn't meant to unnerve him, but it did.

77

He rubbed his palms down his thighs and exhaled heavily. "Ben's accident. My dad died of cancer eight months after that…my family needed me. Someone had to run the ranch. I was the oldest. It was my place."

She clasped her hands together and rested her chin on them, studying him. "That's very admirable."

He glanced away, always uncomfortable when people praised him for taking care of his family; it was the least he could do. "It was what had to be done."

They sat in silence for a few moments and then John decided he had given out way too much personal information without getting any in return.

"What about you?" He rested his forearms on the table and leaned forward.

"What about me?" she replied, feigning ignorance.

"Well, don't take this the wrong way, but occasionally when you talk I pick up a hint of an accent that is not from around here." He flashed his best grin, hoping not to offend her.

She laughed and he was relieved.

"Is it that noticeable?" She grinned and her entire face lit up. John had a fleeting thought that he would do just about anything to see that smile.

"Only about half the time, and when you get angry." he replied.

"Well, it's true I'm not a native. I grew up in Tennessee. That's where I went to school and where my family lives."

"Tennessee?" He leaned back in his chair. "Why that's practically a foreign country. How did you wind up so far away from home in Billings?"

She sipped her water as if formulating her answer before responding. "Dr. Bryan, the head of our department—I did an internship with her. The work she was doing with brain injury patients was just…phenomenal. She was giving hope back to families that had lost so much and I knew that God was leading me to work in that area. I prayed about it, applied for a job, and as they say, the rest is history."

John felt a twinge of guilt when he realized all she had obviously sacrificed to work with brain injury patients here in Montana. All the accusations he had hurled at her filed through his head. He was brought out of his reverie by someone shutting off the lights in the food line.

"Looks like we just shut down the cafeteria." He grinned.

"Another wild and crazy night." she replied, returning his smile. "Your mom mentioned your all were staying a few extra days this time."

"She's excited to spend an extra day with Ben tomorrow. And I've got a meeting bright and early in the morning with a livestock broker. I better turn in, or I'll be so tired I won't be able to negotiate a fair price. " He scooted his chair back from the table, hating to end the evening.

"Yeah, I better head home too," she replied as she stood and collected her tray.

John quickly came around and collected the tray from her and asked tentatively, "Someone at home that will be worried about you?" He prayed his voice sounded as light as he meant for it to.

Jill cocked her head and studied him for a moment. "No, no one at home that will worry about me being late." And then she wasn't sure why but she added, "What about you?"

"Besides my mother?" he teased as he placed her tray on the return carousel.

Jill noticed the way his eyes danced when he was teasing and thought it was probably the most adorable thing she had ever seen. "Yes, besides your mother." She blushed.

"No." he answered softly.

She grinned sweetly at him, struggling to find the words. He seemed to lose control of his himself as he reached up and gently brushed a strand of hair behind her ear. "Maybe we can shut the cafeteria down again?" he questioned softly.

"I'd like that." Her heart soared as he gave her a megawatt smile.

****

Pattie showed up to the hospital early the next morning, a bright smile on her face. Jill immediately began to wonder and worry if Pattie knew about the cafeteria date she and John had enjoyed last night. Not that anything had happened, Jill chastised herself, but to her it had been the best night she had spent in a long time.

79

She couldn't remember the last time she had felt so giddy with excitement. Every time the gym door opened, she jumped in anticipation of a tall, handsome cowboy walking through. All morning she was disappointed when the door opened and John didn't enter.

"I didn't think you were scheduled to work today."

Jill jumped at the voice behind her and turned to face Dr. Bryan.

"Uh… I just thought I'd come in and check on a few patients. Get caught up on some paperwork." Jill didn't make eye contact with the older woman.

"Jill." Dr. Bryan's tone forced Jill to meet her gaze. The older woman studied her thoughtfully. "Don't work too hard," she finally commanded after what felt like an eternity of being under her intense gaze. Jill released a breath she wasn't even aware of holding. She briefly wondered what Dr. Bryan would say if she knew about her cafeteria encounter last night, and decided that for now it would be best if her boss didn't know about her feelings for a certain patient's brother. She stopped short in her tracks. Feelings? Yes, if she got real honest with herself she did have feelings for John; if she didn't she would not be here on her day off hoping to catch a moment with him. She silently prayed that God would guide her way through these feelings.

It was late afternoon before the object of her thoughts finally strolled through the gym doors. She tried to act as if she hadn't held her breath every time the door opened today waiting for him.

He had driven outside Billings that morning to make arrangements for the livestock he would be adding to the ranch. It had taken much longer than he had intended. When he got back to the city, he had stopped by the hotel for a shower and headed straight for the hospital. He wanted to a make a bee line for her when his gaze landed on her on the opposite side of the gym. He glanced around the gym, trying to find Ben and his mother. Not spotting them, he didn't feel the least bit guilty about approaching her first.

As he walked toward her, she glanced in his direction and their eyes held. "Hey," he said softly.

"Hey, yourself," she replied with a grin. She turned to the therapist she had been working with and gave him instructions on finishing the patient's session.

Gathering paperwork, she turned to John and gifted him with a dazzling smile. His heart soared at the sight.

"I think your mom and Ben are in the courtyard if you would like to see them." She gestured toward the door.

"Sure," he replied, thinking that he would follow her just about anywhere.

After a quick stroll through the courtyard with no sign of his mother or Ben, he sat down on a park bench and motioned for her to join him.

"Let's enjoy this sunshine." He gazed up at the trees above them and added, "I can't get used to being indoors all day long."

She realized then how little she knew about his daily life and how curious she was.

"So tell me what it's like, a typical day on your ranch." She took the seat beside him, tucking her leg underneath her so she was facing his profile.

He leaned back and turned to her. "You don't want to hear about that."

She gently pushed his bicep. "Yes, I do. You know all about my job."

He studied her for a moment and then glanced across the courtyard. "Well…it's a lot of early mornings…lot of late nights…really it's twenty-four/seven/three-sixty-five. When you have that many animals and people depending on you…well, there isn't a lot of downtime. We spend the summers getting ready for winter and the winters trying to keep everything alive. And then there are trips like this one, where I need to purchase new livestock, but I also need to be at the ranch."

"Sounds like a lot for one person to handle," she ventured.

He leaned forward, resting his elbows on his knees, dangling his hands between his legs. "Yeah, I guess it is…"

"But you love it," she supplied after a pause.

He looked over his shoulder and found her eyes. "Yeah, I guess I do." The crooked grin he gave her did funny things to her stomach. He looked deep into her eyes and wanted to tell her how lonely a life it was. He wanted to tell her about the burden he felt to provide for his family. For the first time since Ben's accident, he wanted to tell someone everything, he wanted to tell her about the guilt he carried. He wanted to lay his heart open at her feet and wait for her to pick up the pieces and knit them back together. He stopped short of baring his soul. What would she think of him? If he told her he was responsible for Ben's accident; if he finally shared the burden he carried, would she run inside, a look of horror on her face, never wanting to see him again? He could picture the shock on her face when he told her; the hate and disgust that he felt for himself reflected in her eyes. The thought of her hating him stopped him short. He realized then he couldn't tell her. He wasn't sure what was happening between them, but he wanted to explore as far as it could go, and if he told her the truth she would end whatever this was immediately. He didn't want that. The buzzing of his cell phone in his back pocket brought him out of his thoughts.

He frowned as he looked at the number that popped up on the screen. He hit the talk button and said curtly, "Yeah."

He held the phone away from his ear as the voice from the other end sounded frantic. Jill couldn't help but let doubt creep in when she realized the voice on the phone was a woman. He stood and took several steps away from the bench and spoke in short, abrupt tones. He punched the phone to end the conversation and stood there, staring into the sky. The anxiety rising in her chest couldn't wait any long.

"Everything okay?" she ventured.

He continued to study the sky above them so long that she thought maybe he hadn't heard her or that he had forgotten she was there. Just when she was about to ask again, he responded quietly, "No...no, it's not."

He turned and looked at her. The pure anguish in his eyes made Jill's heart trip. She wanted to reach out to him, to comfort him, but something kept her seated on the bench.

Lord, please guide me, Jill silently prayed while she waited what seemed an eternity for him to speak.

He sat down heavily on the bench and released a pent-up breath. He looked at Jill, searching her face. She returned his look and hoped that he could feel compassion through her gaze. She hoped her invitation to unburden was understood even if it wasn't spoken.

"That was my sister-in-law, Amber." He rolled his shoulders trying to relieve the tension.

"Jamie's wife?" she offered, hoping he would feel comfortable enough to continue with the conversation.

"Yeah," he answered, and she was shocked by the bitterness in his voice, "Jamie's wife."

She wasn't sure what possessed her but she reached over and laid her hand on his shoulder in an effort to comfort him.

"Everybody handled Ben's accident differently." He glanced at her hoping to see some type of confirmation in her eyes.

"Of course, everyone deals with tragedy differently." She squeezed his shoulder, trying to piece together how a frantic phone call from his sister-in-law would make him think of Ben's accident. "There is no one certain way to deal with something like this happening to your loved one. Every family has to find their own way."

"We've never found our way. If anything we are all just lost." He bit out the words with a bitterness that came from years of hurt. "It was just too much. Ben's accident and then Dad's dying within a year. It was just too much." He gazed off into the distance. Jill knew he wasn't seeing anything but was lost in memories. "Momma dedicated herself to Ben. I quit my job here and moved home and threw myself into making the ranch successful, and Jamie…well…" He swallowed as if trying to dislodge a huge lump in his throat. Jill waited and prayed for God to give him strength. After several moments, he finally spoke with a broken voice. "Well, Jamie started drinking, and to be honest he hasn't stopped since."

Once he had voiced the problem aloud it was like a dam broke in him. He told her everything, from the first time he had found Jamie passed out in the barn to the numerous times he had dragged him back home from a night of drunken debauchery. He told her how Jamie had begun to stay gone days at a time, leaving the family to worry if he were alive or dead. He detailed, in his opinion, the unnecessary anguish and worry Jamie had caused the family. He explained how after one extended bender, he had brought home Amber and introduced her as his wife, adding someone else for his mother to worry about and one other person John was tasked with taking care of.

"And when he stays gone for a couple of days, she calls me in a panic. Wants me to go track him down and drag him back home." He scrubbed his hands over his face and Jill noticed how tired he looked. "And I do it…but lately…" He searched her eyes as if trying to determine if he had said too much to her.

"But lately?" she prodded him to continue.

"Lately I just want to leave him on his butt. I'm tired of trying to fix everything." Jill thought he seemed a little lighter just having put his burden into words. She contemplated her words before she spoke.

"You can't fix Jamie. And you definitely can't fix Jamie and Amber's marriage. Everyone has to grieve in their own way, but when your grief becomes destructive…maybe it's time to seek professional help. This is not something you can handle alone and expect a good outcome for Jamie or for Amber." She gave him a sympathetic grin.

He studied her and a sinking feeling hit her stomach telling her she had said too much. "I'm sorry, I shouldn't have said anything…"

"No…no, I'm glad to hear someone else say what I've been thinking but…Jamie doesn't think he has a problem," and then he added thoughtfully, "He told me…one time he told me that he drinks because he hates himself."

"Did he drink before the accident?" she questioned.

He sat there pondering her question and realized he didn't know the answer. Just another piece of evidence to hold against him in the case of the worst brother ever. He quickly decided he didn't want to confess that he had been too self-absorbed to know what his brother did before the accident. No, he didn't want her thinking he was a horrible brother and son, he wanted her to realize the sacrifices; better yet, the unappreciated sacrifices he had made for his family. It suddenly hit him why Jamie had made excuses about not visiting Ben this weekend. "He told me he couldn't come this weekend because he wanted to spend time with Amber! He had this planned all along!"

"He's trying to self-medicate himself. Trying to dull the pain." She leaned forward, trying to catch his gaze.

John stood suddenly. "We've all got pain! You just deal with it, you don't go off and leave your wife…your family wondering whether you're dead or alive!"

Jill silently prayed that God would give her the words she needed to help him. "And how do you deal with your pain, John?"

He hooked his thumbs in his belt loops and faced her. "What do you mean? I deal with it and I go on. I don't hurt people because of how I feel."

"Don't you?" She tried to keep her voice as gentle as possible. "I've seen you interact with your family. You may not do destructive things like Jamie, but not being emotionally available to your family causes pain too."

He pierced her with a gaze, but no words would come.

"You are closed off," she continued. "Of all the times I've watched you in the gym with Ben, I've never actually seen you try to speak or interact with him."

He stood there staring at her with his mouth open before releasing a bitter laugh. "That's crazy. I'm with my family all the time. I gave up my career for my family. I am not closed off."

"Being around someone and actually *being* with them, interacting with them, allowing them inside your thoughts and feelings—sharing your burdens—are two very different things." She dropped her hands in her lap.

He turned his back to her and pinched the bridge of his nose tightly. He jumped when he felt her lay her hand on his back.

"I'm not trying to make you feel bad, I'm just trying to say that you've chosen a path of grief that has caused some pain too," she spoke softly.

Jamie's voice floated through his head. *"I just wish I hadn't lost both brothers that day."*

"I am by no means justifying Jamie's drinking, but maybe…maybe you can see where he is coming from?" She reached to turn his shoulders toward her, searching his face. "You've both chosen paths that you thought only caused yourself pain, but that in reality have in fact impacted your entire family."

He felt like he had been gut-punched. He turned and leaned against the nearest tree. If he got really honest with himself, he would admit that he had always looked down on Jamie and the way he had dealt with Ben's accident and their dad's subsequent death; had viewed him as weak for not being able to just stuff his emotions down and keep living. But sitting here in this courtyard, he realized he hadn't handled it any better. Maybe he hadn't taken up drowning his sorrows in booze, but he had bottled up all his emotions and feelings and walled himself off

85

from his family and the world. He hadn't become an alcoholic, but he had also caused destruction in his family. He thought about the pain in his mother's eyes. He thought about the relationship he had with his brothers before the accident. Not only had he caused Ben's accident, but he had continued to cause his family more pain and heartache by the way he had dealt with it. He let out a huge sigh.

"Let's get a cup of coffee," she suggested as she came along beside him, realizing that he had an onslaught of emotions he needed to deal with and hoping to be able to help him without overwhelming him. A diversion, such as a cup of coffee, was needed.

"Yeah," he said on a breath. She prayed that she could be what he needed her to be as a friend and, if she were truthful with herself, maybe more than a friend. She wasn't sure what came over her, but suddenly she found herself slipping her arms around him and giving him a gentle squeeze. He latched onto her and held her tightly against his chest. He dropped his head into her neck and breathed deeply. He briefly thought of how good she smelled and then immediately chastised himself for thinking about her when his family should be the only thing occupying his thoughts.

"It's never too late to start over," she whispered. "God is the God of second chances. You get a do-over; a chance to heal your family."

He raised up and searched her eyes. "I don't know how," he whispered.

"You don't have to have all the answers right now, God has them, just ask him." She gently rubbed her hand across his back.

He wanted to tell her he had asked God numerous times to heal his family and God had remained silent, but he stopped short. Something in her eyes just wouldn't let him ruin this moment.

"Let's get that coffee," he suggested.

"Stop by my office first? I need to wrap up a few things," she said as they turned toward the building, and he slowly let his arm drop from her waist, instantly missing her warmth.

He nodded as he slipped his hand away from her and back into his pocket.

Chapter 11 Wounds Revealed

"He heals the brokenhearted and binds up their wounds." Psalms 147:3

John's eyes roamed her office. He sat across from her desk while she filed paperwork and shut down her computer. He took in the pictures on the walls, the flowers on the desk; this was her space, a reflection of her, and he wanted to memorize every detail. His eyes landed on several picture frames on her desk. One of her and an older couple, he assumed her parents; another of two small children, the final a close-up of a very handsome young man, grinning, happiness evident in his eyes. He stared at the picture, remembering that just last night she had said she wasn't involved with anyone. He studied the picture, barely keeping himself from picking it up. The thought of the young man in the picture being a boyfriend brought an ugly knot of jealousy in his stomach. He glanced up to catch her watching him. She reached over and gently picked up the picture and studied it for a few moments.

She extended the picture toward him. "My brother," she explained, her voice thick with emotion.

"Oh." He hated that he sounded so relieved.

"He…um…he was older than me…quite a bit actually…five years." He looked at the picture and handed it back to her with a smile. She studied it again.

"He was my hero," she whispered softly as she touched the picture gently, and he detected a sense of sadness in her voice.

He cleared his throat. "Was?" he asked quietly.

She leaned back in her chair, keeping her eyes on the picture. "He was in a car wreck when he was eighteen." She set the picture back on her desk and met his gaze. "He had a brain injury, very similar to Ben's. He lived about a year, but died after he contracted an infection. My family fell apart… my parents… they couldn't handle it. They blamed each other and, well, they were divorced in less than a year after he died."

"I'm sorry." He leaned forward and took her hand that rested on her desk.

Tears threatened to spill over. "My family fell apart after my brother's accident, that's why I think it's a blessing when families can stick together through the hard times."

He squeezed her hand and cursed himself for not having the right words to comfort her. She brushed the tears away and sat up straighter. "He's why I went into therapy, why I wanted to work with brain injury patients."

All the accusations he had thrown at her came down on him like hot coals. "I'm so sorry." He caressed her hand gently. "Sorry for all the times I accused you of being cold and uncaring."

She willingly placed her free hand on top of his. It felt good to share her hurts with someone and to find solace in their shared heartache. He involuntarily took his other hand and traced the path the tear had taken down her cheek, searching her eyes.

"I'm so sorry," he repeated, feeling completely inadequate.

She placed her hand over his as it cradled her cheek. "It's okay." She smiled weakly. "God brought me through it and He led me here. I think I'm supposed to use that pain to help others. I'm a firm believer in that. He's got a plan, I just have to trust."

John found he had difficulty swallowing. He had no words he could give her; from his viewpoint the situation was bleak. He admired her ability to trust God and envied her hope even after what life had handed her. He didn't know how to tell her that he had let no one get inside his thoughts for the past four years and yet in a few weeks she had barged in and taken his thoughts captive.

Her smile widened. "We have dealt with some really heavy stuff this afternoon, I think that warrants ice cream instead of coffee."

"What about dinner?" he asked impulsively as he pushed aside the voice in his head screaming that he could not stay away from the ranch for another day.

"Sure, the cafeteria has a soft serve ice cream machine." She reached over to shut off the lamp on her desk.

"No...no, I ... mean like let's go out to dinner." He stood and nervously wiped his hands down his pants and then quickly added, "Two nights in the cafeteria is enough for me."

"Oh...out to dinner?" she repeated, her eyes wide.

"Yeah, out to dinner..." He gave her a crooked grin and then suddenly realized that he might be putting her in an awkward position. "Unless the hospital has some rule against going out with a patient's brother?"

"No, no rule." She smiled shyly. "I'd love to go out to dinner with you."

She gave him directions to her apartment and they agreed that he'd pick her up in a few hours. Then he hurried to his hotel room feeling lighter than he had in years. So light in fact, that he refused to worry about how he would explain the extended trip to his family.

Chapter 12 New Beginnings

"Behold, I am doing a new thing; now it springs forth, do you not perceive it?" Isaiah 43:19

"Hey."

Jill tried to hide the smile the text brought to her lips.

"Hey yourself," she replied and placed the phone back on her desk. It had been several weeks since they had first gone out to dinner. Since that time they had slipped away to dinner or a movie every time he came to see Ben. They would text periodically throughout the day while he was at the ranch and she at the hospital, and at night, after the ranch was quiet and she had arrived home from the hospital, they would spend hours on the phone. She was falling hard for the tall, stern cowboy, and while she felt he was too, he had never mentioned his feelings or even tried to kiss her for that matter. She prayed that she would handle the delicate situation with treating his brother with the proper respect and care.

"What are you doing?" The ding of her phone brought her back to reality.

"Working on paperwork. Stuck in my office, you?"

A moment passed before a beautiful panoramic mountain view popped up on her phone with the text *"This is my office today."*

"Jealous," she replied and then added quickly, *"Heading to the gym. Want me to tell Ben hi?"*

It took several minutes before a reply popped up on her screen. *"Have fun. Talk to you tonight."*

Jill chewed her bottom lip. It bothered her how little John interacted with Ben. She had not had the courage to broach the subject with him again since she first mentioned it in the courtyard. There was no doubt he was devoted to his family and an adamant advocate for their well-being, but he was not engaged with Ben at all and from what she could gather, very few positive interactions occurred between him and Jamie either. She was still wrestling with these worries when she found Ben in the gym.

"How's it going, Ben?" She patted him on the back.

He turned to her voice and raised the hand he had more mobility with.

"I swear, Jill," Sam, one of her most trusted therapists, said as he scratched his head, "it's like some days he is trying…trying to talk."

"I know, Sam, I've thought the same things," she replied as she studied Ben's chart. He had made good progress, more head control, more control of his hands, was even able to feed himself somewhat these days. But there were times when she caught glimpses of more, and it made her heart soar to hear Sam vocalize those same glimpses. She knew brain injuries were tricky and no two were alike. While on the brain scans, doctors might be able to determine what areas of the brain were affected and try to predict what life would be like for the patient, in all honesty, no one really knew. Every brain injury was different and it really was a waiting game to see what skills would return and what skills would remain lost forever. She had read of patients being nonverbal for years and then learning to speak. She had also heard of patients—had even worked with a few herself—who were nonverbal but had learned to communicate through sign language. She had been attempting to teach Ben a few basic signs. She had focused on the signs for "food," "home," and "family." At times he had attempted to imitate her, or so she thought, but nothing to indicate that he could initiate the sign based upon his own cognitive processes.

"Lord, did you bring him here just for me to teach him head control?" she questioned silently as she sat in front of Ben.

"For my thoughts are not your thoughts, nor are your ways my ways." The verse from Isaiah rumbled through her mind.

"Okay, Lord." And she began her daily routine with Ben, incorporating as much of the sign language attempts as she could. She talked to him throughout their session and signed when possible.

****

Ben had been at St. Patrick's for about five weeks when he hit what appeared to be a major roadblock in his therapy. Jill hoped that the planned visit from the family this weekend would bring him out of his slump. He showed little interest in any of the normal exercises that he had previously excelled at. Jill still attempted the basic sign language, even after Dr. Bryan had suggested that she didn't feel that was a feasible plan for Ben. Something continued to nag at Jill about Ben and his ability to communicate. When he looked her in the eye, there was something there, or at least she had thought that until this week. This week had brought its doubts. She stood at the table in the middle of the gym studying Ben's file.

"You know," Dr. Bryan's voice behind her caused her to jump, "it may be time to consider that we've done all we can for him."

Jill let out a dejected sigh, refusing to admit that Dr. Bryan might be right. "He's just hit a little bump in the road."

"Jill…" Dr. Bryan's tone caused her to face the woman. "We went out on a limb bringing him here. He's made some good progress, but I cannot continue to fight the board to keep him here. Not to mention his insurance is going to quit paying if there are no real improvements soon."

"His family is coming in this weekend; maybe that will bring him out of his slump." Jill gathered up her papers and turned to leave.

"Jill, don't let your personal feelings for this family cloud your professional opinions." Dr. Bryan's warning rattled Jill.

"What are you saying?" She turned, her eyes narrowed.

"What I'm saying is that I know you are emotionally involved with this family. Look, I personally think it's great that you've found someone, but Jill, come on, a patient's brother?" Dr. Bryan stepped closer to her. "I've kept this very quiet because I didn't want there to be any implication of impropriety, but you've got to make sure, I mean really sure, that you aren't seeing something in Ben that just isn't there just to please his family," and then she added, "in particular his brother."

Jill stood facing the doctor, her mouth agape. "I can assure you," she began when she finally found her voice, "that I can keep my professional and personal lives completely separate."

Dr. Bryan studied her for a few moments before saying softly, "You be sure that you do."

Jill stood as if glued to the floor, watching the doctor exit the gym. She glanced over at Ben, seated in his chair working with Sam. She thought about Dr. Bryan's words. Was she seeing something in Ben that just wasn't there? And was she doing it so that she could continue to see John on a regular basis?

"No," she said out loud and shook her head. There was something about Ben, Sam had even said it the other day. She took long strides over to Sam and watched a moment of his interaction with Ben.

"Hey, Ben," Sam spoke with a teasing tone, "you better pick up the pace, the boss lady is here."

"How's it going this morning?" Jill hoped that Sam would tell her of a breakthrough.

"I don't know, Jill. Something is just not right...." Sam stopped the manipulation of Ben's hand and studied his patient.

"What do you mean, Sam?" Jill pulled up a stool beside him.

"I don't know...I can't quite put my finger on it. He just stares out the window. It's like...it's like he's sad, you know? But hey, if I'd been in a hospital for five weeks, I'd be sad too." Sam sighed and turned to her. "Do you mind working with him for a while? I've got to take a new patient for an eval."

Jill's mind was running at warp speed, snippets of Sam's comments ricocheting in her head.

"Jill?" Sam studied her. "Did you hear me?"

"What... oh yeah, sure, I'll work with him." She scooted her stool in front of Ben.

She turned her head to follow Ben's gaze. It was fixed on the windows leading outside. In the distance you could see the mountain range. The mountain range that contained the ranch Ben had called home his entire life. Jill considered Sam's words. Five weeks was a long time to be in the hospital. Anyone who had been in the hospital for five weeks straight would have one desire—to go home. She turned Ben's chair so that he couldn't see the windows, but would be forced to look at her.

"Ben," Jill began, "are you homesick? Do you want to go home?"

He looked at her as if he could see straight through her. She sat and studied him for a moment. Suddenly she remembered the picture John had sent her of the beautiful mountain view the other day. She pulled her phone out and quickly scrolled through messages to find the picture.

"I bet your ranch is beautiful, isn't it? Look, John sent me this picture of your ranch the other day." She placed the phone with the picture filling the screen in his line of sight.

She watched as his eyes settled and focused on the screen, studying it for several long moments. She watched his face for some sign of recognition. Moments ticked by and his face stayed emotionless. Slowly he raised his arm, resting his forearm on his chest. He ever so slowly raised his hand until his fingertips touched the side of his mouth, his hand slowly moved upward and suddenly fell to his shoulder. Jill sat, unable to move. Her mind raced, her heart beating loudly in her ears. It had been somewhat uncontrolled, but Ben had just given her the sign for "home." Her mind reeled. He had initiated the sign, it had not been him just copying her movements. She glanced around the gym to see if anyone else had witnessed the breakthrough, only to find everyone busy with their own patients.

She watched Ben's eyes drift from the screen; she quickly hit the home button to bring the picture back up. She placed it in his line of sight again. But this time, there was nothing, no response from him. She tried several more times to get him to notice the picture, but he just looked into the distance.

"*Stubborn….most stubborn person I ever met…*" John's description of Ben floated through her mind.

"Stubborn, huh?" She studied Ben. "Well, guess what? I'm stubborn too." She scooted the stool close to Ben and began his regimen of exercises, more determined than ever.

****

"Homesick?" John frowned as he sat down in his office. "You think he's homesick?"

"Well, wouldn't you be? Five weeks away from home is a long time," Jill countered. She had hatched the idea after working with Ben for several hours. She hadn't told anyone about his use of sign language. She thought it best to keep that to herself until he had a greater hold on the communication tool. But after wracking her brain trying to determine how to break through to him, she decided maybe a trip home was the answer. She had called John and suggested that instead of the family coming to Billings to see Ben, Ben would come to the ranch for the weekend.

John struggled to accept that Ben was homesick. Could Ben even feel such an emotion? John seriously doubted it, but Jill seemed adamant and he knew she had Ben's best interests in mind. John mentally scolded himself for being more than a little disappointed that he wouldn't be able to spend the weekend with Jill if Ben came home.

"What do you think?" Jill asked.

"Well... you're the professional, if you think he needs to come home then I guess he should come home." Then he added, "You might not get Mom to let him go back once she has him here." He tried to hide the truth of his comment with a chuckle.

"Great! I'll get the paperwork started."

"How long will he be home?" John said, glancing up to see Jamie walk through the office door.

"I'm thinking three or four days."

John's mind raced. He ignored the questioning look on Jamie's face as he stood up and quickly stepped outside his office into the barn hallway. "Three or four days, huh? Can he do without therapy that long?"

"Well..."Jill began.

"I just don't want him to lose any of the ground he's gained," John interrupted and quickly added before he lost his courage, "What if you came with him?"

Jamie snickered behind him and John turned to see his brother had followed him into the hallway. John shot him a glaring look that he hoped would send his brother back to the office. Jamie ignored the look and continued to follow John down the hallway.

"Well...I..." Jill stuttered, a bit shocked at John's invitation.

"We've got plenty of room and you could work with Ben while he's here so he doesn't lose anything." John continued down the hall trying to shake his brother; he could hear Jamie still snickering behind him.

The silence from the other end of the line did nothing to calm John's roiling stomach. "Jill?" he finally said when her silence made him think he had lost the connection.

"Yes, I'm here," she said quickly. "Sure, that sounds great. I've got a few days coming my way, I can't think of a better way to spend them."

After making arrangements for Ben's transportation to the ranch, John ended the call and glanced up into his brother's grinning face.

"Not one word," John growled through gritted teeth as he stalked past a laughing Jamie.

"So you and the therapist, huh?" Jamie said to his back, grinning from ear to ear.

"I don't know what you're talking about," John grumbled, as he tried to shut his office door in Jamie's face.

"Come on, now." Jamie stepped forward, placing both hands on the edge of John's desk. "That was more than just concern over Ben's therapy. Guess Amber won that bet."

John snapped to attention. "What bet?"

Jamie sat casually on the edge of John's desk and picked up a magazine, pretending to be interested. "Oh, just a little bet that we all had over what was going on with you and the pretty little therapist."

John glared at his brother as he nonchalantly continued to peruse the magazine. Jamie finally put the magazine down and looked over his shoulder and met his brother's piercing gaze. "I said you didn't have it in you to make a move on her, Momma said you were too busy with ranch business to have a girlfriend, but

Amber…" He paused for dramatic effect. "Amber says she knew the minute she saw the two of you together that there was something there."

John sat down heavily in his chair and rubbed his palm down his jawline. He looked up at his younger brother and remembered a time when they had spoken openly of relationships. A piercing longing for those days hit his chest.

"We've had dinner together. It's not that big of a deal," he finally said and couldn't explain why he didn't want to be honest with his brother.

Jamie raised an eyebrow and gave his brother a knowing look. They stared at each other for several long moments. John was the one who finally broke the silence.

"It's nothing." Jamie continued to give him an "I know you're lying" look.

"I don't have to explain anything to you, Jamie," John countered, but Jamie's continued knowing look finally got the best of him. "If…IF there was something going on, it wouldn't be any of your business anyway."

"You know how I know you're lying?" Jamie answered his own question before John could speak. "Your jaw twitches, always has, even when we were kids."

They stared at each other until Jamie finally tossed the magazine on the desk and folded his arms. "See, what you forget, big brother, is that I know you, probably better than anybody…except of course Ben." Jamie's eyes narrowed. "Even though you hate it, I know you."

They sat in silence, staring at each other. This time Jamie was the one to break the silence.

"Deny it all you want, but I know the truth—shoot, I'm proud of you, big brother." Jamie got up and headed for the door. He threw over his shoulder as he left, "Nice to know you're still human."

John replayed the conversation in his mind. So his family was betting on his relationship status? He wondered how they all felt about it, if they would be happy for him. He had to admit that it felt good to allow himself to feel something for someone again. He glanced through the small window in his office to the main ranch house. He needed to tell his mother that Ben would be home for the weekend and would bring a guest with him.

97

Chapter 13 Home

"For every house is built by someone, but God is the builder of everything." Hebrews 3:4

J ill unclasped and then clasped her watch again for what must have been the one hundredth time. John reached over and gently grasped her hand to keep it from becoming one hundred and one.

"You okay?" he questioned softly. He had driven down to the hospital to collect Ben and Jill and bring them back to the ranch for the next four days. The further they had gotten away from Billings and the closer to the ranch, the more anxious Jill had become.

"I'm fine." She shook her head and tried to grin. She had known John's family for weeks and had spoken to each member individually at some point in time, but she had been Ben's therapist during those conversations, a role she was very familiar with. After John had told her that his family had been excited when he had told them about the two of them, she suddenly had been put in a role she was unaccustomed to; being someone's love interest was a role she hadn't had in years. She glanced at John's profile. Strong. That was the word that came to mind when she studied him; strong. She knew he carried a burden for his family and he had been through a lot in the past four years. She also knew that his family depended on him for support and for provision. She prayed that his family would see her as a positive addition to John's life and not a distraction.

"They already know you and love you, I don't know why you're worried," he said, never taking his eyes off the curvy mountain road.

"Well, they know me as Ben's therapist; now they see me as someone else," she offered.

"You don't have anything to worry about." He grinned at her and brought her hand to his lips to give it a gentle kiss.

Jill's heart leapt as his lips touched her hand. It was the closest physical contact he had initiated in the young relationship. At least she viewed it as a relationship. She wasn't sure what his thoughts were. He made sure they went out to dinner when he was in Billings and he had made the long trip every weekend. They spoke daily throughout the week, but never did they discuss what it was exactly that they were doing. Whatever it was, it made her happier than she had been in a long time.

The three-hour drive from the hospital to the ranch that the Mitchell family had called home for years was nothing short of breathtaking. In the few years she had lived in Montana, she had not ventured far out of Billings. As she watched the landscape slip by she couldn't help but think what an amazing artist God was to create such beauty. The mountain road they turned onto seemed to stretch up to the sky. They continued to climb up and Jill noticed the lack of houses or any other buildings.

"You really weren't kidding when you said you lived in the middle of nowhere," Jill joked.

John chuckled. "We've been on Mitchell land for a few miles now so that's why you don't see any houses. But yes, our ranch is in the middle of nowhere."

"How big is your ranch?" she asked incredulously.

"A little over twenty-six hundred acres that we own. We also have a couple thousand acres of public land that we graze off in the summertime. Roughly four hundred head of cattle, a hundred head of sheep, and a few cowboys at various time throughout the year." Jill could sense the pride in his voice.

"Sounds like a lot for one person to handle." She studied his profile.

He glanced over at her. "It is…occasionally."

She glanced back at Ben seated in his wheelchair and back to John. "Does Jamie help run the ranch?"

"No, Jamie is not much help." John tried to keep the bitterness out of his voice.

"What about Ben? What did he do before the accident?" She hoped John would open up to her.

"Ben was a kid, still in high school. He didn't do much. Besides, I lived in Billings at that time, so my dad took care of everything, just like his dad before him. It's what we do. "

Jill could tell by the tone in his voice the conversation was over. She settled back in her seat and gazed out the window. Just when she thought they couldn't possibly go any further, the road curved and opened up into a valley. There, nestled in the valley, was the Triple M Ranch headquarters. A beautiful log home sat on a rise underneath ancient trees, looking down on a myriad of barns, pens, and corrals. It looked like a scene out of a movie and the beauty of it took her breath away.

John stopped the van as they took in the view of the ranch. "This view never gets old," he whispered and she wasn't sure if he was talking to her or not. She found herself leaning forward, grasping the window ledge, her eyes roaming over the scene, trying to take it all in. She could picture John working in the barns and corrals, and one glance at his face told her that Billings had never truly been his home. His home was where his heart was and that was nestled deep in the mountains of this ranch. He eased the van forward slowly and came to a stop in front of the ranch house.

She scarcely got the van door open before Pattie was standing before her enveloping her in a hug.

"I'm so glad you came!" Pattie whispered emotionally in her ear. Jill leaned into the hug and wrapped her arms around the older woman. "Me too," she whispered.

The embrace was cut short by a piercing squeal. Jill turned to see John lowering Ben's chair from the van. Ben was waving his hand and squealing loudly as his chair reached the ground.

"I've never heard him do that!" Jill exclaimed as she turned to Pattie.

"Me neither," Pattie said breathlessly.

The three of them stared at Ben in disbelief as he once again let loose a loud squeal.

"I guess you were right," John spoke first, "I guess he was homesick."

Pattie laughed as John began pushing Ben up the ramp to the front porch. As Pattie peppered John with details of the trip, Jill's mind began to race. Never had she heard Ben make such a noise and apparently his family hadn't either. She made a mental note to have a speech therapist evaluate Ben when they returned to the hospital in a few days. She had told no one about Ben's use of sign language. He hadn't made an attempt to use it again, but Jill couldn't shake the feeling that with the right help, Ben's "voice" would come out.

Once Ben was settled in his favorite spot in the front windows looking out over the activity of the barns below, John offered to show Jill to the room she would be staying in. She was in awe of the home and felt confident if left on her own she would be lost in its massive rooms and hallways. John explained that the center of the home had been built over a hundred years ago by a Mitchell ancestor. It had been added onto over the years by various descendants.

"We completely remodeled the downstairs after Ben came home. We had hoped that one day he would be able to move his chair around himself, but..." His voice trailed off as she stopped in front of a door just to the right of the upstairs landing.

Wanting to ease the pain she saw in his eyes, she put her hand on his shoulder and tried to offer what comfort she could. "Your home is beautiful. I know you've done all you can to make Ben's life easier. "

For a moment he lost himself in her eyes. The deep green mesmerized him and the caring tone in her voice soothed a hurt a kept buried so deep in his soul, he never believed anyone could reach it. She was here in his home, a place he hadn't brought a female to since he was a teenager. He could no longer lie to himself or anybody else and say that she wasn't special to him.

The intensity of his gaze made Jill's stomach flip. She briefly thought he was going to kiss her and she couldn't quite name the feeling that sliced through her. Was it fear or excitement, or maybe a little of both? "Is this my room?" She gestured toward the door after a moment of silence, ending the moment.

"Uh... yeah," he mumbled, shaking his head to bring his thoughts back to the present.

He opened the door and deposited her suitcase on the bed. The room was large with a bed centered against the wall. She rubbed her hand down the curved wooden footboard, admiring the gorgeous wood and craftsmanship of the sleigh bed. Her eyes roamed the room, taking it all in with a look of childlike excitement on her face. She said something about the bed and the view from her window, but he barely heard her. Conflicting emotions warred inside John's head and heart. He had always kept his love life separate from his family life. While working in Billings, it had been easy to keep the two areas of his life distinct. Since Ben's accident, he had rarely dated and if he did he kept his dates far away from his family. Having her here, around his family, had poleaxed him. Emotions he didn't want to examine too closely were warring in his heart and mind.

"John, are you okay?" She turned from the window and stepped toward him.

"I'm fine," he quickly replied, determined to push the conflicting emotions back down. "I'm fine…just glad to be home."

"I'm glad to be here too."

Their eyes locked as he unconsciously took a step toward her; emotions swam in her eyes. She bit her lower lip and he suddenly found it hard to catch his breath. Had he ever wanted to kiss someone more than he did right now? He reached out and ran his hand down her arm, catching her hand in his and gently pulling her toward him. When their bodies met, he slipped his other hand around her waist, resting it on the small of her back, and gently pulled her tight against his body. Her arm slipped around his neck. His eyes roamed her face, his body memorized how hers felt flush against his. He had a fleeting thought that God had made their bodies a perfect match for each other. He slowly released her hand and touched her face, tracing the planes of her cheekbone with his index finger. To kiss her would change everything, and he could no longer deny that change was exactly what he wanted. He tilted his head and gently took her chin in his hand; a whisper of space separated their lips.

"Hey, John, lunch is—"Pattie stopped in midsentence as she bounded into the room. John quickly dropped his hands to his side and stepped away from Jill as if he was a teenager caught with his girlfriend.

"I'm sorry!" Pattie covered her mouth.

"I…We…We were just on our way down," John stammered, glancing over to see Jill's face glowing with embarrassment. He reached over and took her hand, trying to reassure her that all was okay.

"I fixed lunch." Pattie began to back out of the door. "Again I'm so sorry."

"Lunch sounds great. Thanks. We'll be right there." John wanted nothing more than for his mother to leave the room.

Pattie turned and retreated downstairs as John turned to face Jill, her face still glowing.

"Well, there's the downside of living with your mother and brothers. Nothing is ever private," John said, trying to lighten the mood.

Jill dropped her face into her hands. "I've been here all of five minutes and your mother walks in on us. I'm so embarrassed. She's going to think I'm horrible."

He pulled her into his arms and she buried her face in his neck. He couldn't help but notice how wonderful she smelled and he didn't even try to resist the urge he had to kiss her hair. He moved his lips to her ear and whispered, "Don't be embarrassed. She's probably downstairs doing her happy dance; you know she thinks you're wonderful." He could feel her smile against his neck and warmth spread through his body. "Let's go eat lunch before she comes back again."

Jill could feel the warmth rising back in her face when she entered the kitchen to see Pattie and Ben already seated at the table. A plate piled with sandwiches had been placed in the center of the table. Jill let her inner therapist take over and she began showing Pattie the utensil that had been designed to help Ben feed himself. They fell into an easy conversation that was centered on Ben. Pride shone on Pattie's face as Ben attempted to guide the utensil to his mouth with some assistance from Jill. John took the seat beside Jill and eased his hand to rest on her knee. Jill couldn't help but notice how at ease John seemed to be at home. He seemed to smile more and laugh easier; that is, until Jamie waltzed through the back door.

"Well, well...looks like I'm right on time," Jamie quipped as he slid into the chair across from Jill. She wondered briefly if she smelled alcohol as Jamie took his seat. She could feel John tense as he slipped his hand from her knee, crossed his arms over his chest, and leaned on the table.

"Hey, Jill, sure is good to have you here. I know John is just tickled to death." Jamie winked at John and Jill could feel the tension mount.

"Did you help Buck get those heifers moved?" John did his best to not grit his teeth. Anger just seemed to be the natural emotion that bubbled to the surface when his brother was around, especially when he could smell the beer on his brother's breath from across the table.

"Nope, Butch seemed to have everything under control." Jamie replied as he reached for a sandwich.

"Dang it, Jamie," John bit out, "I asked you to help him while I was gone! What have you been doing?"

Jamie stopped eating and leveled his gaze at John. "I had stuff to do."

"What did you have to do that is more important than making sure this ranch runs? The ranch that keeps you up?" John threw back, biting his tongue to keep from accusing him of drinking the morning away instead of working.

Jamie stood abruptly, his chair flying backward. Pattie quickly jumped up. "Please, you two stop this. Please." She sounded desperate as she glanced from one brother to the other. "Please, not in front of our guest."

Jamie grabbed a sandwich and his hat. "Don't worry, Momma. I just lost my appetite."

Awkward silence descended on the kitchen as he left. John picked at his plate, unable to finish eating. He finally pushed it away from and stood. "I guess I better

103

get down to the barn and check on things." He placed his hand on Jill's shoulder. "Will you be okay if I leave you here for a little while?"

"Sure," she said, trying to sound cheerful, "I need to put Ben through his paces anyway."

He grabbed his hat and quickly made his way out the back door.

Pattie stared at the door for a few moments before placing her face in her hands. "I don't know why they can't get along. Seems as though they have been at each other's throats since Ben's accident."

Jill reached out and patted her arm. "Everyone deals with grief differently. There is no right or wrong way. And the way Jamie and John have dealt with their grief seems to completely and utterly irritate the other."

Pattie gave a small chuckle. "Oh, if you could have seen them before the accident." Her face brightened as she thought of life back then. "They were best friends… in fact, you should have seen some of things they used to get into. Oh, there were days I didn't know if I would survive raising three boys…now I think I won't survive what I raised them to be." She glanced wistfully at the door as if by some miracle her young boys would come tumbling through the door, laughing and joking with one another like they used to.

Jill's heart broke for the older woman. Ben's accident had caused more problems for the family than just the physical ones Ben dealt with. Wounds ran deep and divided the family when they needed each other the most. A verse from Matthew came to her mind: *"Come to me, all who labor and are heavy laden, and I will give you rest."* The burdens this family carried were overwhelming.

The ringing phone broke the silence. Pattie rose to answer and Jill decided she would do all she could to help bear the burdens of this family.

****

Jill rose early the next morning to a quiet house. She slipped on her housecoat and peeked out the bedroom door into the hallway. The door to John's bedroom was open and she couldn't tell if he had woken up even earlier than her or had never gone to bed at all. The faint scent of coffee wafting up the stairs was the only invitation she needed to head downstairs. A quick glance in the dining room that had been converted to Ben's room told her that her patient was still tucked into his bed. It took a second glance to notice Pattie snuggled up on the twin bed beside Ben. It hit Jill at that moment how hard Pattie's life truly was. She worked tirelessly when Ben was home taking care of his needs and when he was away, what was truly a needed break, couldn't be enjoyed because of how much she missed him.

Jill slipped into the kitchen, fully expecting to find John seated at the table. She was slightly disappointed when the kitchen was completely empty except for the gurgling coffee pot. She quietly opened and closed cabinet doors until she found the one holding coffee mugs; fixing herself a cup, she gazed around the kitchen. She could imagine the Mitchell family here; two parents, three strapping boys, laughing and roughhousing, enjoying everyday life together. Her heart ached for what might have been for the Mitchells.

She picked up her coffee with every intention of heading back to her bedroom and enjoying a few moments of relaxation. The pictures in the hall stopped her. She sipped her coffee as she slowly perused years of memories displayed on the walls. She quickly picked out a younger version of John and what must have been his father, Red. She studied John's face, so young, so carefree, no lines of tension, no frown of stress or disappointment shadowing his face. Pictures of John and his brothers laughing and causally resting arms across each other's shoulders brought a pinch to Jill's heart. This family had lost so much after Ben's accident. They had lost more than just Ben's physical abilities; they had lost camaraderie and joy in each other.

She could relate; her family had lost it all after her brother's accident. Her parents, unable to deal with her brother's death, had divorced and quickly moved on to new lives, leaving Jill feeling abandoned and alone. She didn't spend a lot of time dwelling on the demise of her family, but was confident that it had led to her dedication to her career. She had spent years devoting herself to helping others and had never felt anything missing in her life. But lately something had changed and she felt a desire stirring in her soul for something more. She glanced up at the picture of a young John. She would have guessed him to be in his early twenties in the picture. The years had been good to him, she thought; still handsome as ever. She studied the gleam in his eyes in the picture. He had an arm around each of his brother's shoulders and joy seemed to radiate from them. She had to admit the John she knew was not the same person as she saw in this picture. Most days he seemed to carry the weight of the world on his shoulders, not carefree and joyous like the picture.

She slowly made her way down the hallway, studying photos, until she found herself in the expansive living room. A large stone fireplace took up one side of the room; floor to ceiling windows overlooking the heart of the ranch ran along the other wall. She quietly slipped to the windows to once again admire the beauty of the place the Mitchells called home.

The view was like a postcard. Mountains in the distance, panoramic valleys surrounding the impeccably clean and organized barns and myriad pens that seemed to be the epicenter of the ranching operations. It was still early, the sun barely peeking over the distant hills to bathe the ranch in rays of splendor. As she watched the sun creeping over the hill, she noticed a lone figure on horseback, slowly making its way out of the tree line, descending into the valley that held the ranch. She watched the figure closely as it came into view; her mouth gaped when she realized it was John. She glanced at the clock she had noticed on the wooden mantel above the fireplace. *Six thirty*. She watched him disappear into the largest of the four barns and waited for him to reappear.

"If you're waiting for him to come back to the house, he won't."

Jill jumped and let out a startled gasp as she turned to see Pattie standing behind her. She had been so engrossed in watching John, she hadn't heard Pattie enter the living room.

"Pattie, you scared the life out of me!" Jill bent to wipe the coffee she had spilled onto the window frame.

Pattie walked over to gaze out the windows. "He's been up for hours by now. Same thing every morning since he took over after Red died. He rides up into those hills every single morning. I gave up asking him what he was doing up there a long time ago."

Jill studied Pattie for a moment and followed her gaze to the barn below. "Maybe that's his quiet time; when he prays…talks to God."

Pattie cut her eyes to Jill and then back to the scene below. "I use to think that too… Seems to me if you spend that much time communing with the Lord, you wouldn't be so angry all the time." She turned from the window and continued as she sat down on the leather couch, "I worry about all my boys, as a parent that's just part of the territory. I worry about Ben's health, I worry about Jamie's drinking and his marriage, and John… well, with the other two I know exactly what to pray for. John, well, I don't know what eats at him so, but I know something does and as a mother, it kills me to see him so burdened and not a thing I can do about it. "

"What do you think it is?" Jill took the seat across from her.

Pattie rested her chin in her hand and stared out the window. "I'm not sure …something haunts him, or maybe it's just the responsibility of the ranch and all of us" She turned to Jill and smiled softly. "And I don't know how to help him…not that he would let me help him."

Jill moved to sit on the coffee table in front of Pattie. "I know he feels responsible for this family; for every person that works on this ranch."

"I know that." Pattie reached out and took Jill's hand. "He's been through so much, but he doesn't ever let any emotions show. Ben's accident and then Red passing, it was a lot for one family to have to endure in such a short amount of time. Jamie started drinking. He thinks he hides it from me, but I know the truth; and as bad as that is, at least I know what it is and can try and help him. I can't help John when we won't even open up to anyone."

Jill's heart broke for the older lady; too much grief and heartache for one person.

"I lost more than just Ben to that accident. In a way I lost all three of them." Pattie dabbed at the tears that spilled over. Emotions welled in Jill's throat, and any words of comfort that she might have been able to string together died in her chest. Unable to resist, she threw her arms around the older woman and pulled her into an embrace. She wracked her mind trying to come up with comforting words, but everything that flitted through her mind sounded empty and trite.

"Everything okay?" At the sound of Jamie's voice Jill sat back and snapped her head to attention. Pattie quickly wiped her eyes and plastered a smile on her face.

"Yep." Pattie rounded the corner of the couch. "Just so glad to have everybody home. You hungry? Want me to whip up some breakfast?"

Jill noted how quickly Pattie could bury her emotions and put on a brave face. As Pattie took Jamie's arm and directed him to the kitchen, Jill climbed the stairs to change clothes and prepare to begin Ben's therapy.

She had been working with Ben on his hand control when she decided to try sign language again. Ben had been completely unresponsive to sign language since the one day in the hospital gym. Jill had started to wonder if she had imagined the entire event. He seemed responsive to therapy today and eager to work. She sat in the chair across from him and studied his face.

"Are you at home, Ben?" She signed the word "home" as she talked to him. "Do you like being home?"

Ben's eyes met hers before he shifted his head to gaze out the picture window overlooking the ranch. Slowly he moved his hand to his mouth. Jill held her breath waiting for him to continue. His hand fell to his lap. Jill stood up and moved into Ben's line of sight.

"What is this place?" She pointed out the window. "What is this place, this house, to you?"

107

He gazed out the window as if he was ignoring her. She watched him intently for several moments before giving up and beginning his exercise regimen for his lower body. Her mind wandered back to the conversation with Pattie this morning. She couldn't help but let her mind linger on Pattie's comments about John. He had not returned to the house today, not even for lunch. She wondered what he did all day. She had hoped that they would have time alone while she was staying at the ranch, but if her first day was any indication, she would not be spending a lot of time with John.

She had lost herself in completing Ben's lower body exercise. She wasn't sure how much time had passed when she raised her head and found Ben looking at her. His eyes seemed to hold so many emotions. Minutes ticked as they stared at each other. He slowly lifted his hand, thumb and fingers together, and touched his mouth, and then slowly he slid his hand toward his ear.

Jill sat stunned for several moments before she jumped up and grabbed Ben's hand.

"That's right Ben! This is your home!"

She clasped his hand in between hers and squeezed, feeling so joyful that she could have jumped straight up and down. She looked around the room, her gaze landing on the picture in the hallway of the three Mitchell sons. Taking one look back at Ben, she released his hands and quickly walked to the picture, and looking around quickly to make sure she wasn't seen, she took it off the wall.

Returning to Ben, she sat down in front of him. She looked down and studied the picture in her hands before she turned it toward Ben. Ben's gaze fell on the photo.

"Do you remember this picture, Ben?" She moved to stand over his shoulder so she could view the picture with him. "Look at how handsome. And look at Jamie and John." She pointed to one and then the other. "Three very handsome brothers."

She moved around to face him and pointed to each of the faces in the pictures. "Three very handsome brothers," she repeated and signed with word "brothers" as she said it. She repeated the word several times, signing it each time.

She gently reached out and formed an "L" with Ben's good hand, bringing it up to his forehead and slowly down to meet his other hand which rested on his chest. She repeated the movement several times, each time repeating the word "brother." She held her breath, wanting desperately for him to initiate the sign. Each time she let go of his hand, it dropped to his lap.

"Are you two ready for lunch?" Pattie's cheery voice caused Jill to jump. "I'm sorry! I didn't meant to scare you." Pattie walked over to Ben's Chair, "Is Ben ready for a break?" Jill nodded toward the chair unable to stop her mind from thinking of Ben's use of sign language. "You are going to join us, aren't you?" Pattie turned to her.

"Um, yeah, just let me clean up a bit." Jill had no appetite and no desire to join them for lunch. She pressed her forehead against the window and allowed the coolness to seep into her body. She thought back and tried to estimate how long it had taken Ben to use the sign for "home" without being prompted. Weeks, if she remembered correctly without his detailed medical chart in front of her. She shouldn't be discouraged because he hadn't picked up a new sign in a matter of minutes, now should she? Standing here, face pressed against the window, she could admit, at least to herself, that her disappointment was about more than just Ben's lack of progress. She wanted something to lift this family's burden. She wanted to able to give Pattie news that would brighten her world. She wanted to be able to do something for John that would ease his burdens. In short, she wanted to save them, and she quickly understood that she couldn't do that. Only God could save them from themselves and each other.

Chapter 14 Blessed

"Blessed [is] the man that walketh not in the counsel of the ungodly, nor standeth in the way of sinners, nor sitteth in the seat of the scornful."Psalms 1:1

"I thought maybe we could go riding tomorrow? I want you to see the ranch."

Jill's heart leapt at John's suggestion. The trip to the ranch had not been as she imagined. John had tried his best to spend time with her, but it never seemed to fail that someone needed him every second of the day. Her heart broke for him as she realized how many people depended on him and him alone. It also began to dawn on her that every minute he spent in Billings with her put him even more behind at home. He had a heavy load to bear and all she wanted was to be able to help him in some way.

"Oh, I would love that." She threw her arms around his neck as they sat on the porch swing after dinner.

"Good. I have a few things to do in the morning, but I'll pick you up around ten. Sound good?"

Jill bit her tongue, wanting to ask if one of the things he had to do was ride up into the mountains by himself like he had each morning since she had been visiting. Pattie had said it was a ritual, and while he openly discussed his ranch activities with Jill, the early morning ride was never mentioned.

"I'll be ready." She didn't want to ruin the moment by asking about his morning rituals. Tomorrow would be the last day on the ranch before she and Ben headed back to Billings. The fears associated with their return to the hospital tried to creep into Jill's mind. She knew that without progress in learning sign language, Ben showed very little progress in any other area and that his time at St. Patrick's would be coming to an end soon. She didn't want to think about what that meant for her and her relationships with his family. She pushed the thoughts to the back of her mind and focused on enjoying her last day on the Mitchell ranch.

She was ready by nine the next morning and decided to work with Ben until John came to pick her up. She tried several times to get Ben to imitate the sign for "brother" with no success. He seemed to have no interest in using the sign for "home" either. She put him through his normal routine and was intent on his neck exercises to improve his head control when she happened to look up and see John leaning on the door watching her.

When John rounded the corner his breath caught in his throat and not for the first time that week he thought about how right it seemed to have Jill at the ranch. She was lost in the exercises she was putting Ben through. He quietly watched her, taking in the curve of her cheeks, the way her forehead crinkled when she was concentrating, the way she spoke to Ben as if at any moment he would respond. John's heart swelled at the sight of her and he was momentarily breathless.

The emotions she stirred in him were dangerous and he knew it. Those emotions triggered thoughts and questions about the future and they nagged at him. How would this work when Ben came home from the treatment program? What would she do if she knew the truth? The truth that he had been the one who put Ben in that chair? While John had kept anyone of the opposite sex at arm's length for the last several years, he had enough experience with women to know that when she looked at him she had love in her eyes. What scared him more than anything had in a really long time was the fact that getting that look from her didn't scare him at all. All concerns were lost when she looked up and caught him staring at her.

He pushed off from the door and strode toward her. "Hey."

He never took his eyes off hers as he crossed the room. She stood and turned to face him, momentarily forgetting everything else. He reached out and wound his fingers into hers, slowly caressing her fingers with his calloused thumb. "You ready to go?" His voice came out barely a whisper. All Jill could do was nod her head. John released her hand and began to push Ben's chair into the kitchen.

"I fixed you all some lunch," Pattie sang out as they entered the kitchen. Her voice could not contain her excitement.

"Thanks." John released Ben's chair and threw one arm around his mother's shoulders, grabbing the sack with sandwiches with the other. "You ready?" He turned to Jill.

Jill nodded her head and smiled her thanks to Pattie. She patted Ben on the shoulder, letting him know they would complete his exercise routine when she returned, and followed John out the kitchen door.

The sunshine was warm and inviting and she stopped long enough to soak it in. John took the opportunity to wind his fingers into hers again and steadily pulled her toward him. Slinking his free arm around her waist, he pulled her to his chest.

"I'm sorry," he whispered.

"For what?" She tilted her head back to look up at him.

"I wanted you to see the ranch, and it seems like all I've done is leave you here with Ben and Mom." He dropped his chin and cut his eyes toward her.

"John, it's okay. I've had fun and I wanted to see what your life was like here on the ranch and I have." She paused before she finished. "You've got a lot on your plate."

"Yeah, well"—he stiffened and seemed uncomfortable—"it's okay. Somebody has to do it."

Leaving his arm firmly around her waist, he turned and headed to the barn. "Let's enjoy what we have left of your visit."

Within the hour they were saddled and heading away from the epicenter of the ranch. She had watched quietly while he saddled her horse, deftly moving around the animal placing saddle and bridle with an ease that came from years of experience, all the while fielding at last a half dozen questions from his foreman and other cowboys about the tasks that needed to be done today. She was shocked at how much went into the daily management of a ranch and her admiration for John soared to new heights. He checked the security of her saddle one more time and crooked his finger at her. A sly grin spread across his face as she immediately came to him.

With one arm resting on the saddle, he hooked his finger into her belt loop and pulled her so close to him she momentarily lost her breath. "Now remind me, how long has it been since you have been on a horse?"

The pounding of her heart pushing blood rapidly throughout her body, combined with an unexplained sensation that settled in the pit of her stomach at his closeness, was almost more than she could bear. She stared at his lips, concentrating on his words, and tried to form an answer.

"Uh...a while." She was having trouble forming thoughts when he was so near.

"Take this foot and put it in the stirrup." He tapped her hip and nodded toward the saddle. As she stepped into the stirrup his large hands encircled her waist and boosted her up. Breathlessly she stared down at him.

"Good?" He squinted up at her and gave her a crooked grin while resting his hand on her thigh.

All she could do was nod her head yes. In a flash he was in the saddle of his horse and directing them away from the barn.

Through deep green valleys they rode, John pointing out certain features to her, telling her the history behind each mountain and crevasse in view. At times he reined his horse close enough to hers to reach out and hold her hand; other times he challenged her to race across an open field. She had never seen him so carefree. He was in his element; these mountains were his home.

He slowed his horse and sidled up next to her. "There's a place up ahead where we could stop and eat lunch."

"That sounds nice." She grinned, thinking to herself how happy he looked.

He motioned for her to follow his lead up a steep hill. Once they reached the top, he wound his way through pines, twisted and gnarled through the stand of time. He finally reined his horse to a stop and dismounted, and Jill followed suit. He led her to an outcropping that looked over a lush green valley below, dissected by a stream babbling through the middle. Jill's breath caught in her throat. The view could have easily been straight from a travel magazine.

"It's beautiful," she whispered.

"We used to come here a lot when we were kids. It is one of my favorite places on the ranch."

"I can see why, it looks like a postcard," she exclaimed. They stood for a few moments taking in the view, neither speaking but absorbing God's beautiful creation.

"Let's see what Momma fixed for us." John grabbed a blanket and the food he had stashed in his saddle bags and headed closer to the outcropping. They spread the blanket and began unpacking lunch of sandwiches and fruit. While they ate lunch, Jill wished that time would stand still. John seemed so carefree, his laughter came so easily. All his burdens seem to have been left back at the main house. She knew, as she watched him from the corner of her eye, that at some time between him yelling at her the first time she spoke to him and today, she had fallen in love with him. How would he react if he knew how she felt about him? Lost in her own thoughts, it took a few moments for her to realize that he had asked her a question.

"Uh, I'm sorry…what did you say?" she stuttered, embarrassed that she had been caught off guard.

"I said do you want to see another of my favorite places on the ranch?"

"Of course." She grinned as they began to gather up the picnic.

Jill watched him as he gathered their horses and tightened saddles again, wondering again how he would react if he knew how she felt. And if he felt the same way, how would they handle the relationship once Ben left the rehabilitation program?

She thought of the verse from Corinthians: *Love bears all things, believes all things, hopes all things and endures all things.*

She had to believe that if they both felt the way she did, they could bear anything that came their way.

They made their way down from the outcropping, and Jill was surprised when John turned their horses toward the valley they had seen from above. They continued riding, tracing the stream that flowed through the valley seemingly to its source. They rode at a leisurely pace, John moving his horse close to hers so that their legs touched—whether on purpose or not, Jill had to admit she liked it. Their horses began a steady incline, as rocks and bluffs began to shoot from the ground stretching toward the sky. The valley began to narrow after a while, but John continued to lead their horses up. The pines became thicker and the rocks more prevalent. Just when Jill thought they could go no further because of the rocky terrain, John slowed his horse and dismounted.

"We'll have to leave the horses here." He began to loosen the saddle on his mount and then turned to help her down. The look on her face must have told him that she thought he had lost his mind, there couldn't be anything here but rocks and pine trees.

He caught her chin gently between his thumb and forefinger, lifting her face to his. "Trust me it's worth it," he whispered.

John led her up the rocky slope, gently instructing her where to place her feet. Careful to avoid the stream that still trickled through the rocks, they picked their way up the slope. When they reached the top, Jill caught her breath. They had in fact reached the source of the stream. A small waterfall coming from the rocks spilled into a pool. The pool was surrounded by a ledge of rocks which provided a naturally made bench. Pines grew around the pool, providing seclusion.

"It's beautiful," she barely whispered.

"It's a hot spring." John wrapped his arm around her shoulders and pulled her close. "See the steam?"

Barely able to concentrate with his body so close, she turned her face and met his gaze. "I don't think I've ever seen anything so beautiful," she said softly. He studied her for moment before responding.

"I don't think I have either." The way he looked at her, she didn't think he was talking about the hot spring. He placed his hands on her shoulders and gently turned her to face him, sliding his arms down her shoulders and around her waist. Their eyes met and held. He glanced down at her lips and then back to her eyes. He gently cupped her cheek and rubbed her bottom lip with the pad of his thumb. The calloused thumb sent an electrifying tingle through her body. His head dropped, his lips but a breath from hers. He met her eyes one more time and, seeing no reservation in them, he brushed her lips with his. Tingling sensations coiled through her belly as she slipped her arms around his neck and pulled him

115

to her. He pulled back long enough to search her face and then pressed his lips to hers again, this time with more pressure, more demanding.

The kiss ended, but he didn't release her. He traced her cheekbones with his fingertips, leaving a trail of heat on her skin. There was so much that he wanted to say, but the words seem to die in the back of his throat. His chest welled with emotion and he hoped she understood the feelings he couldn't convey through words. Did she know how special she was? He hadn't brought a girl home since high school. Jill opened her mouth as if to speak and fear slammed through his body. What if she were able to put into words the emotions that were volleying back and forth between them? What if she said what he couldn't? Would she still feel that way if she knew the truth? John panicked as he suddenly thought that Jill would probably hate him if she knew the truth about Ben's accident. That his carelessness had caused his brother to be permanently disabled.

"Come on." He grabbed her hand and pulled her toward the pool before she could utter a word. He led her to the rocks surrounding the pool and gestured for her to take a seat. She could feel the heat radiating from the pool and dipped her fingertips in the water to feel its warmth.

"That's amazing!" she gushed when the warm liquid enveloped her fingers.

"We use to come up here all the time when we were kids and go swimming. That pool's about six foot deep right in the middle. In the spring thaw, it was always a dare to see who would get in here first."

She smiled at the memory he shared and leaned toward him and he took the opportunity to slip his arm around her shoulders and draw her close. He pushed his apprehension to the back of his mind. Right now he wouldn't worry about how she would react if she knew he had caused Ben's accident. He would live in the moment and enjoy the time he had with her. Joyous moments were fleeting and even if he didn't feel like he deserved one, he was going to grab this one.

"We had some good times here as kids, but I would by far rather be here with you," and he couldn't help himself as his mouth claimed hers again. Her lips were warm and sweet on his and he wished the moment wouldn't end.

He pulled back and searched her face, gently pushing a tendril of hair behind her ear. "I can't believe I waited until the day before you go home to kiss you."

She dropped her face to hide the heat rising in her cheeks and whispered, "I'm going to miss this, its beautiful here."

"Many times I have wondered how I got so lucky to get to live here." John gazed around at the trees surrounding them.

"Blessed."

"What?" He turned to look at her.

"You're not lucky, you are blessed." She tipped her chin up and smiled at him.

He remembered the last time she had mentioned being blessed; he had argued with her. But today, sitting with the heat from the hot springs wafting over them, his arm around her waist, her lips scant inches from his, there was not a doubt in his mind he was blessed beyond measure, no matter what waited for him back at the ranch.

He leaned forward and rested his forehead on hers. "Very blessed," he whispered before he let his lips claim hers again.

John waited as long as he could before he announced they needed to leave if they wanted to make it back before dark. He held her hand as they descended back to where the horses waited for them. He took every opportunity to lift her over boulders and rocks, pulling her body close to his whenever he could. He thought momentarily that God must have made her specifically for him; her body fit perfectly into his. He helped her onto her horse and let his hand linger on her thigh, holding her gaze for what seemed like endless moments. As they slowly made their way across the meadow and rode underneath the outcropping they had picnicked on earlier that day, he reined his horse as close to hers as possible and reached over to hold her hand.

Jill's heart soared at the attention he was giving her. The way he held her and kissed her, the way he looked at her, it had to mean that he felt the same way that she did. She had thought for a moment that he was going to tell her how he felt back at the hot spring, but something had stopped him. She forced the worry to the back of her mind. She would drink in these moments and live off of them for coming weeks when she returned to Billings.

The closer they came to the epicenter of the ranch, the quieter John became. Jill mourned the carefree John that she had glimpsed today if only for a few hours. It seemed as though the burdens and worries he had been able to forget about on

117

the trip had returned threefold. As they crested the hill and could view the barns and ranch house in the valley below, Jill reached over and squeezed his hand. He gave her a weak smile and sat silently on his horse gazing at her. Releasing her hand, he turned his mount toward the barn. Jill couldn't shake the ominous feeling that she had lost more than just the warmth of his hand as they headed for the barn.

As soon as they became visible to the men at the barn, two riders swung into saddles and came to meet them. John stopped his mount and as they approached they began bombarding him with questions. John quickly made decisions and issued orders, with one cowboy immediately heading back to the barn, the other falling into pace with them, filling John in on a variety of issues that had arisen while John had been away. Jill suddenly felt forgotten, as he zoned in the business at hand. When they reached the barn, he helped her dismount and instructed the cowboy who had ridden in with them to see her back to the ranch house as soon as he had unsaddled her horse. John pulled her around the corner of the barn and dropped a quick kiss on her lips.

"I'm sorry," he whispered, "I've got to take care of some things."

"It's okay." She touched his cheek, wishing again she could take some of his burdens away.

"Today was the best day I've had in a long time." He cocked his head sideways and grinned and Jill felt her heart leap in her chest.

"Me too," she said, grinning back at him.

The cowboy who was to escort her home reappeared and John nodded toward him.

"I'll see you later." He quickly dropped another kiss on her lips and disappeared into the barn.

John had known the day spent away from the responsibilities of the ranch would put him behind. What he hadn't counted on was that every possible thing that could go wrong, would go wrong while he spent time with Jill. Just when he thought he had gotten things back under control, his cell phone buzzed. He watched Amber's number light up his screen. He stepped outside the barn and glanced up at the house. He could see the glow from the kitchen, knowing Jill was there waiting for him. He glanced down at the phone, now showing a voicemail. He knew that if he listened to it, Amber's frantic voice would be pleading for him to help her find Jamie. He sighed and glanced from the phone back up to the house, as if weighing his options. He knew Jill waited for him and he desperately wanted to get back a bit of the peace and warmth he had found today with her while they were alone. He glanced back down at his phone and decided to leave Jamie to fend for himself for once.

Turning his phone off, he got into the truck and headed for the house and Jill. It was time he heeded his mother's and Jill's advice and stopped trying to save Jamie from himself. He had to face the reality that he couldn't appease his conscience over what he had done to Ben by bailing Jamie out of his self-inflicted jams. And while most days his conscience also told him he didn't deserve happiness because of Ben's accident, after today he was ready to grab hold of his chance at happiness whether the universe thought he deserved it or not.

Jill met him at the back door, worry creasing her brow. "Something's wrong," she whispered, glancing nervously back into the kitchen.

Looking past her, John could see his mother on the phone. He stepped around Jill and gave his mother a questioning look.

"Amber, calm down. John's right here. Talk to him." She handed him the phone looking as if at any moment she might shatter into a thousand pieces.

John looked at the phone and thought about how badly he wanted to hang it up and not worry about the latest dust-up between his brother and sister-in-law. She had been crazy enough to marry Jamie, so why did John have to be dragged into every fight? Determined to tell her just that, he brought the phone to his ear just in time to hear, "He's in jail! John, did you hear me? He's in jail."

Rage filled John. He listened to Amber frantically beg him to go and bail Jamie out. He glanced at his mother and saw the worry etched on her face. His gut wrenched knowing how different her life could have been if the accident had never happened. Not for the first time since the accident, John thought how different life would have been if he had only stayed in Billings that weekend. If he hadn't come home, he wouldn't have shot the rifle that caused Ben's accident. Ben would be a normal twenty-something, going to college, bringing home dirty laundry and eating all the food in the house. Maybe Jamie wouldn't have started drinking and

John would be free to chase the happiness he wanted with Jill. And his mother wouldn't have the perpetual look of worry etched across her face.

He didn't hear much of what Amber said as she tried to explain what had led up to Jamie's arrest. Honestly, it didn't matter. No matter how much John wanted to leave Jamie sitting in jail, he couldn't. Duty to his family trumped everything else. He owed them that much after what he had put them through. He had changed everyone's life that day, not just Ben's, and no matter how much he gave of himself to them, it would never make up for what he had taken. He looked at Jill and knew deep in his heart that she deserved better. She deserved someone who would put her first and his guilt couldn't let him do that. He knew he would hurt her someday by placing his family ahead of her, as much as he wouldn't want to. He had been a fool to think he could grab a piece of happiness with her. She deserved so much more. She deserved someone who would make her the center of their world. John had too many people that depended on him for him to be able to do that. His world was this ranch and making sure his family survived, and if that meant he had to sacrifice his own happiness, then so be it. That was the least he owed them.

Something Amber said caught his attention. "Wait, where did you say he was in jail?"

"He's in Fortuna. He just called me…"

John clenched his jaw and gripped the phone. Fortuna was a good three-hour drive away. He glanced at his mother's worried face and then to Jill's.

"Amber." John sternly said her name and she stopped talking. "Fortuna is a three-hour drive. He'll have to spend the night and you can go get him in the morning."

"You mean you would leave your brother in jail all night?" Amber cried.

John sighed heavily. "Yes, Amber, I would. Maybe a night in jail would do him some good."

When she began to scream at him, it was more than John could take. He calmly said goodnight and hung the phone up in the middle of her tirade and turned to face his mother, expecting to have to defend himself to her too.

"Now, Momma, I know you—"

"You're right. A night in jail might be the best thing for him," Pattie said calmly. "Maybe they can make him go get help. Lord knows he doesn't listen to us."

"We'll see in the morning." John wrapped his arms around his mother and caught Jill's gaze. He hoped that she knew how much today had meant to him. The sickening feeling in the pit of his stomach told him that today had been a brief glimpse at what life might have held for him at one point in time. He felt taunted by the universe, as if he had been given a glimpse of happiness just to know that soon it would be snatched from him. As much as he cared for Jill, he couldn't allow himself to explore how deep those feelings might actually run. In the end, his life came down to duty to his family and no matter how hard he tried, he couldn't see a way that he could have Jill in his life and not eventually hurt her. He wasn't sure what love felt like, but he was sure that he never wanted to see her look at him with hurt and disappointment etched on her face, and sooner or later she would. If she ever found out that he had been responsible for Ben's accident, hurt and disappointment wouldn't be the only things he saw there; his biggest fear was that he would see hate in her eyes. There was so much he wanted to say to her, so much he wanted to explain, but instead he just suggested they all go to bed and get a good night's sleep, knowing sleep would elude him for a long time.

Amber was waiting at the back door at 6 a.m. the next morning, obviously angry that John had made the decision to leave Jamie in jail overnight. John had left for the barns before daylight, which left Pattie to try and comfort Amber as Jill packed up Ben's equipment to head back to the hospital today. Amber stomped around the kitchen, slamming cabinet doors.

John stepped inside the kitchen and let the door slam behind him, leveling Amber with his steely gaze. The lack of sleep the night before combined with coming to terms with how little control or choice he had in his life had left him on edge.

"Great, you're here. Can we leave now? My husband—"

"Got himself into jail and if it were up to me would have to figure his own way out," John interrupted, and his tone told Amber this was not the time to argue; unfortunately for her, she didn't listen.

She opened her mouth to argue and John turned toward her. "You have no money, no lawyer, and no means whatsoever to bail him out. You are depending on me to take care of all this mess, so you will do this the way I see fit, do you understand? 'Cause if you don't, I will gladly wash my hands of you and Jamie and you can figure this out on your own. You are living on my ranch, living off my hard work, you will handle this exactly as I tell you to." His tone was firm, words uttered between clenched teeth. He didn't raise his voice, but his tone left no room for negotiation.

Tears welled in Amber's eyes as she nodded and mumbled an apology. John reached out and took her into his arms, whispering something that only she could hear. She pulled back and looked up at him, her eyes full of trust.

Jill knew then why everyone at the ranch depended on him and looked to him for guidance. He released Amber and turned to face his mother and Jill. "Let me clean up and we will get started."

As he passed Jill, he grabbed her hand and tugged her down the hall behind him. He pulled her into the den and wrapped her up in his arms. He buried his face in her hair and breathed in the sweet smell of her shampoo. "I'm sorry," he whispered close to her ear.

She pulled back so that she could see his eyes. She studied him and could see the lines on his face and the worry in his eyes. What she wouldn't give to be able to take away some of his worries, to be able to give him back the peace he had when they had stolen away yesterday.

"You don't have anything to be sorry for," she whispered as she traced his cheekbones with her fingertips.

"I wanted this trip to be…to be more for you…I feel like I've just left you here to fend for yourself…I'm sorry." He caught her hand and held it to his cheek, partly because he didn't want her to stop touching him.

"It's okay. I know you have a responsibility to your family."

His gaze searched her face, memorizing every inch, his heart aching. He leaned his forehead against hers and captured her lips, pulling her body flush against his, not wanting to let her go.

"I have to take care of this mess with Jamie." He pulled back but kept a firm arm around her waist, holding her close to him, his voice no more than a whisper. He briefly wondered if he was trying to convince her or himself that he had no other choice.

"I know you do." Jill held his face in her hands and planted a tender kiss on his lips.

John's steely reserve threatened to come undone at her touch. A wild thought of taking her and leaving the ranch, his family, and all his troubles behind flitted through his mind. He ground his back teeth together, knowing what he had to do. Duty to his family and desire to be with her warred inside his body and he knew if he let the battle wage, desire would win.

He shook his head to clear this thoughts. "It may be late this afternoon before I can get back to take you home. Is that okay?"

Jill studied his face. His sense of duty only made her love him more. As much as she wanted to steal away moments with him even if it was in a car ride back home, she wanted to ease his burdens more.

"Why don't you give me the keys to the van with the lift and I can drive Ben and myself back to the hospital today?"

"No!" He stepped back from her. "What kind of man would I be if I let my…" He paused, not knowing how she would react if he labeled her his girlfriend. "…if I let you take Ben back all by yourself?"

"A man that is very busy and a man that I want to help, not a man I want to cause more trouble for. John, I'm Ben's therapist. I am used to moving him. I can get him in and out of the van probably better than you." She reached for his hand and pulled him back close to her.

He slipped his arms round her again and made soft circles on the small of her back. He dropped his head and Jill waited for him to speak. After several long moments, his voice thick, he spoke. "I feel like I've let you down this weekend."

She thought for several moments, picking her words carefully. "No, you haven't let me down. I wish we had had more time together, but the time we did have was something I will never forget as long as I live."

He knew there was so much that could be said between them. Not wanting to think about the future and how he was going to make all this work, he dropped a light kiss on her lips.

"I really want to drive you and Ben home. Wait for me. I think I can be back by three o'clock."

The desire to be with him outweighed her need to get Ben settled back at the hospital. "I'll wait," she whispered and in her heart she pledged she would wait for him forever.

****

The three-hour drive to Fortuna was tense. John rolled his neck from side to side trying to alleviate the tightness that plagued him. He glanced in the rearview mirror at Amber as she chewed on her fingernails. He couldn't help but notice how young she looked and he briefly wondered how old she was and if she regretted getting mixed up with Jamie. His mother sat silently in the passenger seat, staring out the window. His heart ached for all she had been through. He had tried to convince her to stay at home and help get Ben ready to return to the hospital, but for some reason she had insisted on accompanying him and Amber to Fortuna. She briefly mentioned that he might need her and that Ben was in capable hands with Jill until they returned. He could tell his mother was fond of Jill and wanted him to open up and talk to her about his relationship, but that was the last thing he wanted to do. He didn't know how to label the relationship himself, much less discuss it with his mother.

Fortuna was one of those towns that had grown quickly, but still had that small-town feel. It was big enough to have a big box store and a movie theater, but small enough that people still knew everybody's business. After using his phone's map app, John finally located the Fortuna City Police Department. He told his mother and Amber to stay in the car while he went inside and bailed Jamie out. Amber refused, jumping out of the car before he removed the keys out of the ignition and racing toward the door. John shook his head and followed her. He was several steps behind her, but close her enough to overhear Amber ask the front desk clerk, who looked to be one hundred years old if she was a day, to see Jamie.

Amber's hands shook and she was visibly nervous. John wanted to remind her that this was not the first time Jamie had caused trouble in their marriage and wasn't she used to it by now, but he refrained. Instead he turned his best smile, the one he had used when he was in sales in Billings, to the front desk clerk. "Ma'am, my brother, Jamie Mitchell, was brought in last night and we would like to bail him out."

The front clerk tapped on her computer for several minutes, ignoring Amber and John.

The look she gave John over the top of her glasses told him his megawatt smile had lost some effectiveness over the years. "No bail for Jamie Mitchell," the tight smile on her face gave John the impression that she had enjoyed telling him the bad news.

"No bail?" He gently place his hand on Amber's shoulder and moved around her to be face to face with the clerk.

"Nope. No bail." She began shuffling paperwork and offered no other explanation.

"What?" Amber cried. "You can't do that!"

John spit out between gritted teeth, "Amber, hush and let me handle this." He turned back to the clerk. "Can you tell me why there is no bail?"

The decrepit clerk stared at John over her glasses. "Your brother is being arraigned shortly, no bail will be set until then. If you want any further information you will have to speak to the sergeant on duty."

John stood in front of the clerk, his mind reeling for several moments before he realized he would have to request to see the sergeant. "Well, can I speak to the sergeant?"

"Have a seat." She gestured to a row of straight-backed chairs against the wall. "I'll see if he's available."

An uneasy feeling settled in John's gut as he leaned over in the chair, resting his forearms on his thighs, glancing at the clock on the wall repeatedly. Finally, a gentleman who looked to be close to John's age appeared in the door and scanned the room. His eyes landing on John, he approached.

"Mr. Mitchell?" The sergeant stretched his hand out and introduced himself as Sergeant Anderson.

"Yes." John stood and grasped his hand. "I'm John Mitchell. My brother was brought in last night. I'm just trying to bail him out and get him out of your hair." John's attempt to lighten the mood fell flat.

Amber sniffled behind him and muttered something under her breath. John cut his eyes in her direction and the look he gave her told her to keep her comments to herself.

125

"Mr. Mitchell," The sergeant glanced from John to his mother and then Amber. "Would you all please follow me? I can take you to the courtroom. Arraignment proceedings should begin soon."

"Arraignment? Sir, I'm afraid there has been a big misunderstanding. I just need to bail my brother out of the drunk tank."

"No, I'm sorry, sir, but your brother is being arraigned in just a few minutes." The officer nodded his head down the hall, indicating for John to follow him.

"Sergeant, what is going on?" John refused to move, his hands on his hips.

"Sir, I just came on duty so I don't have all the details, but your brother is being held on charges from an altercation at a local bar last night. If you will follow me, you can sit in on his arraignment." The officer once again gestured down the hallway.

Reluctantly John motioned for Amber and his mother to follow the police officer. He fell in behind them, his mind reeling as to what Jamie had gotten himself into this time.

"John, what is going on?" his mother whispered as they followed the police officer through the door and down a long hall.

"I don't know, Momma, but I think Jamie has got himself in a mess this time," John said tightly.

The sergeant opened a door and held it open for them to enter. John nodded his appreciation and ushered his mother and Amber to a seat before turning back to the officer.

"Sergeant, I think we are a little confused here. My brother called his wife last night"—he gestured toward Amber—"and told her he had been picked up for public intoxication. All this"—he gestured around the courtroom—"seems to be a little bit more than just public intoxication."

The sergeant studied Amber and then turned to John. "I've told you all I know, sir. I am truly sorry I can't be of more help."

"This is ridiculous! Just let us bail him out and take him home!" Amber screamed, her voice echoing around the near empty courtroom, tears rolling down her face.

"Amber, hush." John's tone was stern, leaving no doubt that he meant business. She glared at him and turned back to face the front of the room.

"John, can you find out anything?" Pattie's voice was full of emotion and John regretted bringing them both along.

About that time a gentleman in a suit, carrying a briefcase, entered the courtroom from a side door. "That is the public defender assigned to your brother's case, unless you have other legal counsel. Maybe he can tell you something. I'm sorry." And with that the officer left the room.

John leaned one hand on the wall, running the other down his face.

"I can't believe this!" Amber's voice broke the silence. "They are trying to get money out of us."

John sat down heavily in the chair beside his mother. "Amber, for the last time, hush," John's tone was calm and steady. "And being disrespectful is not helping Jamie out. Tell me exactly what Jamie said to you last night when he called."

"He said he was in jail and to tell you to come to Fortuna and bail him out." She avoided John's gaze and he had an uneasy feeling she was lying.

"Those were his exact words?" He raised his eyebrow and leaned toward her.

"More or less," she mumbled.

"How about exactly what he said?" John demanded.

Amber stared straight ahead for so long John began to wonder if she was going to answer him. "He said that he was in trouble, big trouble, and that he needed you. He just kept saying that it was bad, really bad this time."

"Why didn't you tell me that?" John spat between gritted teeth.

"I was afraid you wouldn't come," she answered quietly.

John studied her. "When have I ever not bailed him out of trouble?"

"You always say one of these days you are going to leave him, I was afraid today would be that day." She didn't look at him, just continued to stare straight ahead.

He couldn't deny her words. He had threatened to leave Jamie high and dry more than once, and while it might be the best thing for him, John knew he would never do that to his brother. He grabbed his phone and scrolled though his contacts, finding the information for the ranch's lawyer. He had a feeling he was going to need him. He held the phone to his ear and mouthed the name "Brent" to his mother when she gave him a questioning look.

After several rings, Brent Tarkinson answered, "Hey, John. What's up?"

John stood and walked to the back of the room wanting to keep the conversation private. "Jamie has got himself in a mess. He's in jail in Fortuna; the sergeant here just said they are going to arraign him in just a few minutes."

"Arraignment? In Fortuna?"

"Yes. Can you help us out?" John hated how desperate his voice sounded.

"Let me make some calls; if you see him tell him to talk to no one but me." John was met with dial tone. He hung the phone up and walked toward the public defender.

The gentleman was busy flipping through files as John approached. "Excuse me, sir." John stretched his hand out. "My name is John Mitchell."

"Hello, Mr. Mitchell." The lawyer looked at John over the top of his glasses. "Am I representing you today?"

"No, no sir, not me but I believe you are my brother, Jamie Mitchell." John gestured toward the stack of files on the table in front of them.

He thumbed through the files, mumbling the word "Mitchell" repeatedly. "Ah yes, there we are, Jamison Mitchell."

"Can you tell me what exactly is going on?" John held his in front of him and gestured toward the stack of files.

The older man licked his index finger and flipped through the manila folder labeled with Jamie's name, making a clicking sound with his tongue. The moments dragged by and John thought momentarily the older man had forgotten what he had been asked.

"Looks like felony assault is the big one." He snapped the folder shut, removed his glasses, and met John's shocked gaze.

"Felony assault?" John said barely above a whisper.

"Yep, among other charges, but that one is by far the most severe." The older lawyer studied John carefully. "You're shocked by these charges?"

"Yeah." John released a pent-up breath.

"But your brother has a record." He picked up the file and thumbed through it again. "Several public intoxication charges."

"Getting thrown in the drunk tank is a far cry from felony assault," John responded. "When can I see him?"

"Oh, probably after the arraignment. This is a formality to bring charges and determine bail if any, set a court date, that sort of thing."

About that time John's phone buzzed and he saw Brent Tarkinson's number on his screen. "Thank you," he mouthed as he answered his phone.

"I've got some bad news," Brent spoke before John could say hello.

"I bet I can guess, felony assault?" John could not keep the anger out of his voice.

"Yeah, apparently your brother punched a police officer when they were trying to break up a bar room brawl."

John's mind raced as he met Amber's and then his mother's gaze. In a matter of moments it seemed that his family was unraveling even further. John did what he knew to do, what he had done for the past four years. He stuffed his own feelings down deep, detaching himself emotionally, and set about taking control of the situation. "What do I need to do?" he asked Brent.

"Well, first off I have an associate on the way. I can't get there in time to make the arraignment, but I pulled some strings and have had it pushed back. When my guy gets there he's going to meet with you and Jamie before he has to go before the judge." Much like John, Brent was efficient.

"What are the chances of getting him out of this?" John asked, his voice eerily cold and calm.

Brent waited so long to answer, John looked at his phone to make sure they were still connected. "John, you need to think long and hard before you go down that road. He is accused of assaulting an officer. There are over twenty witnesses. I'm not sure there is any chance of getting him out of this one." Brent paused to let his words sink in. "Look, we have time to discuss this later, today is just to set bail and court date."

John's mind, always thinking multiple steps ahead, couldn't wait until later to determine how to handle the situation. "What are we looking at….as far as time… jail time?"

Brent sighed heavily. "John, it's a felony; not to mention it involves a police officer. That is not something that is taken lightly. It could be a year, heck it could be twenty."

"Twenty years?" John nearly shouted.

"Well, twenty years isn't likely but remember this is a felony. This is serious. Your family name nor your money are going to mean much in this case, I'm afraid."

John sat down on the nearest bench and rubbed his hand down his face. "Thanks, Brent. I appreciate everything."

"Call me and tell me what happens in the arraignment. After today, I'll handle everything personally."

John tapped his screen to end the call, dreading the idea of telling his mother what Jamie had done. He thought about Jill and he desperately wished she was here with him. Not that she could save Jamie from himself, but her calm, soothing presence would have been a balm to his nerves right about now. He quickly scrolled through his contacts and tapped on her number.

"Hey." She answered on the first ring and John thought nothing sounded sweeter than her voice.

"Hey," he mimicked her.

"Are you headed back? I think Ben's pretty eager to get back to the bright lights of the big city."

"Listen, I'm going to be stuck here awhile."

"Is everything okay?"

"Yeah." He couldn't quite pinpoint why he lied to her, but for some reason he didn't want to burden her with his troubles. "I'm going to call Buck, the guy who helped you to the house after our ride yesterday; he'll make sure you and Ben get back home safely."

"Oh…okay." Jill tried to hide the disappointment in her voice.

"I'm sorry." Knowing he disappointed her ripped at his heart. "If there was any other way, but I just can't today."

"John, it's fine," she replied, trying to sound cheery.

He wanted to argue; wanted to tell her that it was not fine. That he knew that the weekend had been a huge disappointment and that he had let everything else take his time instead of her. He wanted to tell her that disappointing her was more painful than anything he had ever experienced and that if he had a choice he would walk away from the ranch and his family and spend his life making sure she was never disappointed again. But he didn't have a choice; causing Ben's accident had taken all of his choices way. So instead he told her he would call Buck and make arrangements for her and Ben to get home. He looked up and caught his mother's steady gaze on him. Knowing there was no way he could protect her from this, he squared his shoulders and strode across the courtroom.

"What's going on?" Pattie demanded before he could sit down.

John leaned back in his seat and sighed deeply, then catching Amber's worried gaze he quickly leaned forward. "What do you know about all of this?" he demanded.

"What are you talking about? I told you what I know," Amber stammered, dropping her eyes.

John was unconvinced that she was being completely honest and while he was angry that he had walked into the situation blindly, he was in it now and his loyalty to family would ensure that he saw this through to the end.

"Apparently," John said, keeping his gaze riveted on Amber, "Jamie took a swing at a police officer last night during a bar fight." When Pattie gasped he tore his eyes from Amber to see tears welling in his mother's eyes.

"John, no!" Pattie's voice broke as she pressed her fingers against her lips.

"Afraid so." John put his arm around his mother's shoulders. "Brent has gotten the arraignment pushed back and is sending one of his lawyers. But," he added when he saw Amber raise her head, a glimmer of hope in her eyes, "this is a very serious charge. We are looking at jail time here."

"What? No!" Amber cried, tears steadily streaming down her face now. "John, no, he can't go to jail!"

"Amber, assaulting a police officer is a felony. This is serious." John was again struck by how young she looked.

"John, he can't go to jail, you have to fix this." The pleading in Amber's voice was desperate.

"Amber," his said, his voice firm. He waited until she met his steady gaze before continuing, "This may not be something I *can* fix."

Amber sat back in her chair and covered her face with her hands. Pattie slipped her arm around the girl's thin shoulders and pulled her close, looking up at John. "We just have to pray. We have to pray that God will take care of this as He sees fit."

John eyed his mother. Her face was covered in the same determined mask he had seen many times over the last four years when dealing with Ben's accident. He hated that life had dealt her so many curves and he hated even more the fact that his irresponsible actions had caused all of them. He leaned back and pinched the bridge of his nose with his thumb and forefinger. The what-ifs assaulted him. What if he had never come home that weekend? What if that deer had never stepped into the open meadow? What if he hadn't taken the shot? Ben would be a whole functioning human being and Jamie wouldn't have turned to the bottle and his mother wouldn't be sitting here with that steely look in her eye, willing herself yet once again to get through what life had thrown her. Glancing at Amber's tear-streaked face, he realized his decisions had caused havoc in yet another person's life.

He willed the thoughts to the back of his mind and focused on what needed to be done in the present. He called the ranch to make sure Jill and Ben had gotten on the road back to Billings and to delegate ranch tasks. He sat somewhat impatiently waiting for the lawyer Brent was sending. Just when he thought he would lose his mind if he had to wait one more minute, a court officer approached him.

"Mr. Mitchell?" The officer stopped in front of him.

"Yes." John stood hurriedly.

"Your brother's legal counsel is here; he's asked for you to join them." The officer gestured toward the door.

With a glance over his shoulder and a comforting pat on his mother's shoulder, he followed the officer down a narrow hallway into a dark room. John glanced around the room, his eyes landing on Jamie seated on the other side of the table, lip busted and hair disheveled.

Seated across the table was a clean-cut gentleman in a suit and tie who stood as John entered. "John Mitchell, I presume? Nolan Chester, Mr. Tarkinson sent me." The gentleman extended his hand. John took it while eyeing Jamie, who had not met his gaze since he entered the room.

Nolan gestured to the seat beside him. "Let's get started, shall we?"

John took the seat, his steely gaze pinned on Jamie, who refused to meet his gaze.

Nolan flipped through a file. "The charges are public intoxication and disorderly conduct, which we could plea down to fines, maybe community service, if not for the felony assault charge. Jamie, walk us through what happened last night."

Jamie leaned back in his chair, finally meeting John's gaze. "What's the point? He already has me tried and convicted."

Anger surged in John's chest but before he could speak Nolan responded, "It really doesn't matter what your brother thinks, it's up to the court and of course me to defend you, so we need to know the complete story."

Jamie met John's gaze and glanced away quickly. Several tense moments ticked by before Jamie leaned on the table. "I really don't know how I wound up in Fortuna. Amber and I had a fight and I just hit back roads to try and clear my head. Anyway, next thing I know I was here. I stopped in the bar to get a bite to eat."

John snorted. "Sure."

"It's true," Jamie said forcefully. "I ran into some hands from the Circle 3. They bought me a drink—"

"A drink? As in one?" John interrupted sarcastically.

Jamie glared at his brother and returned his attention to Nolan. "Next thing I know, bottles are being thrown, tables being pushed over. People were throwing

133

fists. I guess I just got caught up in it. Somebody grabbed me from behind, and I turned around and swung. I didn't know it was a cop. I swear."

Nolan jotted notes feverishly on a legal pad, occasionally glancing at Jamie and then John. He finished with a flourish and leaned back in his chair. "So you didn't hear the officer identify himself?"

"Mr. Chester, you couldn't have heard a bomb going off in there it was so loud."

Again Nolan wrote on his notepad before addressing the brothers again. "We may be able to use that to lighten your sentence."

"Lighten my sentence?" Jamie leaned back in his chair as if he had been punched. "What do you mean lighten my sentence? A sentence means jail time."

"Well, yes, Jamie." Nolan folded his hands and leaned on the table. "You struck a police officer; the question is not if you will receive jail time, but how much. My firm's job is to make sure your sentence is as light as possible."

"No!" Jamie jumped up, shoving his chair into the wall behind him. "I can't go to jail! You've got to get me out of this." He desperately glanced at John. "John?"

John studied Jamie, hating the gut response he had to try and save his little brother. He was tired of trying to save everyone, tired of everyone's desperate eyes searching his for answers. He rubbed his hand over his mouth. "Jamie, we will do all we can, but you need to accept the fact that we may not be able to get you out of this." He stood and headed for the door, but couldn't stop himself from tossing over his shoulder, "You've made your bed, now you got to lie in it."

Amber peppered John with questions upon his return to the courtroom, which he answered in monosyllables. His mother, knowing what the look she saw on his face meant, kept eerily quiet.

They sat through several arraignments before Jamie was ushered into the courtroom, handcuffed and flanked by two court officers. Jamie searched the room until his eyes found Amber's. John glanced at her in time to see large tears slip from her eyes. He looked at Jamie in time to see him mouth, "It's okay."

Jamie stood behind the podium, Nolan beside him in front of the judge, listening to the charges brought against him.

"Your Honor," the prosecutor, a large man with a droopy white mustache addressed the judge, "considering the severity of charges brought against Mr. Mitchell and the fact that Mr. Mitchell comes from a family of means, *and* was overhead speaking about crossing the border to Canada last night while in custody, the prosecution requests no bail be set and that Mr. Mitchell be held in the county jail until the time of his trial."

John quickly leaned forward, grasping the back of the seat in front of him, mouth agape. His mother put a restraining hand on his shoulder. He glanced at Amber in time to see her jump from her chair screaming, "No!"

Jamie turned to look at her, shock covering his features. He quickly turned to the judge. "Please, your honor, I can't stay in jail. I won't run. I promise. I was just running off at the mouth last night."

"Order! Order!" The judge pounded his gavel until the courtroom became quiet. He pointed his gavel at Jamie and then gestured toward Amber. "One more outburst and I'll hold the whole bunch of you in contempt of court."

He let his statement hang in the air, making sure everyone understood the severity of it, before he continued. He looked at Jamie thoughtfully before addressing the court. "Son, you've had more public intoxications charges than I care to count. And whether or not you meant what you said in the holding cell last night...well, who knows. But, I am inclined to agree with the prosecution. No bail will be set. Hearing will be one month from today at nine o'clock." He pounded his gavel and left the courtroom.

Jamie turned to face his family as the court officers directed him toward the door. John looked at Amber, who had buried her face in her hands and was quietly sobbing. He stood and took a step toward Jamie, who caught the movement and turned to look at John. The desperation on his brother's face caused John's stomach to drop. He nodded at Jamie, hoping to convey strength to him. Jamie dropped his head and let the officers lead him out of the room.

John spent most of the ride home on the phone with Brent Tarkinson—who did not seem surprised that the court had denied bail—and trying to shut out the sobs coming from the backseat.

"Bottom line, John, is that Jamie is in a lot of trouble and as Nolan and I both have told you, we are definitely looking at jail time here. The question is just how much." John thanked him for his time, clicked the phone off, and threw it into the console.

"Wh-what did he say?" Amber stammered, tears streaming down her face.

John sighed, wishing for about the one millionth time that day that he had made this trip alone. "He's going to do all he can, but Amber, you need to prepare yourself that Jamie will have to spend some time in jail."

His words sent Amber back into her incessant sobbing. He groaned inwardly and cut his eyes toward his mother, who sat stoically staring out the windshield. His heart pinched as he thought of the pain and turmoil that Pattie hid behind the blank expression on her face. The vile stench of bitterness crept into his thoughts. Why did she have to go through so much? Why had God caused so much pain in her life? Why did she have to deal with losing her husband and, for all intents and purposes, losing a son, and now having to deal with Jamie's selfish behavior? Anger boiled up inside him and settled in his chest. He remembered a verse from the Bible about people being burdened coming to the Lord because his yoke was light. Where was his mother's light yoke? Where was Ben's light yoke? Where was his? Life kept rearing up and knocking them down time after time and God didn't seem to notice or care about his family or lightening the load they had to bear.

His phone buzzed in the console. He saw Jill's number on his screen and clicked the button to send the call to voicemail. He knew she would try to comfort him, to tell him that God had everything under control, and honestly he just didn't want to hear that. He didn't want to hear her tell him how much God loved him and how everything would work out. Right now he just wanted to wallow in his anger and bitterness.

Chapter 15 Choices

"There is a way that seems right to a man, but its end is the way to death." Proverbs 14:12

He continued to avoid Jill's calls for the next two days, unable to explain why, but just knowing that in her he could find comfort and he didn't want comfort right now, he wanted to be angry. On Wednesday morning, he stood in the kitchen filling his thermos with steaming coffee, mentally planning his day. The phone rang, breaking the stillness of the early morning, sun barely peeking over the distant mountain peaks. He frowned, a sliver of concern slicing through him. The phone ringing this early in the morning usually indicated a problem. He grabbed it and gave a terse hello.

"John?" Jill's voice sliced through him, causing unbidden warmth to surge through his body. He tamped down his reaction and cleared his throat.

"Jill? What's wrong? Why are you calling the house?" He hated how gruff his voice sounded but he couldn't quite explain why he felt the need to keep her at arm's length.

"Well, it's good to talk to you too," she laughed and tried to keep the hurt from her voice.

"I… I'm sorry," he stammered. "It's just when the phone rings this early in the morning, I automatically assume its bad news."

"I've tried to call your cell several times, but you haven't answered. It's just when I call someone several times and they don't answer or call back, I automatically assume it's bad news."

John couldn't help but sense the pain in her voice even as she tried to mask it. He also detected a sense of anger as she threw his words back at him. And didn't she have every right to be hurt? Less than a week ago they had shared their first kiss, connected on a higher level than John had ever connected with a woman, and then he had just shut her out with no explanation.

"I'm sorry." He sighed and leaned against the kitchen counter. "Things have been a little crazy around here."

"Is Jamie okay? Did you get everything taken care of?"

Her voice penetrated his tough exterior, threatening to squeeze away the anger and bitterness he had harbored for the past three days. John briefly contemplated telling her everything, baring his soul and allowing her to comfort him. Something stopped him. Something he couldn't quite name kept him from allowing her into his personal torment.

"Jamie's fine," he lied, grateful that she couldn't see his face.

She waited for him to elaborate, but when he didn't she continued, "Ben has settled back into his routine here."

"Good, that's good." John's anger and bitterness just couldn't let her into his hurt so he kept his answers short.

"John, are you okay?" Jill's voice was thick with concern.

"I'm fine, just really busy right now." He hated the way he was treating her, but for some reason he couldn't stop. He wanted to wallow in his anger and bitterness; the last thing he wanted was for her to comfort him and show him how to let it go.

"Okay, well, I won't keep you. I just wanted to let you know that Dr. Bryan wants to meet with your family to discuss Ben's future treatments." Jill tried to sound professional and John cringed knowing he had hurt her, but the bitterness that had taken control several days ago couldn't be abated.

"Sending him home, huh? No better than he was when he started." Anger welled in him and he spat the accusation into the phone.

Jill sat stunned at John's words. What had happened in the past three days to cause such a shift in him? Was this the same man who had been so sweet to her? Who had kissed her so gently and spoken sweet words to her not a week before?

"Well actually, John…I… this really should be discussed with Dr. Bryan." Jill tried to push her feelings aside and deal with him like she would any other family member of a patient.

"Put her on the phone." John ground his back teeth, knowing that if he stayed on the phone with Jill much longer his resolve would break and so would he. He would confess everything until he was a puddle on the floor and let her pick him up.

"Actually, she would like to meet with you and your mother in person…face to face." Jill waited for his response but was met with silence, so she added, "This Friday at ten?"

John rubbed the back of his neck. He briefly considered sending his mother on her own to the meeting, but quickly knew he couldn't do that. Agreeing to this meeting would mean he would have to see Jill face to face. And if he saw her face to face, he was afraid he would crumple at her feet and beg her to hold him and tell him it would all be okay. And he couldn't allow himself to do that. He had to hold onto the anger because that was the only thing he knew that might get him through this life without being utterly destroyed.

"Friday at ten?" he repeated. "Sure…okay, we can be there."

"Great, I'll put you on Dr. Bryan's calendar." And before he could hang up, she added, "You know, John that I'm here for you, right? If you need anything or just to talk…" Her voice trailed off.

"I know that." He softened briefly. "I'll see you Friday." And he hung up the phone before he lost all composure and begged her to tell him it would all be okay.

John went through the motions of his day with a knot in his stomach. He hated the way he had treated Jill. The thought of hurting her tormented him. More than once during the day he reached for his phone to call her, but something kept him from completing the call. He knew she would be caring and compassionate, and something in him wanted to hold onto his bitterness. He wanted to hold onto his

139

anger, his sense of unfairness. He wanted to wallow in his bitterness. He deserved to be angry. Life had dealt him a bad hand, and he had every right to be bitter. Besides, he didn't deserve her or her compassionate, caring ways; he alone had set his family on this course of destruction. And he alone deserved all that was heaped on him, he just hadn't counted on how much collateral damage his family would have to endure. By the end of the day his mind was a tangled mess. He sat in the ranch office vacantly staring out the window when Amber knocked on the door. He hoped his face hadn't revealed the sinking feeling in his stomach when he saw her.

"Hey, John, I just wanted to see what time we're leaving Saturday morning?" She came in and took the seat across from his desk.

John frowned, briefly confused by her question. He wracked his brain for some appointment he had missed. "Leaving for what?"

"To see Jamie, of course." She crossed her arms, indignation radiating from her.

He studied her thoughtfully, knowing that anything less than complete acquiescence would lead to a fight. He decided he didn't have the time or the energy to be anything less than direct with her. Leaning forward, resting his forearms on the desk, he said, "Amber, I am not going to Fortuna this weekend—"

"What?" she cried before he could finish, tears welling in her eyes.

"Momma and I will be going to Billings to meet with Ben's doctor on Friday," he told her, hoping she would understand.

"And you can see Jill?" She didn't try to conceal the accusation in her voice.

"Yes, Jill will be there."

"So your brother can just rot in jail while you go off to see your girlfriend?" She stood, hands on her hips, anger dripping from her words, and then she added, "We are family, John. Jamie is your family, not Jill. Jamie deserves better than you just forgetting about him while you run off to play house."

John tensed at her accusation. "That's not the case at all, Amber. We have to meet with Ben's doctors, probably to be told that he is coming home. I'll have to get him settled back in at the house and I've already spent too much time away from the ranch. I'm behind schedule and Mother Nature is not going to care that I don't have enough hay put up when it comes time to dump two foot of snow in these mountains." He realized that at some point he had stood and that his voice was an octave below yelling. He composed himself and continued, "You can go to see Jamie if you want, but I am not your chauffeur, nor do I feel the need to put every person and every animal on this ranch at risk this winter because I've spent too much time cleaning up Jamie's messes."

She studied him for a moment before she turned and left without saying a word. He sat down heavily. He opened his desk drawer and saw the worn Bible he had carried in his saddlebag for years. Even after Ben's accident and knowing that he was to blame, he had held out hope that God would help them. He knew that God couldn't possibly forgive him for what he had done to his brother and he also knew that God was probably eternally angry with him, but he had still held out hope that if he begged enough, if he tried hard enough to be all he could for his family, that God would help them in some way. He picked the Bible up and smoothed his hand down its worn cover. Scriptures he had read throughout his life came to his mind. He glanced at his phone and thought of Jill. She would tell him to open the book and let God speak to him, soothe him in his time of trouble. He contemplated it but only for a moment. How long had he begged God to ease their pain and pain just kept coming? No, Jill was wrong, everything didn't always work out for the good. He placed the Bible back in the drawer and shut it, choosing to remain in his anger.

He didn't think Amber would give up so easily, but as he and Pattie left Friday morning for Billings, he realized he hadn't seen or heard from her since she had left his office the other night. Concern for her tried to crowd his brain, but he quickly convinced himself she was pouting and would be fine. He would tell her when he returned to the ranch this afternoon that he would take her to Jamie next weekend. He shifted his focus to the trip ahead and thought about seeing Jill. He longed to see her, longed to rest in her arms and tell her all his thoughts and feelings, yet something held him back. To love was to hurt, that was apparent in his family, and honestly, he wasn't sure how much more hurt he could handle.

The drive to Billings was silent; his mother sat stony-faced beside him. He could only imagine the thoughts running through her head. Probably the same ones that were running through his; Ben was coming home and to be perfectly honest, this program had been a waste of time and money. Ben would be home still bound by his crippled body, Jamie would be in jail, and John would be solely responsible for taking care of everyone. The heaviness of his responsibilities weighed on him. The trip seemed longer than before as they approached Billings, houses and buildings became more frequent, but still the silence remained. The traffic was light when they entered the city, as though the path had been cleared for them. Headed straight for disappointment, John couldn't help but think that disappointment found its way easily to his family. He pulled into the parking garage, and the silence was broken by a deep sigh released by Pattie. They parked and headed to the elevator that would take them to the floor that housed Dr. Bryan's office and the silence hung heavy around them.

They found their way to the familiar surroundings of the floor that housed the rehab program. He stopped in front of the rehab gym doors, knowing that Jill was probably on the other side. He hesitated, not sure of how she would react when she saw him. He couldn't blame her if she slapped him, or worse refused to speak to him at all. Pushing his thoughts aside, he stepped inside the door and scanned the room. His eyes quickly found her. He wasn't prepared for the feelings that overtook him the moment he saw her. She stood leaning against a table in the middle of the room, studying a chart. She absently reached up and tucked her hair behind her ears, her lips pinched between her teeth. The anger and bitterness he had tried to wrap himself in was no match for what he felt for her. Seeing her was the balm he needed to soothe his troubled heart. He pushed every thought and insecurity aside and quickly crossed the gym, slipping an arm around her waist and grinning like a fool at her surprised expression.

She never hesitated as she slipped her arms around his neck and he buried his face in her hair. "I'm sorry," he whispered. His resolve to comfort himself in his bitterness and anger melted at the sight of her. In that moment, with her softly whispering everything would be okay, he knew beyond a shadow of a doubt that he needed her like nothing else he had ever encountered before. More than air or food, he needed to her to survive this life and while he was confident he didn't deserve to be happy, at this moment he was willing to grab his chance and throw caution to the wind.

He raised his head so he could look into her eyes, moving his hands to bracket her face. "I've missed you." His voice was barely a whisper.

Jill slid her hands down his arms, resting them on his forearms. "I've missed you too."

He glanced at her lips and then caught her gaze before he gently leaned in and brushed his mouth against hers. The week behind him, the stress, the anger, melted away when he touched her. The sound of his mother clearing her throat behind them brought him back to reality. Jill's cheeks flushed as she let go of him to embrace his mother.

"Ben's in the other room if you want to see him before the meeting." She released Pattie as she gestured toward the adjoining gym.

Ben sat in his chair, a therapist that John didn't recognize seated in front of him. Personally he didn't think that Ben had improved that much since he had joined the program and had fully prepared himself that Ben would be returning to the ranch today. He stood behind Ben's chair, out of his brother's line of sight, while Pattie knelt in front of him, talking as if she expected him to respond.

"You must be Ben's mother," the therapist who had been working with Ben spoke up. "I'm Steven Miller."

"Yes, I am Ben's mother." Pattie turned to greet the man. "I don't believe I've met you yet."

The therapist shot a meaningful look at Jill, which caused John to briefly ponder if they were sharing a secret. "I'm new to Ben's therapy regimen. Jill had asked me to perform a special consultation for Ben."

"Oh, well, it's nice to meet you," Pattie responded and immediately returned her attention back to Ben, not giving the therapist and his comments another thought. John couldn't shake the feeling that something wasn't being said. If Ben were being sent home, why would he need a new therapist?

"Dr. Bryan is in her office, shall we get this meeting started?" Jill interjected before John could ask any questions. He raised an eyebrow, nodding in the direction of the new therapist when he directed one of the techs to take Ben back to the main gym and joined them as they headed for Dr. Bryan's office.

"Dr. Bryan has asked Steve to join us." Jill's glanced from Pattie to John, but when John caught her gaze and raised an eyebrow to question Steve's presence she quickly looked away, adding to John's suspicion that something was being kept from him.

He waited until Steve and Pattie had turned toward Dr. Bryan's office before he slipped his hand into hers and pulled her body close to his as they walked behind. They found Dr. Bryan seated behind a large mahogany desk poring over a file that John assumed was Ben's. She greeted them enthusiastically, hugging his mother and pumping his hand emphatically, asking them to sit across from her. It didn't go unnoticed when Jill slipped her hand from his and took a seat under the window.

"I'm so excited to see you both! Will your other son be joining us?" Dr. Bryan directed the question to Pattie, who looked at John helplessly.

"No, Jamie won't be with us today. Just the two of us," John responded for her, glancing quickly at Jill and even though it wasn't a lie, he felt guilty at his lack of complete truth.

"Well, let's get on with it, shall we?" Dr. Bryan's eyes shone brightly with excitement as she flipped open Ben's file. "I think we can all agree that on the physical aspect, Ben hasn't progressed as we had hoped. He's gained some improvement in head control and some strength in both his hands, but not to the level we had hoped."

John briefly wondered if they got this excited every time they shared bad news with a family, but he kept quiet and he and his mother both nodded in agreement.

"However, on other levels, I think some day in the future we may call Ben's stay here an unqualified success." She paused and studied them both. "There is an aspect of Ben's therapy that I feel you aren't aware of." She paused to let the information sink in. "Some time ago, Jill began working on sign language skills with Ben."

Pattie looked from Dr. Bryan to Jill. "What? Sign language? Why would that be part of Ben's therapy?"

Dr. Bryan gestured for Jill to explain.

"It was just a hunch I had," Jill said. "Something in his eyes just made me think that he was… I don't know if I can explain it really. Honestly, I think God placed it on my heart to try sign language with Ben. I just kept getting this feeling that his body had failed him, but that Ben, his personality, his essence, was still in this body…trapped. I was here with Ben late one night; I was frustrated and at a loss of what to do next and something just made me try it. He was able to mimic me. At first it was just one sign, actually the sign for 'home,' and then he seemed to pick up another, so we began with simple signs. Just to see what happened."

"At first we thought he might just be mimicking what we were doing," Dr. Bryan offered, "but since he's been back from his trip home, he has shown true initiative."

John's mind reeled at the information. He glanced around the room, being met with bright shiny smiles from everyone. He leaned forward, grasping the edge of the desk. "Wait…wait a minute…what are you telling us?"

"Well, what we are saying is that right now Ben has the ability to use very limited sign language to communicate. Very limited. However, we believe that if the right therapy was applied, he might eventually be able to communicate quite well through sign language." Dr. Bryan leaned back in her chair, giving him a satisfied smile.

He glanced from Dr. Bryan to Jill. "Explain what you mean by limited."

Jill rose from her chair and came over to lean on the desk. "Right now, he tries to tell us if he's hungry or in pain. We feel like he is initiating the signs, not just mimicking what we are doing. Which means that he is having those thoughts and is able to communicate those thoughts to his caregivers."

John looked at his mother, her hand pressed tightly against her mouth, tears welling in her eyes. Jill reached over and squeezed her shoulders. "And while it's great that we've been able to get to that point, we don't have the expertise needed to continue with this type of therapy. That's where Steven comes in."

John's eyes quickly went to the man who had been sitting quietly in the corner, who now spoke. "I know this is a lot to be thrown at you at once. I understand, really I do. Jill called me last week and asked me if I could come do a consult. Upon my examination of Ben, I believe I can help him expand his communication skills through sign language."

Pattie stared dumbfounded for several moments before she could respond. "Communicate….Ben…" She dropped her head in her hands and wept openly, the information just too much for her.

Steven approached, knelt down beside, Pattie and touched her shoulder. "Ms. Mitchell, I don't want to give you false hope. If all we can do is get Ben to the point that he can tell you he's in pain or hungry, wouldn't that be a better quality of life than he has now?"

Pattie looked up and silently nodded, then turned her gaze to John, who sat studying Steven.

"But Jill says he's already doing that, right?" He turned to Jill. "Right, didn't you just say that?"

"Yes, he has used signs sporadically," Jill agreed. "Steven, along with Dr. Bryan and myself, believe he could potentially do more than that."

"How much more?" John watched Jill and Steven share a knowing look, and Jill nodded to Steven.

"Mr. Mitchell, upon my examination of your brother I feel as though his potential to use sign language is significant."

"Significant?" John questioned.

Steven glanced at Pattie. "Again, I don't want to give you false hope, and I can't definitively say at what level Ben could use sign language, but what I can tell you in my professional opinion I think I can help Ben. It may be that Ben learns a few signs that he can use to help you as his caregivers. Telling you he is hungry, in pain, that he's tired. But it may also be that he could become so adept at sign language that he's able to communicate, speak to you, answer questions, carry on a conversation." Steve's excitement built as he spoke and when he finished he was standing in front of them, his face shining. He let his words sink in before he continued.

"I would like to take over Ben's therapy."

John folded his hands, resting his elbows on the desk in front of him, his mind running in a million different directions. After what seemed like an eternity he looked over to find his mother looking at him. He knew from the look in her eyes that they had tapped into her eternal optimism and that as sure as God made little green apples, Ben had a new therapist.

"Walk me through this." He tore his eyes from his mother's and addressed Steven.

"Sure. Ben would become my patient. I would work with him on sign language and sign language only, our goal being improved communication."

"With the goal of Ben being able to communicate with us?" John looked around the room, trying to get his bearings.

"The worst thing that could happen is that Ben isn't able to do anything more than what he is right now," Steven replied honestly and John respected him for that, "and that is a chance that we take."

The room was silent for several minutes before Steven spoke again. "But without giving false hope let's think about the best-case scenario." He turned to Pattie. "What if you could get back the ability to talk with your son…get Ben back through sign language?" Steve touched her shoulder.

The thought sat heavily in the air. Could this man be right? Was Ben, his personality, his essence, trapped inside a body that had failed him?

"Is that what you think?" Pattie's voice shook as she spoke. "Do you think he's in there? That he could be…himself again?'

Steven knelt in front of her, covering her hand with both of his. "Ms. Mitchell, if I didn't think there was something there, I wouldn't offer my services."

"Steven is offering his services at no charge for the first three months," Jill interjected. "We should know in that amount of time if this is something that we need to pursue further."

John stood up. Suddenly the room seemed very small and lacking enough oxygen. He walked to window and leaned against its frame.

"So Ben would stay here?" he asked, not turning away from the window.

Silence filled the room and John turned around. Jill met his gaze and stood to face him. "No, John. Ben wouldn't stay here. Ben doesn't meet the criteria to continue on as part of our program. We focus on physical improvement, and Ben just hasn't made enough of those to warrant staying here. Besides, we aren't trained the way Steven is to teach sign language. Ben would need to be seen in Steven's clinic."

John placed his hands on his hips. "Okay, where is Steven's clinic? Is it in the hospital?"

"No." Jill stepped toward him. "Steven's clinic is an independent clinic in Helena. He isn't associated with a hospital."

"Helena!" He caught his voice before he shouted. The state capital situated southwest of his ranch would be an even longer drive than Billings had been.

147

"You might as well know," Steven said, also standing, "that insurance will not cover my services since they are considered experimental and not pertinent to sustaining life. That's why I am waiving my fees for three months. Also I would need to see Ben every day in the beginning; Ben would need to live in Helena. I have no accommodations to offer you, so you would have to find a place for Ben to live and provide for his care. I am here strictly to work on communication."

John rubbed his forehead, trying to get control of his whirling thoughts. He glanced around the room at the faces looking at him expectantly. He met his mother's gaze and he saw the hope that burned in her eyes. He knew that he could no more extinguish the hope he saw there than he could go back and not take the shot at the deer that set all this in motion.

He stepped forward and placed his hand on Steve's shoulder. "When do we start?"

After completing the paperwork to transfer Ben to Steven's therapy program, Jill agreed to meet John for dinner. His mother had been on the computer since they had returned to the hotel room trying to locate the perfect place for her and Ben to live while in Helena. He stepped from the shower and wiped the steam from the mirror. Leaning against the sink, he studied his face and contemplated the future. With his mother and Ben in Helena and Jamie more than likely to be spending time in jail; he alone would be at the ranch, except for Amber. The more he thought about the situation the more he thought that Amber should go home to wherever it was she hung her hat before Jamie had swooped into her life wreaking havoc. Yes, with Amber gone he could solely focus on the ranch and on his relationship with Jill. He had no idea how they would make it work with his responsibilities at home and her career in Billings, but he would find a way. Finally, things seemed to be looking up for them.

He dressed quickly and drove to Jill's apartment. She was beautiful in hospital scrubs, but she was downright breathtaking dressed for dinner. Pride streamed through him as he placed his hand on the small of her back and guided her to their seat at the restaurant. Despite his previous desire to cling to his anger and bitterness, he found himself sharing every sordid detail of Jamie's arrest with her.

"Oh, John!" She reached across the table and took his hand. "Are you okay?"

His insides warmed to think that she was concerned with his well-being.

"The lawyer I keep on retention for the ranch is handling it. He's good, but he's pretty confident that Jamie will have to spend time in jail." He tapped his fingers against the table and searched her face to see what she thought about his brother being incarcerated.

She squeezed his hand. "I'll be praying for Jamie and for you."

They spent the rest of the evening enjoying each other's company. Every time a worry about how he would handle Jamie's situation or move his mother and Ben to Helena tried to creep in, he forced it to the back of his mind and focused on her. He had been doing just that when something Jill said brought him back to the present.

"I'm sorry, what did you say?"

"I said wouldn't it be amazing if Ben is able to one day carry on a conversation just like you and I are right now? What if one day he is able to talk to you just like he used to? I know that is such a burden on families; the not knowing exactly what their loved one is thinking or feeling. Are they hungry? Are they in pain? What if one day he can tell you exactly what caused the accident? And then tell you everything he's experienced since then?" The excitement shone on her face.

An emptiness settled in the pit of John's stomach. What if one day Ben would be able to tell everyone what happened that day? He would be able to tell everyone, including Jill, that the accident was unequivocally John's fault. And he would be able to tell John how much he hated him. All the burdens John secretly had carried for the last four years would be brought out in the open. Suddenly his appetite was gone. He glanced across the table at Jill as she continued to talk about Ben's therapy and wondered how long before she would be gone as well.

John's mind tumbled into a dark hole, running her thoughts about Ben's therapy over and over through his mind. Sleep eluded him as he returned to the hotel room. He brewed a cup of coffee and sat staring into the dark. What kind of man was he? He should be overjoyed for his brother, and yet all he could think about was that if Ben was able to communicate, then he would be able to tell everyone how much he hated John. John hated himself for his thoughts. He knew beyond a shadow of a doubt that he was a horrible man, and Jill deserved better.

"Can't sleep?" His mother's voice caused him to jump.

He looked over his shoulder. "I hope I didn't wake you up?"

"No, I couldn't sleep." She took the seat across from him. "Too many things to think about."

"Yeah, me too." He sipped his coffee.

"Will you be okay? If I move to Helena?"

"I'll be fine. You don't worry about me." He patted his mother's hand.

"You sure?"

"I'm sure." He forced a smile trying to convince her.

"You're not responsible for it all. You know that, right?"

He raised his eyebrow and took a drink of coffee. "What are you talking about, Momma?"

"You aren't responsible for Jamie, or Ben or me for that matter."

"Momma, I am too—"

"No!" she exclaimed forcefully. "You are not and I don't want you to give up your future to take care of us."

"And what future do you think I'm giving up?"

"A future with Jill." She leveled her gaze at him.

"You think she's my future?" He fingered the handle to the coffee mug.

"I think you are happy when you're with her. Happier than I have seen you in years…well, since Ben's accident." She studied him quietly before she added, "I've always felt guilty that you had to come home."

"We've been through this, I wanted to come home. I had to come home."

"We could have sold the ranch. We could have made it work."

He thought for several moments before he responded, "No, we couldn't sell the ranch and even if I didn't know that then, I do now. It's a part of us. It's home when no other place on earth is."

Tears welled in her eyes as she nodded and he knew that she was thinking of Red. "Momma, that day…the day of Ben's accident… It was…I…" The words caught in his throat. He wanted to tell her, to explain to her that his rifle had caused the accident. He wanted to say the one thing that he had never had the nerve to say out loud to another person.

She reached out and took his hand. "I know…son…I know."

He fell to his knees in front of her and buried his face in her lap, weeping like a child. He wept for the hurt his family had been through and for the loss of his future. He wept because he knew beyond a shadow of a doubt that fate had dealt him the cruelest of blows. He had prayed for Ben to be healed and it looked like that prayer might actually be answered to a degree. But with that answer came fate's cruelest twist. When Jill found out that he had caused Ben's accident and had been too much of a coward to admit it to her, he would lose her forever. And in that moment he knew that God had no intention of ever allowing John to grab onto happily ever after.

He slept fitfully the rest of the night, rising early. Today they would move Ben to Helena, setting him up in a hotel suggested by Steve until they could locate a more permanent location for Pattie and Ben to live in during therapy. The process at the hospital was slow and tedious. He felt as though they had asked for everything but the deed to the ranch by the time they finally had Ben loaded in the SUV. Jill had come in on her day off to help them and offered to follow them to Helena. As much as John longed to accept her support, he knew keeping her at arm's length was the only way he would survive this so he insisted that she stay at home. He had to systematically distance himself from her.

Steve's clinic was state of the art and located downtown. After a quick tour of the clinic, Steve took Pattie and Ben into the therapy room to show Pattie what Ben was already able to sign. John walked around the block looking for apartment buildings; he wanted Pattie and Ben to be close to the therapy center. He was entering the telephone number for a building he had found when his phone rang. Not recognizing the number, he almost clicked ignore but decided he better answer.

"You let her come by herself!" Jamie screamed into the phone before John could utter a greeting.

Jamie continued to yell into the phone and it took John a few minutes to figure out what Jamie was saying.

151

"Jamie," he barked into the phone, "what are you talking about?"

"Amber. I'm talking about Amber and the fact that you let her come here by herself."

John wracked his brain and for the life of him he couldn't figure out why Jamie was so upset. "Jamie, what is the big deal? She drove to Fortuna to see you. That's not against the law."

"No, John, she didn't drive to Fortuna." Anger laced Jamie's voice. "She paid some bartender from the County Line Tavern a hundred dollars to drive her to Fortuna today."

"What?" John stopped in his tracks.

Jamie took a deep a breath. "She doesn't have a driver's license. She paid money to some bartender that she doesn't even know to bring her here because she said you had to run off to see your girlfriend."

"Well, that's not quite the entire story, Jamie." John placed his hand on his hip, taking a defensive stance as though they were face to face. "We had to meet with Dr. Bryan. They are moving Ben to Helena."

"What's going on with Ben? Is he sick?"

"No, it's a new therapy program." John didn't feel like going into details with Jamie at this point so he attempted to direct the conversation back to the current situation. "And she's a grown woman, Jamie, I can't stop her from catching a ride with somebody, and while we are discussing this, why doesn't she have a driver's license?"

Silence stretched for several moments before Jamie responded, his voice calmer. "She has some unpaid parking tickets, that's all."

"That's a whole lot of unpaid parking tickets to get your license revoked."

"That doesn't change the fact that you let her run off with some stranger who could have done who knows what to her!" Jamie's anger seemed to rekindle.

"She's a grown woman, Jamie, I am not her keeper. She can do as she pleases as long as she's on my ranch, I don't have time to babysit. If you want someone to keep tabs on her maybe you should send her back to her parents until we get all this straightened out."

"She can't go back to her parents, John. She's pregnant."

John felt as if someone had hit him in the stomach with a sledgehammer. He leaned against the nearest wall to keep from falling. "Wh-what?"

"She's pregnant, John. That's why she can't go back to her parents, and that's why I can't go to jail."

"Jamie…" John couldn't form his thoughts into words. Suddenly Jamie's anger came into perspective.

"I know I'm asking a lot, but I need you to watch out for her until I can get out of here. I know I don't have any right to ask you for anything, but…I need you to do this for me, John." The desperation in Jamie's voice tore through the years of anger and bitterness that had built between the brothers.

"Of course, Jamie, of course."

"I have to go. I had to do some major bartering to get this phone time. Brent is coming one day next week…"

"I'll be with him…Jamie?"

"Yeah?"

"I'll take care of her."

"I knew you would, John. You always do the right thing."

Chapter 16 Promises

"But he said, 'What is impossible with men is possible with God.'" Luke 18:27

John left Pattie and Ben on Sunday morning and headed back to the ranch. He had them squared away in a hotel until their handicap-accessible apartment one block from the clinic came available next week. The long ride home gave him plenty of time to ponder the curveballs he had been thrown in the past few days. He had decided not to tell his mother about Amber's pregnancy; she didn't need anything else to worry about. He was also determined to double down his effort to convince not only Jamie, but Amber as well, that she needed to go home to her parents until Jamie's legal trouble was over.

He tried to think of all the tasks he needed to complete on the ranch, but instead his mind settled on Jill. An uneasiness swept over him as he once again imagined the look on Jill's face when she discovered he had caused Ben's accident. Not only that he had caused it, but that he had never been man enough to admit that to her or anyone else. Instead, he had dedicated himself to his family to try and make up for his sins. But that would never be enough. Nothing he could do would ever make up for what he had done to Ben. He hated himself for the way he felt. He should be overjoyed by the development in Ben's therapy, instead of dwelling on how it would impact him.

The thought of Jill looking at him with disappointment and disgust caused a sourness to settle in his stomach. How could he manage to see her over the next few months knowing how she would react when she found out his secret? The selfish side of him wanted all the time he could get with her before she found out and hated him. He also knew that the more time he spent with her the deeper in love he would fall with her and then losing her would destroy him. Self-preservation might be his best option in this situation. A deep throb settled in his temples as he desperately wished he had never let his guard down and let the pretty therapist get inside. He would have to return to his "all business, no nonsense, no emotion, the ranch is everything state of mind" if he were ever to survive this.

Hours in the truck gave his mind too much time to wander and as he topped the hill and saw the ranch spread below him, an ache settled in his chest as he finally came to a decision. He would have to systematically remove her from his life because hanging on until the end would be his undoing and too many people depended upon him for that to happen.

John spent the next three days with his head down, trying to fit a week's worth of work into just a few days. He rose before the sun was up and fell back into bed long after darkness had blanketed the ranch. He avoided phone calls from Jill and his mother, listening to voicemails to discover that Ben and Pattie had settled in nicely and that Jill missed him. He checked on Amber periodically to fulfill his promise to Jamie. On Wednesday night he received a call from Brent Tarkinson notifying him that he would be traveling to Fortuna to meet with Jamie the next morning and he thought it best that John attend.

The ride to Fortuna was lonely, with only his thoughts to keep him company. John reached for the phone several times to call Jill. He knew that calling her, hearing her voice, would only make it harder to remove her from his every waking thought. No, he had decided he had to remove her from his life, that way when she hated him he would have the walls around his heart back intact...hopefully. The fifth time he reached for the phone to call her, he tossed it across the truck out of his reach, removing the temptation.

Brent was seated and Jamie was anxiously pacing the floor when John was escorted into the small dank room where they would be meeting.

"Where have you been?" Jamie stopped pacing long enough to confront John. "Brent has called you a hundred times!"

"Uh, sorry, I misplaced my phone," John lied.

"Well, you just tell him that I'm not doing it." Jamie pointed at Brent, who sat calmly at the table. "Go ahead and tell him, John, I'm not doing it."

"Calm down, Jamie. What are you not doing?"

"Both of you sit down and calm down," Brent ordered.

John took the seat across from Brent and waited for the man to explain what had gotten Jamie so upset.

"We've been offered a deal by the prosecution." Brent paused to let the information soak in. "Now there is no question that Jamie assaulted the officer, however, there is some question around whether or not Jamie could have heard the officer identify himself with the bar being so loud, and there is the fact that the officer approached Jamie from behind. Anyway, the prosecution is willing to lessen the charges to misdemeanor assault, which will be about six months in jail."

"That's great!" John exclaimed, clamping his hand on Jamie's shoulder.

"That's not all," Brent continued. "Seeing Jamie's record of public intoxication, the prosecution also demands a minimum of a six-month state-sponsored rehab program. In total, we are looking at about a year total."

"And I'm not doing that!" Jamie jumped up, knocking over the chair behind him.

"Yes, you are, Jamie." John turned to face his brother.

"I can't be away for a year, John."

"If you don't take this deal, they will charge you with a felony and they have more than enough witnesses to convict you," Brent interjected.

"A felony, Jamie." John stood to face his brother. "Do you know how long you will be away if you get convicted of a felony? Twenty years, Jamie. Twenty years."

Jamie looked desperately at his brother. "Brent, can you give us a minute?" John asked, never breaking his brother's gaze.

"Sure."

John waited until Brent had left the room. "Jamie, you don't have an option here. You have to take this deal."

"I can't be a way a year. I can't miss everything. Amber needs me. I haven't always been a good husband, but she needs me now and I need to be there. I need to be there for my kid, John."

"If you don't take this deal, your kid will be grown before you are out of here." John let his words hang, hoping they would resonate with Jamie.

Jamie dropped into the nearest chair, rubbing his hands down his face.

John took the seat next to him. "A year is not that long, Jamie. A year that your kid won't even remember."

"Amber will remember."

"Then after the year is up you can spend the rest of your life making it up to her."

"You don't think I can beat this charge?"

"Didn't you hear what Brent said? It's this deal or be charged with a felony."

Jamie dropped his head and only when his shoulders began to shake did John realize he was sobbing.

"I've messed everything up…everything. I've been so stupid and selfish….Now I'm going to miss my kid being born, miss everything."

John squeezed Jamie's shoulder. "You can't change the past. All you can do is try to make the future better. You have to take this deal. It's best for you and for your family."

Red-rimmed eyes looked up to meet John's and he was transported back to life before Ben's accident. Back to when the bonds of brotherhood had run so deep that John would have given his very life to protect his little brothers. "You'll take care of her?" Jamie whispered.

"Of course."

"I need to be the one to tell her." Jamie stood and began pacing again. "Can you bring her to see me?"

"Of course," John repeated, feeling a shift in his brother, and for the first time in four years he had hope that Jamie might be on the path to healing.

157

Jamie stared out the window for several long moments, seeming to come to terms with his current situation, and turned to John.

"Now"—Jamie took the seat across from him—"tell me about Ben."

****

They agreed that John would bring Amber on Sunday afternoon so that Jamie could tell her in person about his plea deal. She had peppered John with questions since he had returned on Thursday. He had been vague to say the least and he could tell she was frustrated with him. She sat quietly in the kitchen early Sunday morning, while he waited for his second pot of coffee to finish brewing.

He glanced at her, knowing she was angry that he hadn't offered up more information. A twinge of guilt sliced through him. He had information that would impact the rest of her life, but he had withheld it at Jamie's request. He assured himself this was best. She needed to hear the news from her husband. He decided to tackle another topic that had been plaguing him.

"Jamie tells me you don't have a driver's license," John ventured.

Heat visibly crept up her face as she looked at him with wide eyes. "I…um…. I can't believe he told you that."

He scooted the chair across from her against the linoleum and took a seat. "We need to get you a license. I'm not going to be able to drive you everywhere you are going to need to go."

"Jamie will be home; he can drive me." She looked John in the eye and he feared that his face betrayed him. "Right, John? Jamie will be home."

He heard the last gurgle of the coffee pot. He stood and turned his back to her as he poured coffee in a thermos. "We better get going. Fortuna is a long drive."

The ride was silent. John was lost in his own thoughts and barely registered the small country church they passed, parking lot filled with cars.

"John," Amber said thoughtfully, "do you go to church? I know Jamie has told me you used to…"

John released a breath. "Yeah, we used to go every Sunday. Momma still does, but I don't."

"Can I ask why?"

He glanced at her and pondered their situation. As best he could tell, he was going to be responsible for this girl through one of the toughest times in her life. What could it hurt to get to know her a little better? Besides, if he were honest, he was lonely and talking to anyone was better than the silence that plagued him most of his days.

"Uh, well…I moved to Billings when I got out of college and just got out of the habit, didn't have anybody waking me up and telling me I had to go, so I just didn't. Then I moved back to the ranch after Ben's accident and then my dad got sick…well, I got busy with ranch stuff and just never did go back. What about you? Did you go to church growing up?"

"No," she answered quietly, and John couldn't help but feel like there was more she wanted to say. "But I think it would be nice, you know?" she continued. "To have something like that…to have faith that God is looking out over you."

John grunted, not sure how to respond.

"I caught Jill reading her Bible one morning while she was at the ranch and she talked like God was her best friend. She said she couldn't get through the day without God being with her."

John could tell she was studying his profile so he kept his eyes glued to the road and nodded.

"I guess it's easy to have faith when life has always been easy for you," Amber said.

"What do you mean by that?" John glanced at her.

"Well, Jill's life has always been easy. I mean look at her. She's gorgeous, has a good job…not like me. My life has been crap since I was a kid. My dad is an alcoholic and couldn't keep a job, my mom worked herself into an early grave…"

John swallowed the lump in his throat and understood now why Jamie refused to send her home.

"Anyway," she continued, "after my mom died I just got kind of lost… I dropped out of high school and got a job waiting tables at this hole in the wall place. I lied about my age so I could work there… people tip better when they are drunk. That's where I met Jamie."

159

"Oh yeah?" An answer to one of John's many questions about Amber and Jamie was answered at least.

"Yeah, I had known him for a while before he asked me out…if you could call it that. He sat in a booth while I worked and then we shared a six-pack in the bed of his pickup truck. Romantic, I know. We talked all night long; sat there until the sun came up." She turned and studied his profile before she added, "He told me all about you."

"Really?" John raised his eyebrow.

"Yep, you were the big brother that did everything right."

"I doubt that." He gripped the steering, knowing how wrong Jamie's perception of him was.

"He said all three of you—you, him, and Ben—were really close, but that after Ben's accident…well, everything just changed."

John felt uncomfortable with the direction of the conversation so he said the only thing he could think of to change it. "Jill's life isn't as easy as it looks, you know."

"Oh yeah? Looks pretty good from where I'm sitting."

"Her brother was in a car wreck. He had a brain injury like Ben. He didn't make it…he got an infection and died about a year after the wreck. Her parents split after that; they just couldn't handle it. They both remarried…it's like she lost her entire family when her brother died."

Silence stretched between them and John glanced over to see Amber's reaction.

"You can't tell it…that her life is like that…she always seems happy or something." Amber looked at the window. "Do you think her faith in God makes her like that?"

John shifted uncomfortably in his seat. He was the last person that should be giving Amber insight on faith; his own seemed to have failed him.

"I don't know…she seems to think so, I guess."

Amber seemed satisfied with his answer and turned to stare out the window. It wasn't long before he heard her rhythmic breathing and glanced to see she had fallen asleep. Relief washed over him; the last thing he wanted was for her to continue to talk about Jill.

Jill slipped her phone back into her pocket for at least the one thousandth time that day. It had been a week since she had last spoken to John. She had replayed every moment of their time together last weekend trying to determine if anything had happened that might have caused him to be so upset that he wouldn't call her. She analyzed every word, look, and touch, and she could come up with absolutely no reason for John to be avoiding her. Worried that Ben's therapy was not going well and for some reason he was blaming her, she had called Pattie, who had been over the moon with Ben's therapy and their new living arrangements in Helena. Jill had stopped short of asking Pattie about John. No need to be completely pathetic. She kept reminding herself that not only would he now be running the ranch without the aid of his mother, but he was also dealing with Jamie's arrest. The heaviness of his burdens weighed on her. There was no denying her feelings, she was in love with him and she only wanted to help him. Before she could think about it any further, she quickly sent him a text.

Thinking of you. Hope you are having a good day.

She stared at her phone for several minutes hoping he would respond, only to be disappointed. She slipped her phone back into her pocket and decided to solely focus on work, putting John out of her mind until tonight.

Chapter 17 Endings

"Be joyful in hope, patient in affliction, faithful in prayer." Romans 12:12

Amber stared out the window quietly as they made the long drive back to the ranch from visiting Jamie. John wracked his brain trying to come up with words that might comfort her, but had come up short. He thought of Jill, who would have had the perfect thing to say to Amber right now. Absently his hand reached for his phone, but he snatched it away quickly and gripped the steering wheel. He thought of the text she had sent. He needed to talk to her. He needed to tell her that whatever they had together would have to end, but the thought of doing that caused a sickening sensation to settle in the pit of his stomach. He glanced over at Amber to see her wipe a single tear. At a loss for what to do, he reached over and squeezed her shoulder. "It's the best option, and you know that."

"I know," she said quietly, "but a year…." Her voice dissolved into tears.

"We'll get through it. I promise."

He spent the next couple of days with his head down, working from well before sunup to way after sundown. Trying to work so much that he didn't have time to think. He didn't want to think about Jamie, and how he would now be responsible for Amber during one of the most difficult times in her life. He didn't want to think about what would happen when and if Ben was able to communicate how much he hated John for what he had done to him. But mostly he did not want to think about Jill and what he would have to do to her. It was selfish really. He knew that by ending things he would hurt her, but it would save her from looking at him with hate in her eyes down the road when she found out what type of person he really was. He was a coward. He knew that, but the thought of Jill looking at him with disgust and hate was more than he could handle. He sat at his computer early one morning, staring blankly at the screen. He glanced at the clock, mentally noting that Jill would be arriving at the hospital right about that time. He took a deep breath and grabbed his phone, mentally calling himself every derogatory term he could think of that meant coward. That's what he was; a coward. He couldn't imagine her finding out that he had caused Ben's accident and hating him. No, better to end it now, and preserve himself as best he could. He grabbed the phone before he changed his mind and dialed her number, again reminding himself that a real man would do this face to face.

Jill's heart thumped hard in her chest when she saw his number light up her phone screen. She had come in to work a little early and was already in the gym preparing for the day. She paused for only a moment before she answered.

"Good morning," she said into the phone, and John's stomach dropped at the sound of her voice. He realized then how much he had missed her; just the sound of her voice was balm to his roughened soul. How was he going to do this? How was he going to go on without her in his life? He pushed those thoughts aside and cleared his throat. "Good morning."

"I've been worried about you." Jill tried to keep her voice light, not wanting him to know that she had been lying awake at night wondering why he had not returned calls or texts.

"Well, life has been a little crazy lately."

"I'm sure. I hear Ben is doing well." John briefly wondered if she had spoken to his mother.

"Yeah, I guess...that's what Momma says; I haven't been back to see them."

"It's hard with your mom gone from the ranch?" He hated the sympathy he heard in her voice but he took it as his opening.

"Yeah, I guess I didn't realize all she did to keep the ranch running smoothly, lots of bookkeeping stuff that I'm having to do now."

"Anything I can do to help you?"

It was on the tip of his tongue to say yes before he could even think. He bit the word back and leaned forward on his desk.

"Listen, Jill…things have just gone crazy around here. With Momma living in Helena with Ben, and Jamie looking at jail time, my work load has doubled around here. Not to mention Amber is pregnant—"

"What?"

"Yeah, Amber's pregnant. The hits just keep coming." He didn't even try to keep the bitterness out of his voice. "Anyway, our lawyer has negotiated a deal with the prosecutor, but Jamie is still looking at jail time so that means not only am I responsible for all the ranch work but I'm going to be responsible for Amber."

"Oh, John, I'm so sorry all this is landing in your lap. What can I do to help you?"

"Jill…see uh…that's the thing…with all that's going on here and you being in Billings…" He swallowed hard and heard her sharp intake of breath. Seconds ticked by.

"John, don't do this," she whispered into the phone. "We can figure this out."

"I don't see how." John stood and walked to the window. "I've just got too much on my plate right now to play boyfriend." He knew his last comment would hurt her and maybe part of him wanted to cause her pain to keep her from trying to talk sense into him.

"John, I love you. We can figure this out." Her voice trembled and it tore at his heart. He stamped his foot and leaned his forehead against the window trying to compose himself, knowing that she might think she loved him now, but in the end would wind up hating him, and the thought of her hating him was more than he could handle.

"No…" He cleared his throat and fought back the emotion clogging his throat. "No, I don't see how. My responsibilities are here at the ranch and they just keep multiplying. I don't have time to run off to Billings."

Silence answered him so he continued, hating himself for what he was saying, "How was this ever going to work? I will never leave this ranch or my family and your career is in Billings. It just won't work, and it's better that we just end it now."

He heard her sniff and knew he had made her cry. His gut twisted. He didn't deserve her. She was perfect and he was a coward who not only had ruined life for his family, he had made her cry. She would be better off without him.

"Jill?"

"I have to go, John. I'm at work."

"I'm sorry," he whispered as he felt his heart rip inside his chest.

"Me too, John. Me too."

He heard the line go dead just before he threw his phone across the office.

Jill retreated to her office and shut the door behind her. Sliding to the floor, she dropped her head in her hands and sobbed. A dull ache settled in her chest and she knew in that moment that her heart was shattered.

"Oh God, did I hear you wrong? I thought he was the one…I love him," she whispered into the dark office. She sat in the dark thinking of all she had lost. She had lost a brother, and in essence her family after that. Now she had lost what she had thought was the love of her life. She replayed every moment of her time with John. Scrutinizing every word and action to try and determine if he had given off signals that a breakup was imminent and she had been too foolish to notice. As she relived every word, every touch, every kiss, she fell deeper into despair and physical pain spread throughout her body. It was too much, the pain, the loss, it was just too much to bear.

A knock on her office door jarred her back to reality.

"Jill? You in there?" Jill heard the concern in Sam's voice.

"Yeah, Sam." She tried to keep the emotion out of her voice. "I'm not feeling too well…I think I'm going to go home."

"Are you okay? You need me to drive you?"

"No!" she answered a little too quickly. "No, I'll be okay…See you tomorrow."

She prayed that God would forgive her for the lie because deep down inside her heart, she knew it would be a very long time before she would be okay, if ever.

Chapter 18 Bitterness

"Let all bitterness and wrath and anger and clamor and slander be put away from you, along with all malice." Ephesians 4:31

A heaviness settled in the pit of John's stomach, making it near impossible to eat regular meals. He managed to choke down a bite or two at meal time, but mainly had lived off coffee for a week. Amber had taken up residence in the main house and had taken over his mother's role of preparing meals. She wasn't a bad cook—actually she was pretty good at it—and he felt guilty as her face fell when yet again he pushed his plate away with very little having been eaten.

"You don't like it?" she asked for the umpteenth time that week.

"No, it's fine. I just don't have much of an appetite." He stood and poured himself another cup of coffee.

"Are you sick, John? I've not seen you eat more than a few bites at dinner any night this week and you look a little pale."

"I'm fine. And your cooking is good, just got a lot on my mind." He sat back down at the table with his coffee, thinking how awkward their situation was. He was, for all intents and purposes, living with his brother's wife. He couldn't help but wonder how many tongues were wagging in town about their situation.

"John, I've been thinking." Amber fingered her fork nervously and waited for him to meet her gaze before she continued. "I want to go to church Sunday."

The gulp of steaming coffee that John had just taken seemed to lodge in his throat. He struggled to swallow it, coughing as he finally got it down. "What?"

"I want to go to church on Sunday. I keep thinking about Jill." The sound of her name caused John's heart to plummet. "After all she has been through, she is still happy…you know…I mean after you told me about her brother and her family I just can't help but think how strong she is. Makes me think it has to do with her faith in God."

He nodded, unable to speak about Jill.

"Well, I just think I could really use some of that faith right about now." She absently looked down and John knew she was thinking about her unborn child.

He studied his coffee, turning over options in his head. He had promised Jamie he would take care of her, but did that include taking her to church? He was leaning toward no when she raised her head and he saw the tears mingled with hope in her eyes.

He sighed. "I'll drop you off."

He quickly saw the horror in her face. "But John, I don't know anybody…you know everybody. I was hoping you would go with me."

"Amber, I haven't been to church in years."

"I know, but you used to go…plus everybody in this county knows you and respects you." She bit her lower lip and tears threatened to spill down her cheeks. "I'm afraid to go by myself."

John released a breath and let his shoulders slump. He thought about Jamie sitting in a jail cell for the next six months and despite the animosity that had developed between them over the last few years, he loved his brother deeply and wanted to help him if he could. Helping Amber meant helping Jamie. He could hear his own voice in his head, promising Jamie he would take care of Amber as long as he agreed to take the deal. He glanced up and saw the fear and uncertainty in her eyes, and he couldn't help but think about Jill. Here was his chance to make at least one woman in his life happy, even if he had failed all the others. Knowing what he had to do, he stood up from the table. "We will go to church on Sunday, then."

Jill went through the motions of her day, an emptiness invading every cell in her body. Her usual easy smile seemed to have disappeared and coworkers noticed no matter hard she tried to hide her broken heart. She had many people at the hospital that she deemed her friends, but none so close that she felt she could share her broken heart. She spent hours in the chapel after work, pouring out her heart to God, offering him all the pieces of the heart John Mitchell had shattered. Days turned into weeks and she still felt broken and splintered. She prayed and read Psalms and prayed some more. She identified with David's bleakness in many of the Psalms as he lamented how broken he was. She clung to her faith that just like David, God would piece her back together and she would sing praises again. She prayed for John as well. She prayed that he would be able to find peace and happiness and that whatever the reason for their brief relationship she prayed that something good would come out of it. God reminded her that something had; Ben had been helped. Jill wondered if she would have been as dogged about Ben's therapy if it had not been for her affection for John. Had there been other patients that she could have helped more if she had been as determined as she was with Ben? She pledged to herself and her future patients that she would give everyone the same level of dedication she had given to Ben.

Dr. Bryan found her sitting in the chapel one day after her shift more than a month after the breakup.

"Jill." Dr. Bryan's voice was gentle as she touched Jill's shoulder.

"Oh, hey, Dr. Bryan." Jill jumped at the contact.

"I didn't mean to startle you. Do you mind if I join you?"

"No, not at all." Jill gestured to the seat beside her.

The doctor whom Jill had always admired turned a concerned gaze toward her. "Jill, I'm worried about you."

Jill dropped her gaze to her lap, hoping that she could keep the tears from spilling over her cheeks.

"While your work is as impeccable as always, you seem…different…sad."

Jill sniffed and looked up, avoiding Dr. Bryan's piercing eyes.

"I'm guessing it has something to do with a certain cowboy that doesn't come around anymore."

"Am I that obvious?" Jill finally met the other woman's gaze.

"I'm so sorry, Jill. I had a really good feeling about you two."

"Yeah, me too." Jill's voice cracked.

"God heals the brokenhearted, Jill."

Jill nodded, her voice thick with emotion, and she thanked God for not the first time that He had placed the godly doctor in her life.

"If you need me…"

"I know. Thank you." Jill nodded and the fight to keep the tears away was lost as one slipped down her cheek.

After the first Sunday at church, Amber was hooked. John grimaced as he thought back to how they had been swarmed by churchgoers the first Sunday they had attended. The word *busybodies* came to mind as he heard several women pry into their family business under the guise of being concerned. He was sure most of the people had heard about Jamie's incarceration, but luckily no one who knew of it had come right out and asked. Amber had met several young women her age and had started attending Sunday school as well.

Over the past month, John had learned a lot about Amber and they had fallen into some type of routine. He still felt very uncomfortable about the two of them being alone in the main house, so he spent most of his nights sleeping on a cot in the barn. But with her driver's license being suspended, he still had spent quite a bit of time with her taking her to church, the grocery store, and finally the doctor's office. He mostly sat in the truck waiting for her on these trips. At her doctor's appointment she had eagerly run to the car to show him an ultrasound picture. She claimed there was a baby in the picture; he would just have to take her word for it. She had proudly displayed the picture on the refrigerator, and repeatedly said she couldn't wait to show Jamie. She seemed as happy as she could be under the circumstances and he felt some modicum of relief knowing he was keeping his promise to Jamie.

As he sat in the church parking lot waiting for her once again, he made a mental note that he needed to check with Brent Tarkinson about getting her driver's license reinstated. Not only did he have responsibilities at the ranch that were falling to other people, but all that sitting around and waiting gave him too much time to think about Jill. Every song that came on the radio reminded him of her, every blonde woman who walked past him made his heart skip until he was able to convince himself it wasn't her. The long moments spent waiting in parking lots also gave his mind time to think of all the what-ifs. What if he hadn't come home the weekend of Ben's accident and insisted on his brothers going hunting with him? What if he had met Jill under different circumstances? What if he had just been honest with her from the beginning? What if he had just told her the first time he met her that he was responsible for Ben's accident? But all the what-ifs in the world didn't matter now. He had ruined any chances he had at happiness when he had walked away from her.

Lost in his own thoughts one Sunday, he didn't even notice the pastor of the church approaching his truck until the other man rapped on his window, causing John to almost jump out of his own skin.

"Pastor Rick." John nodded as he rolled down his truck window.

"John, good to see you. You know you could come in for small groups too." The preacher laughed and John squirmed in his seat.

"Uh, yeah…well… I usually have things I need to do. Ranch work never ends."

"Really? I thought I had seen you sitting out here before while Amber attends small group."

John glanced at the clock in his truck, hoping that it would be time for the preacher to go inside to prepare for his sermon.

Pastor Rick slapped John on the shoulder and chuckled, obviously finding John's discomfort amusing. "I'm giving you a hard time, John."

The relief must have shown on John's face as the pastor continued, "We would love to have you join a small group when you are ready, but I am so happy just to have you attending church. It's been a while."

"Yeah, a while," John said tightly, bracing himself for a lecture.

"Well, like I said, good to have you. Your mother seems to be doing well."

"Yes, she is." John was relieved at the change of subject. "Anything that helps Ben makes Momma happy."

"That's understandable. John"—the pastor's face turned serious—"how's Jamie? Your mother is very concerned about him."

John briefly wondered how often his mother spoke to Pastor Rick. "He's doing okay."

"And Amber?"

"She seems to be holding up okay."

"She's a very special young lady. The church has just fallen in love with her in the short time she's been here. We would love to help any way we can."

John studied the pastor, a little shocked by his offer. "I think we can manage, but thanks anyway."

"Well, if you change your mind you know where to find me." Pastor Rick turned and headed toward the church, then suddenly stopped and turned to face John. "That offer extends to you as well, John. If there is anything I or the church can do to help you, all you have to do is ask."

John nodded and pressed the button to raise the window, not exactly sure what to think about the preacher's offer.

Chapter 19 Thankful

"I will give thanks to you, LORD, with all my heart; I will tell of all your wonderful deeds." Psalm 9:1

Despite Jill's feeling that time had stopped on the day John had ended their relationship, days and weeks slipped by, and before she knew it the holidays were right around the corner. As always the therapists had decorated the gym with plastic pilgrims and turkeys, and while a festive mood seemed to hang in the air, and Jill plastered a smile on her face and helped with the decorations, her heart just wasn't in the holiday spirit.

She had gotten up each morning since that fateful day and prayed for strength, and God had provided. Slowly God was knitting her heart back together, but there were days, less frequent than before, but there were still days that she wondered what if. What if she and John were still together, how would they be spending the holidays? But as soon as the thought came, she pushed it out of her mind. No need wasting time thinking about things that would never happen. She had volunteered to work over Thanksgiving. She could eat her frozen turkey and dressing dinner any time. She would just have spent the holiday alone in her apartment, might as well be at work.

Several coworkers had stopped by to wish her a happy holiday as she sat at a desk in the gym finishing up charts. And while she could dwell on being alone for the holiday, she decided to thank God for allowing her to have such a good work family. She smiled thinking about her coworkers and what they had meant to her, especially in the past few months.

"Jill?" The sound of her name being called by a familiar voice caused her to glance up from her chart. The voice was familiar, but she didn't immediately know who it belonged to until she saw Pattie Mitchell crossing the near empty gym, pushing Ben in his chair.

"Pattie?" Jill stood and closed the space between them, and without even thinking she enveloped the woman in a hug. "Hey, Ben!"

"I hope we aren't bothering you. We are on our way home for Thanksgiving and thought we would stop by and say hello to everyone." Pattie touched Ben's shoulder and he signed hello to Jill.

"Hello, Ben," Jill signed back to him, feeling an overwhelming sense of joy. "You seem to be doing well." She glanced behind them as her heart betrayed her soaring with hope that John would be with them.

"He's doing great. Making strides every day. We can never thank you enough, Jill." Tears of joy filled Pattie's eyes.

"Oh, Pattie, you don't need to thank me. I really didn't do anything. Ben and Steve have done all the hard work." She patted Ben on the shoulder.

"But you gave Ben a chance when nobody else did and for that I, well our entire family, will be eternally grateful."

Jill dropped her gaze, confident that at least one member of the family would not be eternally grateful to her. In fact, she imagined that John wished he had never met her. Pattie must have sensed that her thoughts were on John.

"Have you spoken with John lately?" Pattie's voice was soft.

"Uh, no." Jill forced a smile but avoided direct eye contact to keep herself from crying.

"Jill, he's a complicated man. I know he cares about you deeply." Pattie touched her arm and Jill could no longer keep the tears away as a single solitary drop rolled down her cheek.

"It's fine, Pattie. He was right, it would just never work." She brushed the tear away and forced a smile.

Ben signed something to his mother and Jill couldn't quite decipher it.

"Hush, Ben." Pattie turned her gaze to Jill. "I never thought I would get to say that ever again; telling him to hush." Pattie brushed happy tears away. "In case you were wondering, he just said John was stupid."

Jill reached over and squeezed Ben's hand. "Tell me all about therapy. Don't leave anything out."

****

The smells of holiday cooking wafted from the kitchen as John sat in what once had been Red's office, working on his laptop. He preferred working in the office in the barn, but his mother's crestfallen face when he had announced he was going to the barn had caused him to retreat to Red's old office in the house instead. He stared at the spreadsheet in front of him without seeing anything. If Pattie had mentioned their stop by St. Patrick's once, she had mentioned it a hundred times. Each time he had nodded and did his level best not to ask about Jill; of course he didn't have to ask because his mother told him every detail of their visit.

The door to the office opened and his mother slid in holding two steaming mugs. "I thought you might like some coffee."

"Sure. Thanks." He took the cup and sipped the hot liquid. He had avoided being alone with his mother since her arrival yesterday knowing that she would want to discuss his breakup with Jill.

"Amber seems to be doing well." She sat down across from him, sipping from her own mug.

"Yeah." John leaned back in the chair and rubbed his hand down his face. "Brent thinks he will have her driver's license reinstated before Christmas."

"That's good. Maybe free up your time a little bit."

"I've got plenty of things waiting to fill it up." He nodded toward the computer.

"Maybe you will have time to go to Billings…"

"Momma, don't." John set his mug down with more force than intended and hot liquid sloshed over the side, burning his hand.

"John, I just don't understand. She is perfect for you and I know you care for her."

He studied his desk for several moments before responding, "Sometimes it takes more than that, Momma."

"Like what, John? Talk to me, tell me what happened."

"It just didn't work out, that's all. No one's fault, just not meant to be."

"So you both agreed to this? Both thought this was the best decision?"

John nodded, avoiding his mother's all-knowing gaze.

She stood and turned toward the door, stopping short before she slipped from the room. "For two people who thought this was the best decision, you both look horrible. Neither one of you look like you've had a decent meal in months." She let her words hang and then left the room, closing the door behind her.

John double-downed on his efforts to focus on the spreadsheet in front of him, refusing to allow himself to think that Jill was as miserable as he was.

John tried to get out of going with the entire family to see Jamie the next day, but the disappointment on his mother's face spurred him to join them. They had been allowed to spend their time with Jamie in a meeting room, not separated by glass. Jamie and Amber had been glued to each other's side, while Ben impressed him with the sign language he had learned and they discussed baby plans with Pattie. John sat in the back feeling like an outsider, unable to get his mother's comments about Jill out of his head. A knock on the door indicated that the visit was coming to an end. Amber clung to Jamie's neck, silently weeping. Jamie whispered something in her ear and set her away from him.

"Let me talk to John…alone." Jamie looked around the room, his gaze landing on John.

John straightened and held the door for Pattie as she maneuvered Ben's chair, telling her he would be right out. The door closed behind them and the brothers were left alone.

"John, I just wanted to say thank you. Thanks for taking care of Amber and…" He swallowed and looked away before continuing, "Thank you for making me take this deal."

"Jamie." John took the seat across from his brother, unsure of what to say next.

175

"I just wanted to say that and to let you know that I'm doing well. Really good."

"That's great, Jamie."

"Six weeks and I head to rehab, and I'm not sure if you believe this or not, but I'm looking forward to it."

"What? And leave all of this?" John gestured around the drab room, trying to lighten the mood.

Jamie chuckled. "Yeah, it's real nice here."

"I'm glad you're looking forward to rehab, that's a good sign."

"I want to get to the bottom of this, you know? Why do I feel like I have to drink to handle things?"

Silence stretched between them and John sensed Jamie had more to say. He sat quietly studying his brother.

"I've been seeing a counselor in here." Jamie met his brother's gaze as if looking for acceptance.

"Really?" John tried to keep the shock from his voice.

"Yeah, and Pastor Rick has been coming to see me too. They've really helped me a lot. Made me realize it's not my fault."

"What's not your fault, Jamie?" John leaned forward, forearms resting on the table.

"Ben's accident." Jamie's words hung heavily in the air as John recoiled. How could Jamie believe the accident had been his fault when it was clearly John's? His heart hammered in his chest as a sickening feeling filled his stomach.

"Why do you think Ben's accident is your fault?" John's voice was barely above a whisper.

Jamie looked around the room as if trying to find something to draw strength from, he closed his eyes and dropped his head before he spoke, "I was drunk that morning.

"What?" John's mind reeled at his brother's admission.

"I know you and Momma think that my drinking problems started after Ben's accident, but they didn't. I had been drinking all night; snuck back in about an hour before you came to wake us up." Jamie glanced at this brother to see how he was responding to the news. "I was still drunk when it happened. I've spent the past four years wondering if something I did caused it or if I could have done something to change it. Maybe something I did and didn't even realize it caused the accident."

"Jamie, it's not your fault," John said softly. "You can't do this to yourself."

"Well, I'm working on it, you know? With the help of the counselor and Pastor Rick I've really started to forgive myself and see it for what it was, an accident, and if I could have done something, I would have. He's my brother. I love him." He paused for a moment. "I love you too, John."

"I love you too, Jamie." John surprised himself at how quickly the words rolled off his tongue.

They stared at each other silently for a few moments before Jamie spoke. "Well anyway, I just felt like I needed to say all that to you."

John nodded. "We're good, Jamie. You focus on getting better and coming home."

Jamie cocked his head to the side. "You doing okay? Amber mentioned you and Jill had broken up."

"Yeah," John scoffed, trying to keep his voice light. "Just one of those things...no big deal."

"No big deal, huh? You look rough, John. When's the last time you ate a meal or got a decent night's sleep? I'm in jail and I look better than you."

Making a mental note to force himself to eat, he pulled his hat lower. "I'm fine."

A corrections officer stuck his head in the door. "Time's up."

John hugged his brother and left, thankful that the conversation hadn't gone any further.

Chapter 20 Unwelcome

"Trust in the LORD *with all your heart, and do not lean on your own understanding. In all your ways acknowledge him, and he will make straight your paths." Proverbs 3:5-6*

Jill eased the rental car to a stop in front of her mother's house. She sat for a few minutes, gazing at the house. A wreath hung on the front door and a tree stood in the front window, lights twinkling merrily. She took a deep breath, exited the car, and walked to the front door. She paused, unsure of what to do. This was her mother's home, along with her stepfather and his three teenage children, but it had never been her home. Did she knock, or just open the door and announce her arrival? While she had been around her stepfather and his children quite a bit, she didn't quite feel comfortable just barging in. She knocked and waited for someone to answer. She could hear noises through the door; a television, a dog barking, muffled voices. Her youngest stepbrother, Jody, opened the door.

"Jill!" He stepped back to let her enter the house and called over his shoulder, "Dad, Mom, Jill's here!" It felt strange hearing this young man refer to her mother as "Mom," but as Jill had calculated earlier, Jody had only been four years old when his father and her mother had married. Now ten years later, of course he would refer to her as Mom, she had fulfilled that role.

Susan Morgan Walters hurried down the hallway, wiping her hands on her apron, to meet her daughter. Her husband, Roger, close on her heels.

"Jill!" her mother cried, gathering her in her arms. "It's so good to see you!"

She hugged her mother, breathing in her familiar scent that seemed to ground her no matter how long they had been apart. Her stepfather patted her on the shoulder and wished her a Merry Christmas.

"We are just finishing getting dinner ready, come on in." Her mother turned and ushered her down the hall. "After dinner Jody is in a Christmas musical at his school, you don't mind going, do you?"

Jill was exhausted from her trip, but she plastered a smile on her face. "Not at all. It will be fun."

Roger's other children, a nineteen-year-old daughter named Melissa, and a sixteen-year-old son named Nick, entered the kitchen and casually greeted Jill. She asked her mother how she could help and was instructed to set the table. Given the silverware and napkins, she began, quietly listening to the family banter. They spoke of the upcoming ballgame, and mentioned names she did not recognize. Melissa threw in some comments about needing to go shopping before she returned to school.

"Oh, and I picked up some of that soap you like, Melissa, I had a coupon." Her mother smiled and Jill felt strangely out of place in her own mother's home. She briefly wondered if her mother knew what her favorite soap was. The conversation was lively, but Jill contributed little more than a smile or nod throughout dinner, picking at the food on her plate.

"Do you not like it?" Roger asked, nodding toward her plate.

Jill looked at the chicken casserole she had moved around her plate. "Oh no, it's good." She hoped God would forgive her for the white lie.

"It's one of your mother's specialties." Roger beamed at his wife. "We just love it."

"Mom, where is my dress shirt?" Jody yelled from the stairs, having excused himself to get ready for the concert.

179

"Oh, Lord, that boy couldn't find his head if it wasn't attached to his shoulders," her mother grumbled as she rose from the table to assist him.

The house was chaotic from that point forward as preparations were made to leave for the concert. Melissa announced she would drive herself, planning to leave a little early to go see friends while she was in town. Jill rode with her mother and stepfather, squeezed between Jody and Nick in the back seat. She appreciated her stepbrothers' attempts to include her in the conversation, but really what did she have in common with two teenage boys?

They entered the crowded auditorium and Jill followed Susan and her stepfather as they headed down the main aisle.

"Oh, Jill…"Her mother's tone let Jill know that something was off.

"What's wrong, Mom?" Jill asked, standing behind her mother.

"Well, um, you see… we only have four reserved seats and well…I just didn't think…you know, about you being here." Her mother blushed.

As Jill watched Melissa, Nick, and Roger file into their seats, realization dawned on her. "There is no place for me to sit."

"Oh dear, I am so sorry…" Susan said hurriedly. "You can sit in the balcony, it's open seating."

Jill felt heat rising up her cheeks. "I can just leave, Mom."

"Nonsense." Susan scanned the auditorium, catching a glimpse of someone over Jill's shoulder. Susan waved the person down and mouthed, "Are you sitting in the balcony?" Jill glanced around the room, her feet glued to the floor by humiliation.

Jill turned in time to see a woman nodding her head yes. "See? There you go, you can sit with my friend Sandy." The stranger waved enthusiastically, as Susan gestured that Jill would be joining her.

Heat rose up Jill's neck as she made her way to the woman waiting for her at the balcony stairs.

The woman offered her a hug and smiled as Jill fell in step beside her. "I'm Sandy."

"Hi, Sandy. I'm Susan's daughter Jill."

"Well, I didn't even know Susan had another daughter. What a treat to meet you."

Jill's heart sank. She had never felt as alone as she did at that moment sitting in the middle of a crowded auditorium filled to capacity.

****

Jill lay in the makeshift bed on the pullout couch in her mother's basement. Glancing at the clock on her phone every few minutes, she was convinced time had stood still at 4:33 a.m. central standard time on this particular day. Her bags were packed and she was fully dressed, lying under the covers waiting until time for her to leave. The trip to her mother's had been nothing if not eye-opening. Her mother had walked into a ready-made family when she had married Roger and early in the week Jill had begun to wonder if there was room for her in that family. Only after she had scoured the house to find only one small picture of her and her brother siting on a shelf in the dining room did she realize there was no room for her or the family her mother had once had. She prayed that she would not be angry with her mother. Jill knew firsthand the hurt her mother had been through. Perhaps this was the best way her mother knew to deal with it. To try and put it out of her mind, and by doing that she had put Jill out of her mind as well. Jill's heart hurt and a tear slipped from her eyes. She couldn't lay all the blame at her mother's feet. She had stayed away as well, wrapping herself in her career.

She called her father to see if she could begin her visit with him a few days early. Unfortunately, he had been on a cruise with his wife and would only be arriving home today. She had planned lunch with them in Nashville and then, citing work problems, had proclaimed she would be ending her trip a few days early to head back home.

Home. Jill sighed as she thought about that word. She had always felt as though Tennessee was her home; being with her parents was being home. She flopped on her side and shoved her face in her pillow, fighting the urge to scream, because the one place that popped into her mind when she thought of home was the wide open valleys ending in towering snow-peaked mountains, riding alongside a tall, taciturn cowboy. And in that moment she knew that she would never be home again.

****

John stepped out of the barn and turned the collar on his barn coat to keep the wind off his neck. They had made it through the holidays and January was right on track to bring more snow to the mountains than they had seen in years. While the snow-covered landscape made it hard on ranchers, John secretly loved it. He inhaled deeply, taking in the crisp air. He felt lighter today, as if somehow he had begun to heal from his heartache. The dull, sickening feeling in the pit of his stomach had haunted him for months. But this morning as he scanned the snow-covered land surrounding his home, he felt as if it had subsided, or maybe he was just becoming accustomed to it.

The snow crunched under his boots as he made his way to his truck. He glanced over to see the few cowboys he kept employed full time during the winter standing around a pen. They had been tasked with thinning the horse herd and getting the best horses primed and ready for spring round-up. They seemed deep in conversation; John let the truck door slip from his hand and headed in their directions.

"What's going on, fellas?" John leaned against the top rung of the corral fence. He felt a camaraderie with the handful of men he kept on full time, and as he often did he likened it to what he had felt with his brothers at one time. He shoved the thought to the back of his head. So far today was shaping up to be a good day. He did want to ruin it by getting lost in his thoughts.

"Just checking out these horses, John." Buck leaned his arm on the top rail; he had been with the Mitchell family for as long as John could remember and was his most trusted employee. John never questioned Buck's decisions and in the months since Jamie had gone to jail and Pattie had moved to Helena, Buck had been vital to John.

John looked through the horses they had corralled, mostly older mares that had been with the ranch a while. "Might as well thin some of these out, John. That riding school over in Cutler County will take them off our hands lickety-split."

A flash of red caught his attention, bringing back a memory that he had worked hard to forget. Before he could think about what he was doing, John stepped up on the bottom rung to get a better look. "Bring that little sorrel over here."

As one of the cowboys herded the horse John had requested out in the open, his heart plummeted. He thought he had recognized the mare, but seeing her up close confirmed it. This had been the horse Jill had rode the day of their picnic.

The day he had kissed her; the day he had finally admitted to himself that he was head over heels in love with her. He stood, staring at the horse, everything else fading into the background so that all he noticed was this sorrel mare.

He wasn't sure how long he had stood there watching the mare, allowing memories that he never allowed himself to dwell on flood his mind. He could still feel her hand in his, her lips on his. He could still close his eyes and smell her perfume, feel her close to him. Six hard months of shoving down every emotion he had for Jill Morgan came crumbling down. His heart surged with emotion and he knew that he loved her just as much today as he had on that picnic. So much for having a good day.

"Whaddya say, John? Want me to call that fellow over there at the riding school? We've sold to them before, or there is that summer camp place a few counties over…I could call them." Buck's questions brought him back to reality.

"Either one is fine with me, just keep that little sorrel mare," he tossed over his shoulder as he turned to leave.

"John, are you serious?" Buck asked incredulously, "Why she hasn't seen a round-up in five years. Can't remember the last time she threw a foal that we actually kept."

"I don't care. Keep her." The tone in John's voice left no room for debate as Buck instructed the other cowboys to return the mare to the herd.

John slammed the truck door, cranked the motor, and jammed the truck in gear, throwing gravel as he left the barn. Anger surged through his body. He knew keeping the mare was irrational, but something in him could not let the animal leave his ranch. He hated how the very sight of the mare had brought back emotions he thought he had buried over the last six months. He had thought he had turned a corner; had begun to heal from his self-inflicted heartache. People had stopped asking him about her; his mother had stopped badgering him about calling her. Amber hadn't mentioned her name in weeks and the last time he had visited Jamie, they had made it through the entire visit without her name coming up. If people had forgotten then he hoped that maybe in time he could too.

But the sight of the sorrel mare had proved that those memories were far from forgotten. He might have successfully buried those feelings temporarily, but they were still there, simmering under the surface, waiting to explode with more depth than ever before. He hated himself for how quickly he could go back to that moment at the hot springs. He could close his eyes and feel her body, her lips, smell her fragrance.

He had no idea where he was going as he sped up the lonely mountain road that led away from the ranch, he just knew he had to be alone; had to get as far away from the sorrel mare that now would be a constant reminder. In his mind's eye, he could go back to the first day they met in the clinic. He remembered every word, every touch, and every look. He pressed the gas harder, hoping he could outrun the memories. He remembered the nights he had dragged back to the ranch in the early hours of the morning just because he had wanted to spend one more hour with her. He remembered how right it felt to have her at the ranch, in his home, among his family. His heart pinched when he remembered the exact moment he had realized he had never felt that way about anyone before. He could still hear her voice in his head telling him that she loved him. He remembered every word of their last conversation. Sweat beaded on his forehead as the phone call played through his mind.

He reached up to readjust his hat and wipe his brow. He must have closed his eyes momentarily, hoping to will away the emotions. When he opened them he had crossed the yellow line and was headed straight for another car. He swerved to miss the blue sedan that blared its horn at him, overcorrecting the wheel. His truck careened off the highway, bouncing across the snowdrifts accumulated on the side of the road before, with a final jerk, the truck came to a halt, the hood buried in a snowbank.

John wasn't sure how long he had been sitting in the truck when he realized he needed to get back to the main road and try to get help. He reached for the door handle and quickly determined the door was stuck. He pushed with his shoulder and even tried trying to kick it open to no avail. He slid open the back sliding glass and shimmied through the small hole to exit the truck. He surveyed the damage and determined he would need a tow truck to remove the truck from the snowdrift.

He took his hat off and slapped it against his leg, chiding himself for allowing his emotions to cloud his thinking. This was exactly why he had kept his emotions tamped down for the past six months. Letting his emotions take control caused him to do stupid things, like keeping horses around for sentimental reasons, running into snowbanks, or, even worse, stalking the hospital's website a few nights ago in hopes of seeing a picture of her. He glanced back up at the road and wondered how long it would be before someone passed along this lonesome piece of highway. He patted his jacket and pants pockets trying to locate his cell phone to no avail. He was just about ready to crawl back in the cab of the pickup to search for it when he heard a voice calling from the road.

"You need some help, John?"

John turned quickly to see Pastor Rick slipping down the embankment toward him. Of all the people that could have just happened by, it had to be the preacher. John shook his head at his luck. This day just kept getting better.

"You okay, John? Do I need to call an ambulance?" The preacher reached out and touched his shoulder as he drew near, his eyes roaming over John looking for injuries.

"I'm fine, Preacher. Just a little embarrassed and mad at myself for doing something as silly as running off a road I've driven my whole life."

"Accidents happen, John. You sure you are okay?"

"Yeah, I'm fine, just not so sure about my truck." John glanced at the front of his pickup buried in the snowdrift.

"Trucks can be fixed or replaced. As long as you are okay, that's all that matters." Pastor Rick walked to the front of the truck and let out a low whistle. "Man, you must have been going along at a pretty good speed to get buried this deep in the snow."

"I think I hit a slick spot up there." John jerked his head toward the road and hoped the preacher didn't immediately sense that he was lying. "What you are doing out this way?"

Pastor Rick turned to face John. "I was coming to see you."

"To see me?" John repeated dumbfounded, hoping that the wreck hadn't scrambled his brains.

"We've been missing you at church these past few weeks." Pastor Rick reached out and patted John's shoulder. "We got used to seeing you there and then you went MIA."

Since Brent had gotten Amber's license reinstated around Christmas, she had been able to drive herself to church, leaving John to hide out at home by himself.

"Ranch work never ends," John mumbled, avoiding the preacher's gaze.

"Well, it looks like God sent me at the exact right moment when you needed some help. Isn't God good that way? Always sends people into our lives when we need them the most."

John nodded, not sure what to say. Pastor Rick walked around to the front of the truck and let out a low whistle. "That's buried deep. I think we will probably need a wench or tow truck."

"If you could just give me a lift back to the ranch, I've got a tractor that can pull it out." John didn't like having to ask for help and honestly wanted to get away from the preacher as quickly as possible.

"Sure." The man slapped John on the back as they turned to climb back up the hill. "Jamie's heading to rehab next week right?"

"Yeah, next week." John knew that Pastor Rick visited Jamie at least once a week. The pastor knew Jamie's schedule better than most. They climbed in the truck and John relished the blast of warmth.

"And the baby will be here soon?" Pastor Rick turned the pickup around slowly.

"Uh, yeah, around March." John shuffled in his seat.

"Jamie sure is excited."

"Yeah, he seems to be." John wasn't sure where this conversation was headed.

"John, it seems to me that you have an awful lot riding on your shoulders." Rick glanced over at him. John bristled at the remark. He had protected and provided for his family since Ben's accident and Red's death.

"Nothing I can't handle." John stared straight ahead.

"We are always here for you, John, me and the church. We love you and your family. You don't have to do everything by yourself."

John clenched his jaw and kept his gaze averted. The last person he wanted to discuss his responsibilities with was Pastor Rick.

They topped the rise that opened into the valley that held the ranch and John breathed a sigh of relief. "If you can just drop me at the barn, I can take it from there. Thanks, Pastor."

Before John could jump from the truck, Rick reached over and squeezed his shoulder. "I meant what I said, John, you don't have to deal with all of this alone."

"I appreciate that, Preacher." John shut the door and turned to find Buck.

For the remainder of the week, Pastor Rick's words bounced through John's head. They continued to torment him as he drove to Fortuna for his last visit with Jamie before he was moved to a rehabilitation center. Snippets from past conversations played through his mind. Pastor Rick telling him he didn't have to carry the burden alone. His mother telling him he didn't have to take responsibility for everyone. He drove, quietly pondering the words. How could he just lay this burden down? How could he just stop being responsible for everyone? The thought was appealing, but John was unsure if it was even possible.

Chapter 21 Alone

"Turn to me and be gracious to me, for I am lonely and afflicted." Psalm 25:16

"You're awful quiet." Amber broke the silence in the truck and John glanced over at her. Three months from delivery, Amber was glowing. He had witnessed a subtle change in her. It had not happened overnight, but over the past several months he had watched her develop into a content, mature young woman. Gone was the woman who had looked to Jamie to complete her in every way. In her place was a strong, confident young woman, who if asked would immediately give credit for her change to her growing relationship with God. John could not deny that attending church had been good for Amber. She had made friends, felt accepted, and gained some independence. In fact, she had become so independent that she had refused John's suggestion that she move to Helena with Pattie and Ben until after the baby was born.

"You aren't mad because I don't want to move to Helena, are you?" She placed her hand protectively on her protruding stomach.

John dragged his hand down his face and tried for what seemed the millionth time to word his argument so Amber could see it as the only logical solution. "Amber, it just makes sense. If you went into labor at the ranch, it would take us a long time to get to the hospital, not to mention that we still get major snowstorms in March. What if we are snowed in and can't get you to the hospital?"

Amber snorted. "I've never seen a snowstorm that can keep you in the house."

John rolled his eyes. "That's different. I don't want to take any chances with trying to get you to the hospital. I promised Jamie I would take care of you and that's what I'm trying to do."

"By sending me to Helena? Where I don't know anybody? Away from my friends and my church family?"

"Momma will take care of you, and it's not like it would be permanent, just until after the baby is born."

"She has her hands full with Ben, not to mention my doctor isn't in Helena." She leaned back and crossed her arms. "We'll be just fine, John."

He took the ball cap off his head and resettled it, choosing not to argue with her. He would see if Jamie could talk some sense into her. The thought of her going into labor at the ranch terrified John, and as soon as those terrifying thoughts came, he would hear Pastor Rick's voice telling him he didn't have to do it all. Maybe he could send her to live with the pastor until after the baby was born. He remained quiet the remainder of the trip and hoped that Jamie convinced her.

He was surprised by how much he looked forward to visiting Jamie these days. The change in his brother had been nothing short of remarkable. As he watched his brother greet Amber, he noticed a spark between them, a loving gaze as they held each other's eyes that had not always been present in their marriage. John briefly felt like an intruder as the couple greeted each other. And while his heart soared that his brother seemed to be well on the road to recovery and happily married, he felt a slight pinch when he thought about his own future. Life seemed to be looking up for everybody but him. In six months Jamie would be coming home from rehab to a wife and baby. Ben was progressing daily and his communication abilities were growing beyond what they had ever hoped. John felt like he was stuck in a gut-wrenching in-between. Would he ever be able to hear her name and not feel like he had been kicked in the stomach? Would he ever look at a happy couple and not feel a twinge of regret or a thoughts of "what if"?

They visited with Jamie for the better part of an hour. John contributed to the conversation when he was expected to, but his thoughts had dived deep back into the regrets of the past. He had done what he thought was best. Better to be without her than to have her hate him when she found out he had caused Ben's accident.

John snapped to attention when he heard Jamie tell Amber to give them a few minutes alone. Amber stood and clung to Jamie. He whispered in her ear something that John couldn't hear. She looked up at him through tear-filled eyes and reached up on her tiptoes to press her lips to his. His hand rested on her stomach and they gazed into each other's eyes. John again felt like an intruder and averted his gaze.

"I'll wait for you in the lobby, John." Amber's voice was no more than a whisper, her eyes never leaving Jamie's.

Jamie watched her leave and continued to stare at the door for several moments before he took the chair across from John. He studied his older brother for several long minutes before he spoke.

"You look like ten miles of rough road," Jamie finally stated.

"Well, thanks, brother." John leaned back in his chair and avoided Jamie's steady gaze.

"When are you going to give this up?" Jamie leaned forward.

"Give what up?" John snapped.

"This act that you put on. This act where you try to convince everyone you aren't dying inside because you made the biggest mistake of your life cutting Jill loose."

John met his brother's gaze for several minutes before he spoke. "You don't know what you're talking about."

"Don't I?" Jamie raised an eyebrow.

John leaned forward and snapped angrily, "Do you ever stop and think about all I am responsible for right now? I'm running the ranch single-handedly. We've had one of the worst winters I can remember; Momma's in Helena; and I'm taking care of *your* pregnant wife, who refuses to listen to reason."

"And you have always thrived on that kind of stuff. You have always loved playing the hero." Jamie leaned back in his chair and then added, "And I was never any help at the ranch anyway, it's not like you weren't running it by yourself even when I was there."

John grunted and rubbed his hand down his face. "Well, that's true."

"When are you going to admit that you still love her?"

"I don't love her." John hated the way the words tasted as they left his mouth.

"You are such a liar," Jamie chuckled. "Well, when you are ready to admit how stupid you are behaving about all of this, then I'll be here to help you."

"I don't need any help," John quickly retorted.

Jamie leaned across the table and pointed his finger at John. "And see that…that right there is your problem. We all need help, John. You don't have to go through all of this alone."

"Why do people keep saying that?" John raised his voice and stood up quickly, causing his chair to tip over and clang loudly against the concrete floor.

"Because the weight of the burden you are carrying is evident to everyone but you." Jamie stood and rounded the table, reaching out to squeeze his brother's shoulder. "Pastor Rick says you haven't been to church in a few weeks."

"Are you kidding me right now?" John braced himself, both hands on his hips. "You and Pastor Rick have been discussing me? You're the one in jail, Jamie. You are the one headed to rehab. I'm the responsible one that always cleans up your messes and takes care of everything and you two have been discussing me?" John was yelling by the time he finished.

"You're right. I can't argue with any of that. I am in jail and I am headed to rehab. But I've changed, John. I know that I can't do this alone and I also know that God is here helping me every step of the way. I don't have to shoulder the burdens of what I've put our family through, what I've put Amber through, alone anymore. God is walking me through this and showing me how to forgive myself for everything I've done. He can help you too."

"I haven't hurt our family the way you have." John regretted the words the minute they left his mouth.

"True, you haven't. If anything, you stepped up for the family, but John, there is something inside of you that causes you to push people away. God didn't make us to be alone. God can heal that, whatever it is."

Silence stretched throughout the room as John studied the toes of his boots.

"Listen, I want you to drive me to rehab next week without Amber, please?"

John looked up to meet his brother's gaze.

"It would just be too hard on her to have to leave me again. Can you do that for me?"

"Sure, you know I will."

Chapter 22 Diversions

"Therefore do not be anxious about tomorrow, for tomorrow will be anxious for itself. Sufficient for the day is its own trouble." Matthew 6:24

J ill looked around the empty bedroom and turned to the Realtor behind her. "I'll take it."

"Great!" The Realtor clapped her hands. "I knew you would love it."

Jill walked out to the upstairs landing and watched as her Realtor descended the steps to the front hallway of the newly constructed home. Jill glanced out the picture window in the foyer that faced the mountains in the distance. She touched the glass wistfully, thinking that somewhere nestled in those mountains was the ranch and the man who had captured her heart and refused to return it.

"You are going to love it here!" her Realtor enthusiastically called up the steps.

"Already feels like home," Jill whispered, unable stop the tear that slipped from the corner of her eye. She hoped that the physical move would help her move on in her heart and mind as well.

****

You cannot imagine how good it feels to be outside, to be in a truck again, and to be free." Jamie grinned as he stretched his legs out in the truck seat beside John.

"I bet." John grinned, allowing Jamie's infectious good mood to brighten his own. "I wish you could come home for few days before going to rehab."

"It's better this way," Jamie responded after a few moments. "If I went home I might not want to leave, and I do have to go to rehab."

John thought back to the desperate Jamie who had gone into jail six months ago. That person was a distant memory compared to the responsible, level-headed man who sat beside him now.

"You've come a long way, brother." John glanced over at him.

"Still got a long way to go, but I'm getting there. Wouldn't be anywhere without God, though. Every time I want to give up, every time I want to go back to my old ways, God sends…something; he sends help. You know what I mean? He sends a word by someone to help me get back on track."

John grunted, not wanting to encourage this line of conversation.

"He does the same for you, if you would just look around."

"I don't need any help." John gripped the wheel and was regretting his agreement to drive his brother to the rehab facility two hours away from Fortuna.

"And once again, there is your problem." Jamie laughed bitterly.

John clenched his jaw. "I don't believe you want to get into a discussion about each other's problems. I'm not the one that just got out of jail today." John immediately regretted his words.

"Oh, if it were a contest to see which of us had the most serious problems, I'd win hands down for sure. My problems are many, but at least I'm not trying to hide them anymore. At least I'm man enough to admit I need help."

"I don't need help," John repeated and resettled his hat low over his eyes, hoping to end the conversation.

"We all need help, brother. I knew I needed help to stop drinking, but I had no idea the extent of help I really needed until Pastor Rick really started counseling me. I have a drinking problem. I've had one for a long time and I used it to cover up the guilt I felt over Ben's accident. I've spent the last four years blaming myself for Ben's accident. Pastor Rick helped me see that it wasn't my fault and that even if I had caused Ben's accident, I could walk in forgiveness. He showed me how God forgives me and how I needed to forgive myself. God used Pastor Rick to show me that I could still have a good life even after Ben's accident. We don't have to spend our lives punishing ourselves because Ben had an accident that changed our lives."

"That's great, Jamie; really it is. But me and God...we're good...I don't need counseling."

"Being good with God is more than just salvation, John. It's more than just confessing Jesus as Lord and Savior. It's about walking with Him every day. It's about letting him in and letting him work in you and through you." Jamie paused momentarily before he added, "Jill was a great example of that."

Rage filled John and he punched the dash of the truck. "Is that what this is all about?" he demanded angrily. "That is over and none of you can let it go. It never would have worked between us but that doesn't mean that I need counseling or need help or need anything for that matter."

"I never said you needed counseling, I said God sends help to us all. But since you brought up your relationship with Jill, how about explaining to me why it wouldn't have worked."

John glanced over at his brother, wanting nothing more than to wipe the devious grin off of his face. "I didn't feel....I didn't have feelings for her...I didn't love her. It wasn't going anywhere. No need to drag it out." He almost choked on the words as he forced them out.

He felt Jamie staring at him and finally, after several long moments of silence, he glanced over at his brother. Jamie waited until their eyes met to respond. "Liar."

"So since you've spent six months in jail getting counseling you think you can read my mind? You think you know how I feel?"

"No I don't, but anybody with two eyes could tell that you loved her. I've never seen you look at anyone the way you looked at her. I know you, John. When we were kids, you were my hero; I wanted to be you. I watched every move you ever made and tried to do the same thing. I watched you with girlfriends from high school to college. You never acted like you cared whether they were around or not. You were different with Jill. You know it, I know it, everybody knows it. You brought her to the ranch—"

"Ben needed therapy," John interrupted defensively.

195

Jamie snorted with laughter. He doubled over in the truck guffawing. "Oh, you actually thought we bought that excuse? Oh, that's precious."

John glanced at the clock on his dash, hoping that by some miracle time had passed and they would be nearing the rehab facility soon. He was disappointed to find out that they had only been in the truck about twenty minutes.

"You loved her and I didn't need counseling to be able to see that." Jamie let his words hang in the air before he added softly, "And I know she loved you too."

John resettled his ball cap on his head. The anger he felt couldn't quite overtake his curiosity at Jamie's comment. "How do you know that?"

"Like I said, brother, anybody with two eyes could tell how you felt about each other."

John stared out the windshield, mulling over his brother's words. He cleared his throat and finally spoke. "Well, that was then, and if we did…" His throat tightened and he couldn't force out the word *love* without breaking so he chose his words carefully. "If we did care for each other, that's all over now. She's better off without me."

"Maybe you should let her decide that."

Jamie didn't mention Jill again during the two-hour ride. They spoke of ranch business and what Jamie's role would be there when he graduated from rehab. When they approached the facility, Jamie grew silent. As they registered and Jamie was shown to his room, John couldn't help but notice how calm his brother was. A year ago, Jamie would have been ready to fight at every step of the way, now he seemed almost eager to begin the rehabilitation process. He hugged his brother fiercely when he was finally checked into the facility and John had been told gently by the attending physician it was time for him to leave. Jamie would not be allowed any visitors or contact with his family for the first several weeks of the program.

"You take care of Amber and the baby." Tears welled in Jamie's eyes as he gripped John's shoulders.

"I will, Jamie. I promise." John fought his own emotions as his throat constricted.

"And you promise me you will go to church?"

"Yes, Jamie, I promise."

"And promise me you will think long and hard about Jill before you completely close that door?" Jamie didn't release John's shoulders until he met his gaze.

"Jamie, quit worrying about me and just focus on you. Six months and you are home. Then we can talk about this."

"Six months may be too late. Don't waste time like I did. I did a lot of horrible things to Amber and wasted a lot of time with her that I'll never get back. I'd give anything to have that time to do over again."

John caught the physician's gaze once again. "I gotta go. I'll see you in a month."

Chapter 23 Redemption

"When these things begin to take place, stand up and lift up your heads, because your redemption is drawing near." Luke 21:28

"How's the new house?" Sam asked as he and Jill leaned against the gym station charting files together at the end of their shift.

"Good. It's good." Jill didn't look up from her file to meet his gaze.

"What made you decide to buy a house?"

Jill sighed as she closed the file with a little too much force. "Why does everyone around here keep asking me that? Is it so strange that a grown woman would purchase a home? I mean it's a sound financial investment."

She had been in her new home a little over a month and she was still fielding questions from her coworkers and friends about her somewhat spontaneous decision to purchase a home in a suburb of Billings. She had repeated the same response when questioned, hoping that eventually people would stop asking. What she didn't tell them, or rather, what she couldn't tell them, was that the sole decision to purchase the home had been completely spur of the moment. She had found herself driving around an area outside of downtown one afternoon. She had stumbled upon a housing development quite by accident. It was nestled away from the main highway with tall pines flanking each side of the entrance. The homes were all Craftsman-style homes with exposed wood and pine shutters and shingles. It had reminded her of John's ranch house. She felt a warmth spread through her body. She parked her car and strolled down the sidewalk, studying each home. The view of the mountains in the distance only added to the feeling of belonging.

She had found herself several days later driving through the subdivision again, and then again the next weekend. One of the homes just happened to be set up for an open house that day. She had instantly fallen in love with the exposed wood accents and stone fireplace in the living room. But what had sealed the deal, what had caused her to make one of the biggest decisions of her life, had come from the fact that from the upstairs window there was a breathtaking view of the mountains. And in those mountains, somewhere out there was the man that she had come to realize she would always love. If she couldn't have him, at least she could have the mountain view. She would find herself at times gazing out the window thinking about him. What was he doing? Did he ever think of her? Did he ever lie awake at night and wonder what she was doing? And when she was really brave she would allow herself to consider if he had moved on and was dating someone else.

She grabbed the next chart, hoping the conversation was over with.

"Hey, I think it's great that you bought your own house. I guess we all just thought that...well...you know."

She closed the file slowly and eyed Sam. "No. No, I don't know." She mimicked his tone. "What are you talking about?"

Sam looked over his shoulder and then stepped closer to her, dropping his voice to a whisper. "Well...you know, we all thought that you'd be leaving us soon, not buying a house."

"Why would I be leaving here?"

"To ride off into the sunset with the cowboy," Sam said matter-of-factly. "I mean we did have a betting pool about when you all were going to get married."

Jill felt as though she had been kicked in the gut. Had her feelings for John been so apparent? Maybe that was why he had ended the relationship? Maybe he had gotten tired of her obviously apparent feelings toward him; feelings he didn't return. She gathered up the rest of her charts. "I won't be riding off into the sunset with anybody."

"Hey, Jill…I'm sorry," Sam called after her as she headed for her office.

She turned to face him as she backed out the gym door. "It's nothing; don't worry about it." And only after the gym door closed behind her did she let the tears she had been fighting slip from her eyes.

****

It had been almost a month since John had dropped Jamie off at the rehabilitation facility, and try as he might he couldn't forget the conversation that had taken place on the drive. Bits and pieces of it played over and over in his mind. It had brought all of his feelings for Jill, which never seemed too far away, surging to the surface. He put his head down and threw himself into his work. He kept his promises to Jamie as best he could, going above and beyond in his efforts to take care of Amber. He drove her to church every Sunday and sat dutifully beside her. He kept replaying Jamie's words in his head.

"I've spent the last four years blaming myself for Ben's accident. Pastor Rick helped me see that it wasn't my fault and that even if I had caused Ben's accident, I could walk in forgiveness."

If it were possible for Jamie, was it possible for him too? In brief moments he dared hope—if he could find forgiveness from God and his family, might it be possible for Jill to forgive him as well? He found himself listening intently to Pastor Rick, jotting down scripture references and looking them up when he returned home. He dusted off the Bible that had ridden in his saddlebag for years, and he pored over the scriptures from Pastor Rick's sermons. Could he walk in forgiveness too? Could not only God forgive him, but could he forgive himself? And what about Jill? Her face tormented him in his periods of fitful sleep at night.

Plagued by the thoughts for over a month, he found himself in no better shape than he had been immediately following his breakup. His appetite, which had slowly made a resurgence, had been lost again, and sleep that had finally brought him sweet relief from his thoughts once again eluded him. The stress of the ranch and Amber's impending labor gave him even more reasons to worry. By mid-February, John was hesitant to leave her for more than a few moments, fearing she would go into labor. The only small blessing he found in his concern over Amber was that it kept him from obsessing over Jill.

He wasn't exactly sure when he had come to the decision. Maybe it had been during one of his Bible readings or maybe on one of his early morning rides where he spent time pouring his heart out to God. But at some point he had decided that once Jamie came home and took over his role as protector and provider for Amber and the baby, John would go to Billings. When he thought of what would happen when he saw Jill again face to face, his stomach quivered. He pushed the thought out of his head and focused on the present. He would think about that later; it was enough right now to know that he would at least attempt to talk to her. To offer his explanation for his behavior and if she sent him back to the ranch with his tail between his legs, then he deserved it. But until he spoke with her, until he knew once and for all if she could still love him, could forgive him or if she couldn't, he would never have peace.

But having made that decision didn't immediately cease his heartache. He sat one evening pushing his food around his plate, hoping to deceive Amber into believing he had actually eaten it, and watched in real time as one of his fears took form. The small kitchen TV played in the background and something caught John's attention. He stood and took two long strides to cross the kitchen, turning the volume up just as the weatherman forecast one of the biggest snowstorms of the year bearing down on them in the next few days.

****

John slammed the kitchen door behind him and slapped his hat against his leg. Despite his most sound arguments, Amber refused to leave the ranch. With one of the biggest snowstorms of the year bearing down on them, John had plenty to do to ready the ranch, and the last thing he needed was to have to worry about her going into labor. Not for the first time he thought of how glad he would be when Jamie came home; maybe he could talk sense into her. Of course by then it would be too late. Amber's latest doctor's appointment had only added to John's worries when the doctor announced that she could deliver at any moment. She, however, resolutely argued that no one knew her body better than her and she was confident the baby was still a month away from making its appearance. He slammed his pickup truck door and glanced up at the increasingly gray sky. He hurriedly threw his truck in gear and headed for the barn. Animals were easier to deal with than his stubborn sister-in-law.

He wasn't sure when the plan took form. He had spent the day putting out extra hay for the herd and making sure the animals and barns were secured for the impending storm. But sometime during the day, the thought had come to him that possibly Pastor Rick might be able to convince Amber to leave the ranch until after the baby was born. He knew that Amber had a deep respect for the man and

201

he hoped he would be able to persuade her. He had plans to call the pastor as soon as he returned to the house. Pastor Rick had offered to be of help many times and John had turned him down; he prayed that the offer still stood.

The sun had settled behind the mountains hours before John returned to the house, and the snow had begun falling about the same time. It had come in waves, at times so heavy he could barely see his hand in front of his face. He and his men pressed on, fighting the snow and biting wind to do their best to protect their livelihood. Mentally and physically he was exhausted. He had done all he could for his ranch to prepare it for the storm. Now he would just have to wait and see what happened.

He vaguely remembered his father standing in the front windows as a norther would hit, watching it assault his home. He could close his eyes and hear his father praying. Calling out to God to spare his family, his workers, and his animals. As far back as John could remember, the ranch had not seen severe damage or felt dramatic loss because of a storm. His father had been the strongest man he had ever known. John had admired him all his life. Something inside of John stirred; if his father called upon God for protection, maybe John needed to as well. He felt unprepared for the days ahead and he had begun to doubt his ability to protect his ranch and his family. Reaching down deep into his memory, he recalled the words his father spoke. He paused before he entered the kitchen and repeated them, staring up at the darkened sky, heavy with snow.

"God, I know I don't have any right to ask you, but please protect us. Please help me keep Amber safe." He swallowed the knot that formed in his throat and continued out loud, the words falling out of his mouth as if a dam inside him had broken. "I need help, Lord. I can't do this all by myself. I can't do this without you. I need you, Lord. Help us." He remembered the verse his father would quote as he prayed and John repeated it. *"The Lord is my rock and my fortress and my deliverer; my God, my strength, in whom I will trust…"*

"John." Amber's quivering voice from behind him stopped John from finishing the verse. He knew before he turned around that she was in trouble. He opened his eyes and saw snow falling heavily from the sky; turning, he saw his sister-in-law clutching her stomach, her face contorted in pain.

"Amber…" He felt as if the wind had been knocked out of him momentarily, but quickly gathered himself. Now was no time to let fear take over. "How long?"

He stepped into the kitchen, taking her by the arm and easing her into the nearest chair.

Amber winced as pain swept over her. John knelt in front of her and he could see her stomach contract violently. "Most of the day," she answered between gritted teeth.

"What!? Why didn't you tell me?" John demanded and then quickly changed his tone as another wave of pain flashed over her face. "No, I'm sorry, I shouldn't have left you alone."

"You had to get the ranch ready for the storm, I didn't think it was serious." Her eyes met John's and he could see the fear there. "What are we going to do?"

John studied her face and remembered his prayer only moments before. He thought of Jamie and his words. *"Every time I want to give up, every time I want to go back to my old ways, God sends…something; He sends help. You know what I mean?"*

"God sends…something; He sends help."

The words reverberated in John's mind as he tried to fight the wave of panic that wanted to overtake him. He met Amber's eyes and squeezed her hand. "Looks like we are going to have a baby."

He smiled at her, trying to reassure her that all would be okay. He immediately knew what he must do. He reached for the telephone and dialed the sheriff's office in town that doubled as the 911 office. With each unanswered ring, his calmness faded. His plan was to get the sheriff or the ambulance to come and get Amber. That way, even if they couldn't make it to the hospital, someone with some medical training would be there. He had never anticipated that no one would answer. He assumed the office was overloaded with calls with the severity of the storm bearing down on them.

He glanced out the kitchen window and could barely make out his truck under the security light, the snow was falling so heavily. He glanced back at Amber and saw her gripping the kitchen table, her knuckles white as she rode the wave of pain. He had seen enough horses and calves born to know that her time was short. He mentally calculated how quickly he could drive to the hospital. Flipping on the television, he prayed that the weather would be forecasting a break in the snow; instead, he was met with the gut-wrenching news that the snow would continue until the early hours of the morning, dropping an unprecedented amount of snow on the area this late in the winter. As the weather forecaster began listing the roads that had become unpassable, he glanced back over his shoulder and met Amber's gaze. The last thing he wanted was to get stuck on the highway, unable to get her to a hospital. A baby born outside in these conditions would be immediately at risk for frostbite or worse. He knew what he would have to do. He turned and knelt in front of Amber.

"Amber, how far apart are your contractions?"

"About five minutes…." Her breathing was labored as she clutched her stomach.

"Amber…" He waited until she met his gaze. "We will never make it to the hospital. You're going to have the baby here."

Fear clouded her eyes and he squeezed her hand. "I'm here, Amber. I'll take care of you."

"Do you know anything about delivering babies?"

He couldn't help himself as he let a chuckle. "Well, I've delivered plenty of calves and foals. Can't be too different, right?"

"That's comforting," she said sarcastically as he helped her rise from her chair.

He took her to the closest bedroom, which blessedly had a fireplace. He thanked God earnestly as he remembered the cord of firewood Buck had stacked at the back door just last week. After getting Amber settled in bed, he ran to the back door and flung it open. The wind whipped around him violently as snow bit into his skin. He grabbed an armful of wood and hurried back to the bedroom. He began stoking a fire in the fireplace as the lights flickered above. He again thanked God for the provision of fire. If the lights went out, he would at least be able to keep her and the baby warm. He ran back to the rick of firewood, quickly being covered over with snow, and continued to bring in stacks of wood to the bedroom. Within moments he had a roaring fire going in the fireplace as he caught Amber doubling over in pain once more. He went to comfort her, but stopped short of touching her, noticing the dirt from the firewood on his hands. He quickly assessed his clothing, covered with dirt from the barns, and determined he needed to be clean before he delivered his niece or nephew. He explained to Amber he would be right back. He took the quickest shower of his life, leaving the door open, listening intently for her cries. He ran to her room and rifled through drawers until he found a nightgown. He stepped back into the room and gently laid the gown on the bed.

"Thought you might need this." He turned his back so as to give her privacy.

She slipped on the nightgown and the low guttural groan that escaped her lips told John to turn around. He knelt by her bedside, assessing her from head to toe. He vaguely recalled movies where water being boiled and sheets ripped into rags had appeared to be standard order for delivering a baby. He couldn't for the life of him figure out why. He thought back to all the calves and foals he had delivered and tried to convince himself that this wouldn't be that much different. The sharp cry of pain that escaped between Amber's gritted teeth told him he was a liar.

"I need to push, John," Amber said on a ragged breath.

His first instinct was to tell her no, but a sense of calm took over him as he thought her body would best know how to handle this.

"Amber, I'm going to have to look." He gestured toward the sheet covering the lower half of her body.

"At this point, I think we are beyond being embarrassed around each other, John. Do what you have to do." Amber barely got the words out before her body curled forward, taking on the natural posture to push the baby into the world.

John hesitated momentarily before he gently lifted the blankets. The lights flickered before giving way to complete darkness. The glow from the roaring fireplace kept them from being plunged into complete darkness. John looked up at Amber, who seemed completely oblivious to their loss of power. He quickly jumped to shut the bedroom door, hoping to keep the warmth from the fire from escaping.

"God help us." He breathed a prayer before returning to the bed. He gently lifted the cover, shocked to find the head of his niece or nephew crowning.

"Okay, Amber, I see the head." He began to roll the sleeves of his shirt up and he could feel the tension leave Amber's body as she fell back on the pillows behind her. It took but a moment for the pain to sweep over her again and she began to push.

In the days and weeks to come, when he thought back to this time, he would recall it as if it were an out-of-body experience. An unseen force seemed to take

205

over as he coached her gently, taking her hand as she felt the excruciating pain building and gently comforting her with soft muddled tones as she labored through the pain. The waves of pain became continuous as he coaxed her gently. As the shoulders appeared he gently guided the tiny body and with a determined groan Amber pushed the final time. A tiny, perfectly shaped baby girl slipped into his hands. He held her in his palms, staring at her perfection. Finally, remembering something he wasn't sure how he knew, he took his pinky and swept her mouth, causing her to gasp her first breath and release an earth-shaking wail. He glanced up to see Amber's frightened and expectant face. He quickly wrapped the baby in a blanket and took her around the bed to her mother. As he watched mother and daughter meet for the first time, he was confident he had never felt such a wide range of emotions before. Caught up in the headiness of those feelings, it took him a minute to realize someone was shouting his name. His eyes and Amber's met at the same time as recognition dawned on them. The door opened as Pastor Rick stepped into the room, followed quickly by a man neither of them recognized.

"John!" Pastor Rick quickly crossed the room. John was off the bed enfolding him in an embrace.

"Pastor, I have never been so happy to see you in my life."

"John, this is my nephew; he's a medic in the Army, home for a visit. Something just told me you needed help."

John clamped the man's shoulders, overtaken by emotion and unable to speak. Pastor Rick patted John soundly on the back. "It's okay. Everything is going to be okay." He helped John sit in a chair by the fire as he turned to his nephew, who had immediately begun assessing Amber and the baby.

John stared blankly as the men turned their attention toward Amber and the baby. He had no concept of time—even now after it was over, he couldn't recall how much time they had spent in that room. In the months and years to come when he thought about this time, he would never be able to decipher if they had spent only minutes or hours in the room. Time had stood still. Many would tell him later that instinct or Mother Nature had taken over in those moments; some arcane ability in human DNA left over from caveman days to preserve the human race. He would smile and gently let them know that the only thing that had gotten them through the most frightening and at the same time most beautiful experience he had ever had was the grace and presence of an almighty God.

Chapter 24 Awakening

"As for you, always be sober-minded, endure suffering, do the work of an evangelist, fulfill your ministry." 2 Timothy 4:5

"Well, she's perfect," Pattie announced, cuddling her granddaughter from the rocking chair seated at the foot of Amber's hospital bed.

John peeked over his mother's shoulder at the sleeping baby and his heart soared. He had known from the instant he first held her that he would share a special bond with his niece. He glanced up to see Amber grinning at him. He would also share that bond with her mother.

"I can't wait for Jamie to see her." Amber resettled her blankets.

"Well, so much for him getting out on good behavior," John joked. After finally arriving at the hospital, John had been able to call the rehabilitation center to inform Jamie he was a father to a beautiful baby girl. Jamie had sheepishly admitted, after John had assured him repeatedly that Amber and the baby were fine, that after watching the emergency weather alert for their area he had threatened to whip every person in the facility unless someone got him in touch with his wife. His behavior had been frowned upon by his counselor.

"He was just worried about us; me and little Faith." Amber grinned, announcing the baby's name for the first time. "Faith Johnna Mitchell." She watched John's reaction to his niece's name. "I couldn't very well name her without acknowledging the uncle that helped bring her into the world."

John's throat tightened and he nodded to Amber, unable to speak for fear of his emotions spilling over. He reached down and gently took the baby from his mother and walked to the window, turning his back on the watchful gaze of his mother and sister-in-law. He searched the sleeping face and felt a love so deep it hummed through every ounce of his body. The only other time he had ever felt a love so deep was when he was with Jill. He suddenly ached for her. He wanted to share with her everything that had happened over the past twenty-four hours.

"John." Pastor Rick's voice as he entered the room brought John back to the present. "Do you ever let anybody else hold her? Every time I walk in the room, you are the one holding the baby."

John passed the baby to the preacher silently, beaming proudly as if she were his own daughter. Time passed quickly as various church members drifted in and out of the room, fawning over baby Faith.

John stifled a yawn as the pastor sat beside him. "Been a pretty tiring day, huh?"

"Yeah, about as exhausting as I've had in a while," John replied. He wanted to thank the man for all he had done and wanted to ask him exactly what had led him to show up at the ranch in the middle of a snowstorm just in the nick of time. "Can I buy you a cup of coffee, Pastor?"

"Of course you can."

Seated in the hospital cafeteria, John rolled his shoulders and eyed the other man. "So what made you come to the ranch?"

The older man studied his paper coffee cup thoughtfully and for so long John thought momentarily he hadn't heard the question. He finally looked up and met John's gaze. "John, it's the strangest thing I've ever experienced and without a doubt it was God." The man proceeded to tell him how he had been dogged all day of thoughts of John and Amber. He explained how he had prayed for them repeatedly throughout the day. His nephew had arrived the day before for a visit and had gotten stranded by the storm. Finally in the evening he had felt an overwhelming urge to check on them. He had tried to call, but had not been able to get through.

"John, it's like God just told me to go to you. It's like I could hear you asking for help."

"That's just...crazy." John rubbed his hand down his face. "But Preacher, I promise you this. God was in that room with us. He had to be, there is no way I can explain it any other way."

Pastor Rick sat back and assessed John. "I'm glad to hear you say that, John. Maybe all those prayers that we've been praying are starting to work."

John glanced up see the pastor's grin and returned the smile. He fingered his coffee cup, studying the dark liquid. He wasn't sure how long he had been silent when the pastor cleared his throat. "John, is there something you want to talk about?"

John shrugged, not sure if he was completely ready to bare his soul.

"You seem as if you've got something on your mind. I've been told I'm a pretty good listener."

John eyed the man and sipped his coffee, letting the steaming liquid scald his mouth. He swallowed and felt the warmth slide to his stomach. Deciding it was now or never, he gathered his courage and asked the preacher the question that had been plaguing him.

"Preacher," he began, pausing briefly to look around the cafeteria before continuing, "do you think there is a sin you can't be forgiven for? Something so bad that God can't forgive you?"

Pastor Rick leaned back in his chair. "The Bible does speak of an unforgiveable sin, John, but the fact that you seemed worried about this tells me you haven't committed it. Let me ask you this, John, do you want to be forgiven for this sin you've committed?"

"More than anything in the world, I want to be forgiven. To put it behind me and start living my life again without this cloud hanging over me." The words tumbled out of John's mouth before he could even think them through.

"As long as we desire forgiveness and know where it comes from, I believe there is nothing that can separate us from the love of Christ." Pastor Rick met

209

John's steady gaze. "Why don't you tell me what you've done that you think God can't forgive you for?"

John tapped the paper cup on the table and leveled his gaze on the pastor. Then he spoke the words aloud that he had never spoken to anyone else. "I caused Ben's accident."

The words hung in the air, and as much as John was confident the pastor would hate him for his admission, the relief he felt at finally speaking the truth was liberating. Once he got the initial sentence out, it was as if a dam broke inside of him. He spoke to the preacher in detail of that fateful morning, explaining the timeline of events as he believed they had happened, drawing the only logical conclusion that the report of John's rifle had spooked Ben's horse, in turn causing the accident.

Pastor Rick listened raptly to John's story, occasionally nodding his encouragement for John to continue.

When John had finally finished his story, the pastor, resting his elbows on the table, tented his fingertips and studied John. The trepidation in John's stomach reached a boiling point as he waited for the preacher to tell him what a miserable, vile person he was. Finally Pastor Rick reached to pick up his coffee cup, pausing but a moment to ask a question before he took a sip. "John, have you ever shared this story with anyone else?"

"No, you are the only living soul I've ever told this to."

John thought his heart would explode out of his chest waiting for the preacher to respond.

"Well, John, even if this story is the exact way the accident happened, it's not something that God couldn't forgive you for. What happened to Ben was an accident. A horrible, terrible, life-changing *accident*." He emphasized the last word.

"I've never told my family what happened. I've closed myself off from them to punish myself. I don't even have the courage to look Ben in the eye, because I know I will see hatred there."

Pastor Rick leaned forward, resting his elbows on the table. "John, do you remember the first time you ever rode a horse?"

John stammered, "N-no. I think I was born on horseback."

Pastor Rick chuckled. "I remember one time, I came out to the ranch to see Red and he had you out in the pasture with him. You couldn't have been more than four or five, but man, could you handle that horse. There you were handling those reins all by yourself, turning that horse around and trotting around. Red was beaming with pride."

John couldn't help but smile. "Dad put us to work at an early age. Always joked that he had us to be free labor for the ranch."

"Did Jamie learn to ride that young too?" the preacher asked.

"Oh yeah, Dad made sure we all knew how to ride at an early age."

"But not Ben?" Pastor Rick questioned.

"Oh no, Ben too. He was a daredevil. Always trying to keep up with us."

"Oh, I see…" And then he added, "Didn't Ben rodeo a little bit in high school too?"

"Yeah, he did, won a state buckle." John let his mind wander back in time to the moment his brother had reached that particular achievement.

"Have you ever fallen off your horse, John?" Pastor Rick raised his eyebrows.

"More times than I would like to admit," John replied on a laugh.

"Whose fault was it?" Pastor Rick leaned back in his chair.

"What?" John was caught off guard by the question.

"Whose fault was it that you fell off your horse?"

"It was nobody's fault…" Realization dawned on John.

Pastor Rick read John's expression and continued, "John, don't you see, it wasn't anybody's fault that Ben fell off his horse and was hurt. He was an excellent rider. I'm sure he had fallen off his horse more times than he wanted to admit too. It was an accident, pure and simple. Nobody's fault. Not your fault, John. If you think you've done something that God needs to forgive you for, then ask Him and He will. Then you need to forgive yourself. Stop punishing yourself for something you didn't do."

John felt a slight lessening of the tightness he had carried in his chest for years. It would take time to completely work through all of his feelings about that fateful morning, but for the first time since the accident, a small ray of hope lit in his chest. He knew he needed to speak with his mother and Jamie about what he had been feeling for the past four years and how he had kept them at arm's length as a form of self-inflicted punishment. He wanted to see Ben; to apologize to him for the years they had lost because of John's distance. But hope coursed and soared through John as he thought that maybe, just maybe, forgiveness could be his.

"Thank you. You seem to always come through for me." John cleared his throat as his emotions, rubbed raw from exhaustion, seemed to rise to the surface once again.

"It's not me, John. It's God. He always comes through for you and He always will." The pastor glanced at his watch. "Well, I better get going. I'll be around to the ranch as soon as you all get settled."

John stood, stepping into the older man's path; words failed him so he embraced the pastor in a fierce hug. "Thank you just doesn't seem adequate for all you've done for us."

Pastor Rick returned the hug with just as much force, finally releasing John and gently cuffing him on the shoulder. "You can pay me back by volunteering at the church's Spring Carnival."

"Consider it done."

****

"You're sure you can get them home safely?" Pattie asked for at least the one hundredth time. After spending two nights away from Ben, who was still in Helena with Steven, Pattie reluctantly was leaving her brand new granddaughter.

"Momma, I delivered her in a snowstorm with no electricity. I think I can drive them home from the hospital," John tried to reassure her.

"We are never going to hear the end of this story." Pattie looked past John to meet Amber's laughing eyes. John had never seen anyone more openly joyful than Amber after giving birth.

"We will be fine, Pattie. And it's just for few days, right?"

"That's right," Pattie cooed as she picked up Faith from her hospital cradle. "Grandmommy will be home in two days with Uncle Ben. He can't wait to meet you!"

Pattie kissed the baby's head and handed her to her mother. "Walk me to my car?" She glanced at John.

He nodded and fell into step behind her.

He could tell there was something she wanted to say. She waited until they were in the parking garage before she spoke. "You seem…different." She touched his arm and he turned to face her.

"Different how?" He crossed his arms over his chest.

"I don't know….it seems if that little black storm cloud that is usually over your head isn't quite so big." She clicked the button to unlock her car.

John leaned against his mother's car and studied her. He thought about all she had been through in the past four years and he knew he had added to her hurts.

"For a lot of years I blamed myself for what happened to Ben—"

"Oh, John, it's normal for family members to feel guilt." Pattie touched his arm.

"It was more than that. I had convinced myself that my rifle spooked his horse and caused his fall. And maybe it did…I don't know, I guess we never will. But I've been going to church with Amber and talking with Pastor Rick…" His voice trailed off.

"And?" his mother demanded.

"And maybe it's time to forgive myself, ask Ben to forgive me."

Tears welled in his mother's eyes and before he lost his nerve he continued, "I'm sorry, Momma. I pushed you and Jamie and Ben, especially Ben, away. I closed myself off. You know I've never looked Ben in the eye since the accident? I haven't been much of a brother or a son in the past few years."

Pattie reached out and touched his cheek like she did when he was a boy. "Ben has always known how much you care for him. Jamie and I do too. You gave up so much to take care of us when we needed you."

John shrugged his shoulders. "It's what families do."

"You know Ben misses you." She wiped her eyes on a Kleenex dug from the bottom of her massive purse. "Wants to know when you are coming to see him."

John crossed one leg in front of the other and studied his boots, choosing his words carefully. "I need to talk to him, to try and explain."

"I think he would love that."

****

John stood in the hallway of Stephen Miller's therapy clinic, watching Ben through the plate glass window. He wasn't sure how long he had been standing there, but long enough for three different employees to ask him if he needed help. He cleared his throat and rolled his shoulders, trying to steel himself to walk in the room and look his brother in the eye for the first time in four years.

"John, good to see you." Stephen approached from behind and offered an extended hand.

"Hey Stephen, good to see you too." John shook the man's extended hand and hoped that his nervousness didn't show.

"I was just heading in to see Ben. Come on; he will glad to see you." At that point John had no choice but to follow.

"Ben, you've got company. John is here." Stephen announced. John watched from behind, not yet ready to face his brother, as Ben used his hands to communicate with Stephen. Stephen moved a chair directly in front of Ben and gestured for John to take a seat. John wiped his sweaty palms down the front of his jeans and took a step. He kept his head down until he was seated, breathed a small prayer and then looked up to meet Ben's gaze. They stared at each other for a few moments. John's mind raced as he wondered what Ben might be thinking about him. Ben slowly moved his hands.

"He said he's happy to see you." Stephen interpreted the movements. Ben moved his hand some more and Stephen chuckled, "He also said it's about time you showed up."

John's shoulder's relaxed as the burden of four years' worth of guilt and shame seemed to roll off of them. He reached out and grasped Ben's shoulder, struggling to keep his emotions in check it took him a few moments to find his voice and when he did, it was no more than a whisper, "I'm sorry, Ben." He sniffed, cleared his throat and tried to continue, "I'm sorry this happened to you and I'm sorry for the way I've treated you for four years. I just thought…" John's voice cracked and he stopped to compose himself before continuing, "I just thought it was my fault, your accident was my fault and I figured you hated me."

Ben moved his hands hurriedly and Stephen interpreted, "He said it's wasn't your fault. Just an accident. He said he remembers that morning in the ravine. He was so scared, but when he heard your voice he knew you would take care of him, just like you always had, just like you still do."

Tears pooled in John's eyes, unable to find his voice, he patted Ben's leg trying to show him everything he felt without words.

Ben moved his hands again. "He says he loves you and he's missed you."

John's shoulders shook as emotion overtook him. When he finally composed himself, he looked up to meet Ben's tear filled gaze. "I love you too, Ben. And I've missed you too."

Chapter 25 Full Circle

"As for you, always be sober-minded, endure suffering, do the work of an evangelist, fulfill your ministry." 1 Thessalonians 5:1-28

The morning rays of the late June sun beamed through the window as John slipped into Faith's nursery to find her staring in awe at the swinging mobile hanging above her. It had become his ritual whenever he had a moment to seek out Faith and cuddle her. He gently picked her up and cuddled her as he sat in the rocking chair near the window.

"How's my best girl? We had the prettiest little pony born early this morning and she's going to be all yours one day. How would you like that?" he cooed to the baby as she gazed at him raptly.

"One of these days, I'm going to video you talking to her like that. No one believes me when I tell them." At the sound of Amber's voice, John's head snapped up. "And she's too little for a pony."

"Gotta do something to make sure she remembers me." John looked down at the Faith's sweet face. "Daddy will be home next week and I bet he won't put you down. I'll have to sneak in here in the middle of the night just to hold you."

John glanced up at Amber to see her smile. "I can't wait for him to be home, for us to be a real family."

"I know," John said quietly. He cleared his throat and gestured for Amber to sit down. "I've been thinking, Amber, you and Faith are all settled here in the main house and with Momma and Ben coming home for a few weeks, I know she will want to be around Faith all the time... Why don't you and Jamie just move in here...permanently?"

"Are you serious, John?" Amber sat across from him, fingering the baby blanket she held.

"Yeah, this place is huge and who knows how long before Momma and Ben come home to stay."

Tears welled in Amber's eyes as she whispered, "Thank you, John."

"I'll get some of the hands to get the rest of your stuff from your old place."

Excitement danced in Amber's eyes. "I can't believe we are all going to be together next week."

"Yeah, Ben's excited too." John grinned at the thought of his brother.

"Did you two FaceTime again last night?" Amber asked as she adjusted Faith's blanket.

"Yeah... he told me a joke." John grinned as he remembered.

"Was it funny?"

"Well, he thought it was."

They sat in silence for several long moments, each lost in their own thoughts. Amber was the first to speak. "You know, John, with Jamie coming home next week...maybe you won't be so busy all the time...Jamie can help with the ranch work..." Her words faltered and she bit her lower lip as if afraid to continue speaking.

"What are getting at?" John narrowed his eyes as he interrupted her.

"Well...I mean...you've just been so good to me...I want to see you as happy as Jamie and I are."

John raised his eyebrows and she rushed on. "See, there is this woman I met in my Bible Study, she's from the next county over, but she's real sweet—"

John held up his hand to stop her. "No."

"Why, John?"

John gazed out the window as his throat tightened; he gritted his teeth. "Because I said no."

Amber reached out and touched his knee. "You can't pine away for Jill forever, John. She's gone."

"I'm not pining." He ran his hands through his hair and met Amber's gaze. If he had learned anything about Amber in the time they had spent together, it was that she was just as stubborn as he was, if not more. He took a deep breath and decided the only way to stop her from pestering him about the woman from Bible Study was to tell her the truth. "I've been thinking that once Jamie is home, I might go to Billings for a few days." His stomach flipped over as he waited for her response.

"Billings? To see Jill?"

"Well, I don't have any other reason to go to Billings." John half laughed, trying to lighten the mood.

Amber stood and left the room, leaving John with his mouth open. He gently placed Faith back in her crib as he followed Amber from the room. He found her in Red's office, rifling through a stack of mail.

"What are you doing?" he asked as he approached the desk.

Finding what she was looking for, she shoved a postcard invitation in front of him. "She's gone, John, or at least she will be after today."

John took the invitation and stared at it. It was from the rehabilitation program at St. Patrick's.

SHHHHH…It's a surprise!

Join us as we say goodbye to Jill Morgan!

When: June 28

Where: St. Patrick's rehab gym

Time:2:00-4:00
Jill has accepted a position with Vanderbilt Hospital in Nashville, TN.

He sat down heavily in the nearest chair. She was leaving. He felt as if the air in the room was scarce as his head began to swim.

Amber knelt in front of him. "I thought you knew… I thought you had seen the invitation."

"She's leaving," John said out loud more for himself than for Amber.

Amber searched his face. "You still care her, don't you?"

John fell back in the chair, still gripping the invitation. It took him several minutes to answer and when he did his low voice broke over the words. "I…she's never far from my mind."

"Go!" Amber jumped to her feet. "Go to the party. Tell her how you feel."

John looked from the invitation to Amber and then back to the invitation. He jumped up and headed to the kitchen, grabbing his keys from the counter as he passed by.

"John!" Amber called from behind him, stopping him as he stepped out the door. He turned to see her bright smile. "Change your clothes first."

He looked down at his dirty work clothes, and decided Amber might be right.

Chapter 26 Confessions

"Do to others as you would have them do to you."
Luke 6:31

"Surprised?" Dr. Bryan took the seat beside Jill, balancing a plate of cake in one hand and punch in the other.

"Yes." Jill smiled at her soon to be former boss.

"Now I know you said you didn't want us to make a big deal out of your last day, but Jill...we just had to. You've been a very special part of our family here and it just wouldn't seem right to let you leave without letting you know that."

"Thank you." Jill stared into her punch glass, praying that she could keep the tears that threatened from spilling down her cheeks.

"So when's your flight? Got all your packing finished?"

Jill silently thanked God that the doctor had changed the subject. "My flight is Saturday morning and I've still got some packing to finish."

"I bet your parents are excited that you're coming home." Dr. Bryan took a bite of cake and looked at her expectantly.

"Yeah." Jill tried her best to make the grin seem real. "Excited."

Dr. Bryan studied Jill as she chewed, wiped her mouth and set the cake plate aside, reaching for Jill's hand. "You know, Jill, things that we are running from have a tendency to find us no matter how far away we may go."

Refusing to meet the doctor's penetrating gaze, Jill studied their entwined hands and replied, "I'm not running, Dr. Bryan, just need a change of scenery."

"Well, if you change your mind, you always have a job here." The doctor collected her thoughts for a moment before she continued, "Jill, I need to tell you—"

The doctor was interrupted as Sam reached for Jill's hand and began the chant for her to give them a goodbye speech. Jill grinned and tried to pull her arm out of Sam's grip. Her coworkers gathered around her, continuing the chant until she nodded. "Okay, okay," she shouted over their chant.

"I...I really don't know where to begin...I'm so thankful that I had the opportunity to work with each of you." As Jill spoke the gym door creaked as it opened behind her. Probably just some wayward hungry employee from another department who had smelled cake. Jill didn't bother to turn around, continuing with her speech. "You all are so special to me..." Her words trailed off as she looked at Sam to see his eyes had widened as he stared behind her.

Jill slowly turned to see the man who haunted her nights and a huge part of her day standing a mere six feet behind her. Time stopped as she stared at him. The crisp white button-down shirt accented his deep tan, tucked into creased blue jeans that encased his long muscular legs. He stood there, weight settled on one leg, looking as if he had just stepped out of scene from a western movie. The only cue that the quintessential cowboy might be feeling a small portion of the emotions that volleyed through her was the constant turning of his cowboy hat in his hands.

"Jill." Her name slipped from his lips, no more than a whisper, but in the deafening quiet of the gym, it seemed to echo.

Jill felt as if her feet were glued to the floor. She stood there as minutes ticked by staring at him with her mouth agape. Finally she turned her back to him and met her coworkers' shocked and curious gazes.

"I have to go," she mumbled as she quickly made her way to the side door of the gym, escape being her only thought.

"Jill!" she heard him call after her, but she didn't stop. She made it through the gym door and turned toward her office when she felt him gently grab her arm, stopping her escape.

"Jill, please."

She turned to face him. She had spent hours wondering what would happen if this moment ever arrived. What would she say? Would she cry? Would she scream at him? She had planned speech after speech, orchestrating words so as to magnify their potential to hurt him as he had hurt her. She was utterly disappointed in herself because in the actual moment, no words came to her.

"Jill, please, I need to talk to you," he pleaded, still gently clasping her elbow.

"What are you doing here?" She managed to croak out the words and hated herself for sounding so weak.

"I came to see you." He reached in his back pocket and produced the invitation. "I was invited."

"I didn't send that." She jerked her arm from his grasp.

"I didn't think you did." He slipped the card into his shirt pocket and rested his hands on his hips, looking very much like he did in many of her dreams. Her stomach flipped and in that moment she hated her traitorous body. "But somebody did send it to me. Maybe somebody thinks we have some unfinished business and I agree…we do."

Jill narrowed her eyes, remembering the last conversation they had. "I think we've said all we need to say."

John released a breath he didn't realize he had been holding. "Please, Jill…" He glanced around the busy hallway, where several people had stopped to watch them, not to mention the faces of her coworkers pressed against the glass in the gym door. "Can we go somewhere private and talk?"

"It's been a year, John. If there was something that needed to be said, I think a year is plenty of time to say it." She turned to leave him but before she could take a step, he jumped in front of her.

"I know you're upset with me—"

"Upset?" she interrupted angrily.

"Okay." He held his hands up in front of her. "Angry with me; probably furious. I know you're furious with me and you have every right to be, but...but if you would let me try to explain."

"There is no explaining what you did, John." She continued to try to pass him.

"Agreed, there is no excuse for the way I treated you. But if you would just let me try to explain..."

The desperation in his voice chipped away at her hardened heart. She sighed, knowing she was close to giving in to him. She purposefully recalled all the nights she had cried herself to sleep, all the days she had spent hurting and aching for him. No, she would not give in so easily.

"I have to work." She brushed past him.

"Have dinner with me?" he called after her. "That Italian place over on Broad...the one that we went to after we got caught in that rainstorm."

She stopped dead in her tracks, his words taking her back to the exact spot, the exact memory.

"We went to the park to watch a movie under the stars. A downpour came right in the middle of it. I gave you my jacket to try and keep you dry. You tried to hold it over both of us and we wound up getting soaked through to the skin. We were laughing so hard when we got to the truck..." He was close to her now. She could feel his presence without turning around; when he spoke again she could feel his breath on her neck. "I wanted to kiss you that night, but I didn't. I've regretted it ever since. We saw the lights from Mauricio's Restaurant. They had that big fireplace and we sat beside it to dry out. I remember thinking you were the most beautiful thing I had ever seen, sitting in that firelight."

His fingertips touched her shoulders, brushing her hair back to reveal her neck. His fingers skimmed her neck lightly as he moved to turn her chin toward him. She followed his command with his hands and turned to face him. They were chest to chest when she turned and she gazed up into his eyes.

"Say yes," he whispered.

Emotions warred inside her. Her heart screamed yes with every fiber of its being but her mind could not let go of the hurt he had caused. She wasn't sure how long she stood there, but she became aware of the audience around them that had grown.

"I have to finish some things here." Her heart flipped as a grin split his face and she cursed its weakness when it came to him.

"I'll pick you up." He slipped his arm around her waist and tried to pull her close. She placed both hands on his chest and pushed him away.

"I moved. I'll meet you at the restaurant. Seven thirty?" she said as she backed away from him.

He nodded as he mouthed the words *seven thirty*. She turned her back and walked briskly down the hallway, never looking back.

****

John arrived early to the restaurant. He called as soon as he had left the hospital to reserve the exact table they had dined at before. He nervously tapped his fingertips on the table waiting for her to arrive. He briefly wondered if she would show, but his mind was put to ease when she glided through the front door. He watched her speak to the hostess and a lump formed in his throat. If she was beautiful in hospital scrubs, she was downright breathtaking in the short summer dress she wore. Her long blonde hair fell in soft waves down her back, and he found it difficult to breathe as she approached him.

He stood and held her chair for her, telling her how beautiful she was.

Jill thanked him, taking her time to settle in her chair and fold her napkin in her lap. She refused to meet his gaze at first. She had to compose herself quickly if she were to make it out of this dinner without damaging what healing had occurred in her heart. With thoughts of dinner consuming her all afternoon, she had devised a plan. She would play it cool, explaining her emotions this afternoon as just the shock of seeing him. She would attempt to direct the conversation away from their breakup and would end dinner as soon as possible, retreating to her house to cry herself to sleep.

They exchanged pleasantries and comments about the restaurant, both seemingly hesitant. Jill took this as her cue to direct the conversation.

"How's your mother?" Jill asked, hoping her voice sounded light.

John seemed to be caught off guard. "Um…she's good."

"Still in Helena, I'm assuming."

"Yeah, Steven thinks a few more weeks for intense therapy and then maybe they can start splitting their time between Helena and the ranch." He sipped his water and Jill hated how she studied his fingers, remembering their touch.

"Jill," he began as he set down his water, only to have her interrupt him.

"And Jamie? How's Jamie?" she asked a little too brightly.

"He's good." John leaned his forearms on the table. "He will be coming home from rehab next week. He's really come a long way. He's working hard to turn his life around."

"That's great." Jill didn't have to fake the joy she felt at Jamie's good fortune. She was truly happy for him. "And I'm sure Amber will be glad to see him. I guess she's had the baby by now."

John reached in his pocket for his phone, flipping to a picture of Faith. As he passed the phone to Jill, she couldn't help but notice the way his face lit up at the sight of Faith; another piece of the wall around her heart chipped away and she doubled her efforts to keep that wall erected.

"She's beautiful," Jill whispered as she studied the picture. She instinctively swiped the phone to the next picture. And another chunk of her heart wall crumbled as the next picture to fill the screen was a very handsome John grinning down at a tiny pink bundle snuggled in his muscular arms. She quickly swiped back to the original picture and handed the phone back to him.

"Beautiful," she repeated, unable to keep the emotion from her voice.

"I delivered her." John buttered his bread as if it were a completely normal part of his day to deliver babies.

"You did what?" Jill's eyes widened. The waiter had the worst timing as he approached to take their order. Jill quickly ordered and repeated John's statement. "You delivered her?"

"Yeah…she decided to make her appearance in the middle of a late winter snowstorm. It was kind of crazy."

She raised her eyebrows and it was all the encouragement he needed to dive into the story of Faith's birth. For a moment in time they fell into the old familiar feelings. She asked questions as he relayed the story, laughing at times, gasping in

225

disbelief at other points. They were interrupted briefly when the waiter brought their food.

"So what did Amber name her?" Jill asked at the end of his tale.

"Faith." John couldn't stop the grin that split his face just at the sound of her name. "Faith Johnna Mitchell."

"Johnna," Jill repeated. "After you?"

John nodded.

"That's very sweet." Jill stirred her food around her plate. "And that is an amazing story."

"Yeah, it was pretty surreal." John straightened his shoulders and put down his fork. "I thought of you a lot during that night."

Jill's face drained of color as her fork clanged against her plate. She weakly asked, "Me?"

He reached over and gently covered her hand. "Yes…you. It's what I do. When something happens, whether it's good, bad, or amazing, I think about you. What would you do? What would you say?"

She took her free hand and pinched the bridge of her nose to keep tears from clouding her vision. "John, please," she whispered.

"Jill, I have so much I need to say to you… so much I want to try and explain to you, and I'm afraid if I don't get it out right now, I never will and I will regret it for the rest of my life." He rubbed gentle circles on her palm as she dropped her free hand in her lap and looked around the restaurant desperately.

He lifted his hand across the table and gently wiped the stray tear that slipped down her cheek.

"I have no right to ask you to listen to me," he said softly, "but I'm asking anyway. Please just hear me out and if you still want me to leave you alone after that, then I will. It will be the hardest thing I've ever done, but I will."

She looked deep into his eyes, steadying herself with a deep breath before she whispered, "Not here, I can't do this here."

"Okay, where?" he questioned softly as he continued to rub the pad of his work-roughened thumb across the back of her hand.

The caress caused her mind to spin and without thinking she quickly suggested he follow her home. He stood silently and motioned for the waiter to come over, handing him a large bill and telling him to keep the change, much to the waiter's surprise. He settled his hand on the small of Jill's back and guided her out of the crowded restaurant and to her car. It occurred to Jill as she let him guide her that he had done what he always did. He swept in and took control of a situation. Jill stepped away from his hands as she quickly opened her car door before he could. She couldn't let him take control of this situation. If she wanted to come out of this unscathed, she would have to keep her wits about her, and John's hands off of her.

****

John prayed as he followed Jill to her home. "God, give me the right words."

He pulled his truck into the driveway behind Jill. As his boots landed on the concrete, he studied her home. She watched him study the For Sale sign in her yard, and she hoped he didn't start asking questions about her decision to buy and then quickly sale her home.

"Nice house," he offered as he followed her up the front steps.

"Thanks."

"When you said you had moved, I didn't think about you buying a house."

"I just got tired of renting. Can I get you something to drink?" She gestured for him to take a seat and desperately hoped to change the topic of conversation. She shifted her weight nervously as John walked slowly around her living room.

He shook his head no and reached for her hand, pulling her down on the couch beside him.

"Jill," he began as he held her hand tightly, "I…I, uh." He dropped her hands and rubbed his palms nervously up and down his thighs. "I've rehearsed this a thousand times…what I'd say to you when I saw you… and now I'm here and I can't seem to find the right words."

She bit the inside of her jaw as she watched him stand and turn toward the fireplace.

He stood with his back to her for a long time. Jill panicked as she thought of the framed picture of a view from their picnic sitting on her mantel. She prayed he wouldn't notice it.

"For a long time I thought…" He swallowed hard, trying to find the words to continue. "I thought I was to blame for Ben's accident." He turned to gauge her reaction to his words. His eyes searched her face as he saw her still seated on the couch, eyes wide, lips parted.

"From the moment I saw him lying at the bottom of that ravine, I knew it was my fault."

"John, it's normal for family members to feel guilty that they weren't the ones injured." She cleared her throat, trying to make her voice sound strong.

"No." He crossed the distance between them quickly and sat on the coffee table in front of her, his legs brushing against hers. "No, I didn't feel guilty because I had escaped injury, I felt guilty because I knew…I knew the moment I saw him that my rifle had spooked his horse. I had gotten in a hurry to shoot that buck and I didn't give them enough time to put distance between us. I caused the accident. In my mind I was convinced of that."

"John, it was an accident, just an accident. It was not your fault." Jill couldn't stop herself from reaching forward and covering his hands with hers.

He looked down and studied the floor. When he raised his head and met her eyes, she could see the emotion in them that he worked so hard to keep in check. He threaded his fingers through hers and squeezed. "I know that…now." Fighting the emotions back he continued, "Most days I know that…I know it was an accident. But for a long time"—he stood and paced the floor in front of her—"for a long time, I was convinced that it was all my fault. I had caused my brother to be hurt, I had caused my family to be hurt. I convinced myself that I didn't deserve anything good in my life because I needed to pay for what I had done to Ben, to my family."

"John." She said his name quietly, pressing her hand against her lips.

He ignored her and continued, "I convinced myself that God hated me and could never forgive me." He turned to face her then, to meet her gaze. "And I convinced myself that if you knew the truth, if you knew that I had caused Ben's accident and was too much of a coward to admit it, that you would hate me too."

She leaned forward and dropped her head in her hands. He came back to his seat on the table in front of her. "When I found out Ben could possibly use sign language…well, I hated myself because all I could think of was the day that he would tell you that I was the reason he was in that chair and you would look at me with hate in your eyes. I couldn't even be happy for my brother; all I could think about was myself, and I hated myself for it."

He gently clasped her chin between his thumb and forefinger, lifting her head to look in her eyes. "I was a coward. I used all that was going on with Jamie's situation as an excuse to distance myself from you." He slipped to his knees in front of her and cradled her face in his hands. "All my life, I've thought I was tough, thought I was brave. Anything life threw at me I could handle…I put my head down and I put feelings aside and I get through it. I did it when Ben got hurt, I did it when my dad died. I just put my head down and closed off my heart and got through it. But I knew…" He took her hand and brought it to his lips, kissing it softly. "I knew that if you ever looked at me with hate in your eyes, I wouldn't be able to get through it. It would kill me. So I ran. I hurt you and I ran."

She turned to keep from looking in his eyes. He gently took her chin and turned her face so their eyes met. "And if you give me a chance, I'll spend the rest of my life making it up to you."

Inside, her heart screamed, *Yes!* The words she had lain awake at night dreaming to hear from him were tumbling from his mouth. Any yet her brain refused to let her heart take the lead. She remembered the pain of the past months. Memories of the days she had barely been able to get out of bed because she had spent the night weeping over him and what might have been all came flooding back.

She jumped and stalked to the window. She stared out into the dark, unable to take his pleading gaze for another second. She could see him in the reflection moving toward her.

"Don't." She turned, holding her hand up to stop him. "Just, don't."

She headed for the kitchen, trying to put distance between them. She needed some space to form what she wanted to say to him. She turned to find him leaning on the bar separating the kitchen and living room, studying her.

"It's been a year," she began calmly but as she continued her voice grew louder. "A year, John, and not one word from you. You didn't call, you didn't text, you

229

sure didn't drop by, and now you expect to just walk in here and all of that will just be forgotten?"

"I know—"

She didn't wait to hear his explanation. "Why now? Just because I've decided life can go on without you, because I've decided to make changes in my life that don't include you, you…you…" She struggled to find the right words. "You just swoop in here and expect to flash a grin and everything will be okay?"

"No, I don't expect that," he said.

"What do you expect then?" she demanded angrily, hands on her hips.

He came around the corner of the bar and stepped toward her. Jill took a step back to keep distance between them. A look of pain flashed across his face and he dropped his hands to his side. "I don't know what I expected." He paused, running his fingers through his hair. "When Amber showed me the invitation this morning something in me snapped; I just got in my truck and started driving. I knew I couldn't let you leave without talking to you." He rubbed the back of his neck and gazed at her hopefully before he continued. "Ever since I realized that I wasn't to blame for Ben's accident and that even if I was I could be forgiven, I've wanted to talk to you. I kept putting it off because…well, like I said before, I'm a coward. I kept telling myself that when Jamie got home, when there was someone there to look after Amber and Faith, I would come see you."

"Oh, so when the ranch was in good hands and when Amber and Faith were taken care of, *then* you would come." She spat the words at him.

"No, I didn't mean it like that."

"And what about the next time there is some crisis at the ranch or with your family, you'll toss me aside again."

"No!" he said forcefully between gritted teeth. "No, I've learned my lesson. I'll never put the ranch or my family drama in front of you again."

She studied the floor, choosing her next words carefully. "John, I've moved on with my life. I have a new job, a new house. I'm catching a plane Saturday morning and I'm starting over in Nashville." She could see the hurt in his eyes, but she forced herself to continue. "It's really late and I have a lot of errands to run in the morning. I think it would just be best if you left now."

"Jill, don't do this….you know what we had was special. We shouldn't give up on something like that so easily."

"Easily?" Jill's voice rose an octave and she struggled to gather herself and appear calm. "Nothing about this past year has been easy, John. But that's just it, it's been a year and I…well, in hindsight maybe what we had wasn't so special." She clenched her jaw and met his gaze.

He stared at her, unable to form words. He opened his mouth several times as if to speak, only to close it just as quickly. He finally shook his head and stepped toward her. He moved swiftly and caught her off guard as he swept her up in his arms. He buried his face in her hair, and, breathing deeply he whispered, "Let me see you tomorrow."

"No." she said firmly, trying to dislodge herself to no avail. "It's better this way. No need to drag it out."

"What have you got to lose?" He leaned back enough to look her in the eyes, but close enough to keep her securely locked in his arms. "You've made up your mind. You're getting on a plane Saturday morning. Just give me one day. One day. It may not have all that special to you, but it sure was to me. Let me have one day," he whispered as he traced her cheekbones with the tips of his fingers.

She was lost for a moment in his eyes and her traitorous body relaxed into his. Not for the first time in her life she thought of how wonderful it felt to be in his arms. She let her arms slip up and around his neck, tugging him ever so slightly forward. He grinned wickedly at her and she quickly came back to her senses, shoving against his chest to free herself.

She shook her head to clear it and took a few steps backward. "I have an appointment with my Realtor at eight in the morning…if you want to come by some time after that…I'll be here."

"I'll see you then." And before she could stop him he pulled her back into his arms, placing a gentle kiss on her forehead before releasing her quietly, turning, and letting himself out the front door.

Sleep eluded Jill most of the night. She shot out of the bed at the sound of the doorbell ringing, instantly chiding herself for oversleeping. She jerked the front door open, expecting to see Pam, her real estate agent, standing there. Instead she found a very handsome cowboy, who seemed to have rested well the night before based on the grin on his face.

"I brought breakfast," he announced as he held up a sack from a local restaurant.

"What are you doing here so early?" She stepped aside to let him in and couldn't help but notice how good he smelled as he passed.

"You said you had a lot going on today," he said, shrugging, "just wanted to be sure you got it all done. Plus I only have one day with you…I want to make the most of it."

Jill snatched the offered bag out of his hands and stomped up the stairs to get ready.

An hour later she found herself following her real estate agent around the house as she offered suggestions to ensure the house sold quickly.

"Honestly, Jill, I'm not sure why we haven't had more inquiries about this house. It's beautiful and the houses in this neighborhood have all sold quickly."

Jill cast a nervous glance in John's direction, hoping that he hadn't overhead the Realtor's statement. Her house had been on the market for over a month with very few inquiries and none leading to an offer. Pam offered her a few suggestions for staging the house after she moved her things out and Jill thanked her as she showed her to the door. She closed her eyes and steeled herself to face him. She knew he had heard the Realtor's comments and if he had paid attention he could have easily picked up on the fact that she had purchased the house less than six months ago. To her surprise when she turned to him, he just grinned and asked her what was next on the agenda. In fact, he escorted her around town all day while she made the final preparations for her move, being the picture of a perfect gentleman.

It was only during their late lunch, sitting on the restaurant's patio, that he mentioned her house.

"When did you buy your house?"

"Um…February."

"February," he repeated. She nodded, trying to avoid his penetrating gaze. "So let me get this straight, you bought a house in February and you're selling it so you can move across the country four months later?"

"Things change," she said, clasping her hands in her laps, frantically trying to piece words together that would satisfy his curiosity about the house. "I went home for the holidays and really connected with my family. When the opportunity came to move home, I jumped on it."

"Can't blame you there. Family is important."

She silently thanked God that John didn't push the conversation any further. It was late evening when they arrived back at her house. She turned to him as they approached the front door.

"I just really think it would be best if you didn't come in," she announced, trying to make her voice sound stronger than she felt.

"Oh," he breathed, and she could read the hurt and disappointment on his handsome features.

"I have an early flight in the morning and—"

"Don't go," he interrupted, reaching for her hands and pulling her to him. He rested his forehead against hers and repeated softly, "Don't go. We can work this out. I love you."

Tears threatened to spill down her cheeks and she dashed them away roughly. The words she had ached for had been said and a part of her wanted to throw all the hurt and pain to the wind and jump at the chance to be with him. She searched his face and her thoughts swirled out of control. She could see hope building in his eyes and something inside of her broke.

"I can't do this, John." Her voice no more than a whisper. "I just can't. I have to leave. It's too late for us."

"What can I do to change your mind?"

She gathered herself and hoped she sounded more confident than she was, "Nothing. There is nothing you can do. I'm leaving, John. Whatever we had is over and it's been over for quite some time now."

She turned and ran up the steps, stopping only when he called her name as her hand touched the doorknob. She turned to find him still at the bottom of the steps, hands in his jean pockets.

"I love you, Jill. I know I haven't always treated you like I did, but I do love you. I've known since that day at the hot spring when I kissed you for the first time, that you were the only woman in the world for me. That God made you specifically for me." He shrugged his shoulders, releasing a pent-up breath before he continued, "And I know I've hurt you. I know I shattered your heart in a thousand pieces…and if that felt anything like what I'm feeling right now…a thousand 'I'm sorrys' would never be enough."

She sniffed back tears that threatened but couldn't force herself to look away from him. He slowly stepped up on the porch until they were inches from each other. "If you have to go," he said, reaching out and tucking her hair behind her ears, "if that's what you have to do to be happy, then I love you enough to not try and stop you anymore. But I want you to know that I will always love you. No matter where you go in this world, no matter what happens to you, no matter how many guys you date or marry, I will always be here…loving you. Praying for you… waiting for you."

She tried to speak and he touched his finger to her lips. "If you ever change your mind, I'll be here waiting for you. If it's two weeks, or two years, or twenty years…I'll be here. I'll be here praying and waiting for you."

He brushed his lips lightly across hers and she couldn't stop herself from returning the kiss. He cupped her face in his hands and studied her for several long moments before dropping another light kiss on her lips.

"Goodbye, John." She hoped her voice sounded stronger than she felt.

"Goodbye, Jill," he whispered as he turned and headed for his truck.

Chapter 27 Restoration

"I will restore to you the years that the swarming locust has eaten, the hopper, the destroyer, and the cutter, my great army, which I sent among you. You shall eat in plenty and be satisfied, and praise the name of the LORD *your God, who has dealt wondrously with you. And my people shall never again be put to shame." Joel 2: 25-26*

"We are so happy to have you on staff, Jill." The managing therapist squeezed Jill's shoulder as she left her with a stack of charts to review.

After days of watching human resource videos and filling out paperwork, Jill was thrilled to be back to seeing patients. She flipped through several files, deciding to read the file of a twenty-eight-year-old female who had suffered a brain injury in a car wreck six months ago. She studied her file, reading it from front to back, before she made her way to the patient's room.

Jill softly knocked as she stepped into the doorway of the brightly decorated room. She knew from the chart that Kristen, her patient, had been in a coma since the accident. Orders stated that Jill was to put her through range of motion exercises to keep her muscles from atrophying more than they already were. She found Kristen much as she expected, lying in bed with various machines beeping and whirling. Seated beside the bed was a young man.

"Hello, I'm Jill. I'll be Kristen's therapist today," she announced as she approached the bed.

The man nodded at her and stood over the bed whispering softly. "Baby, it's time for your exercises." He softly caressed her hand before he turned to Jill. "I'm Seth, they tell us you're a miracle worker." Glancing over his shoulder, he added, "I sure hope so."

"Well, I'm not a miracle worker, but I know someone who is." Jill smiled.

Jill knew better than to become attached to her patients and their families, but something drew her to Seth and Kristen. She saw Seth frequently as he made visits throughout the weekdays, stopping in on his lunch breaks and after work. On the weekends he would arrive early and stay until the wee hours of the morning. Jill found herself stopping by Kristen's room just to chat with Seth. They fell into an easy friendship, something Jill needed desperately. Moving back to Nashville had not been without its issues. Now more than ever, it was glaringly obvious that neither of her parents could be counted on to play a major role in her life. Both had moved on with their lives after her brother had passed, and Jill had the impression that she was a reminder of a painful past for both of them. In the three months she had been in Nashville, she hadn't seen either of them more than a handful of times. Plus there was the constant ache in her chest when she thought of John. She had hoped that by now the ache would have dulled somewhat, but if anything it seemed to be more persistent than ever. When Seth asked her to join him for lunch in Kristen's room one Saturday, Jill promised herself it would only be this one time. Within a month, it was a regular occurrence. One particular Saturday Seth suggested they enjoy their lunch outdoors in the secluded garden not far from Kristen's room. They sat in the garden soaking up the rays of sun filtering through the trees that surrounded them. Jill felt a camaraderie with Seth and she decided to find out more about him.

"How long have you and Kristen been together?" Jill asked the question that she had avoided for weeks.

Seth's cheeks reddened as he intently studied his plate. He took several minutes and cleared his throat. "Well, technically we're not." As he looked up and met Jill's puzzled gaze he repeated, "We are not a couple, at least we weren't when the accident happened."

"Seth…" Jill dropped her hands in her lap, sensing her friend's hurt, but unsure of its source.

Seth leaned forward. "We had dated for about a year. We got into a fight and we broke up. After a few months, I still couldn't forget about her…but…" He looked away. "I let my pride keep me from calling her. We had each said things to hurt each other and I was determined I was not going to be the one that made the first move."

Jill watched as Seth struggled with keeping his emotions under control. He swallowed hard and composed himself before he spoke again. "It had been about six months since we broke up. I still wasn't over her. Suddenly one day her number shows up on my phone. I can't even explain to you how I felt. I just knew it was her calling me to tell me she wasn't over me either; I felt pure joy answering that call." He fiddled with his cup, and Jill could tell by the look in his eyes that in his mind he was back there in that moment.

"But it wasn't her. It was her mother telling me about the accident, and I've been here ever since. At first I didn't leave her side. I took a leave of absence from work, I let all my other obligations slide, but the bills kept coming even though my life had all but come to a stop. I eventually had to go back to work, but I still try to come every day."

"Seth, I am so sorry." Jill touched his arm. "That is the saddest thing I've ever heard."

"Well, she's my one and only, you know? And even though she's…." He shrugged, unable to finish his sentence. "She's still mine. I still love her. I can't leave her."

"She's very lucky to have you." Jill wiped a tear and couldn't help but think of John.

Seth sat quietly for a few moments, composing himself before he spoke. "Now, can I ask you something, Jill?"

"Um, sure." She pushed her plate away from her, knowing that her friend needed a change of subject.

"Why Nashville? Why did you move here?" He studied her, waiting for her response.

"I think I've told you before; my family is here." Jill shifted uncomfortably.

"So why were you in Montana?"

"I followed a doctor there. A doctor I had interned with."

"Oh, a doctor?" Seth raised his eyebrows. "Good for you."

"Oh no! Not like that." Jill shook her head vehemently. "Dr. Bryan was a woman and a good friend."

Seth studied her some more. "So let me ask you this; have you ever been in love, Jill?"

Jill glanced around the garden, briefly contemplating what it would feel like to talk to someone about John. She had never shared her feelings with anyone. She turned and met Seth's gaze and answered quietly, "Yes. Yes, I have."

"I'm guessing it didn't end well?" He took a drink, never taking his eyes off her.

"What makes you say that?"

"Well, you are here eating lunch with me. You work all the time. I've never heard you mention a guy, and don't take this the wrong way, but you kind of have this heartbroken vibe going on."

Jill bit the inside of her mouth in an attempt to keep the tears away and nodded in agreement.

"Was he a good guy?"

"Yes," Jill answered without thinking. "Yes, he was…he is a good guy."

"Tell me about him." Seth leaned back, waiting.

"What?" she asked incredulously.

"Tell me about him. What's his name?"

"John. His name is John." Jill hated the way heat rose on her cheeks as she said his name. Seth nodded for her to continue and once she began she couldn't stop. She told him everything, from their first meeting, their first date, even up to their last conversation.

Seth leaned forward and rested his arms on the table. "Do you still love him?"

Jill met his steady gaze, biting her lower lip. She thought about this question and knew there was only one answer. "Yes. I wish I didn't, but yes, I do still love him." Her voice was barely a whisper.

"Does he still love you?" Seth's voice was soft.

Jill looked up at the sky above them and exhaled. She studied their surroundings before composing herself enough to answer. "He says that he does." Her voice was ragged with emotion.

Seth sat quietly for so long that Jill finally looked at him. He held her gaze, and tenderly reached over and took her hand. "Then I only have one question." He didn't even give her a chance to respond before he continued, "Why are you here? If you love him and he loves you then why are you in Tennessee and why is he still in Montana?"

"It's complicated," she whispered as a tear slipped own her cheek.

"Then make it uncomplicated." Seth's voice was stern. "Jill, if I have learned anything from this accident, from this nightmare, it's that you don't take love for granted. If you love somebody and you are blessed enough that they love you back, you don't take that for granted. Whatever makes it complicated, you must set that aside. You don't let something as precious as love slip through your fingertips because of pride."

"Seth, you don't understand…"Jill hated how emotions bled through her voice.

"Maybe I don't understand your exact situation, but Jill, let me tell you this. If the woman I love was anywhere and I mean anywhere other than laying in that hospital bed"—he pointed toward the building for emphasis—"nothing—absolutely nothing would keep me from her."

****

John took the bandana from his back pocket and wiped his brow. It was an unseasonably warm day for late September in northern Montana, but as his eyes scanned the mountains surrounding his ranch, he knew that winter was just around the corner. That was why he had insisted the ranch medicate all of its calves today. It had been a monumental job to round up the calves and separate them from their mommas. He was surrounded by pens of calves bawling incessantly. He worked

239

at a feverish pace, causing the other men to struggle to keep up with him. Most of the men admired his zeal for work, but Jamie, ever present since he had returned home, eyed John suspiciously as if he knew that John's drive had more to do with what he was trying to outrun than anything else. John reached for the reins of his mount so that he could bring in the next batch of calves.

"John, it's one o'clock." Jamie grabbed John's reins. "Amber has been holding lunch for almost an hour for us. Why don't we take a break?"

John studied his younger brother and at once was amazed and annoyed with him. He was thrilled that Jamie had turned his life around and had become a doting husband and father, but it annoyed him how Jamie could see right through him. He knew John better than anyone and he knew that John's heart was broken into a million pieces and he also knew that was exactly what drove John's relentless work pace.

"Yeah, you go on and take the boys up to the house and eat, I'll just get this next group ready." John reached for his reins once again to no avail.

"You need to eat too, John. Coffee is not a sufficient meal."

"I will. I'll get something later." John slapped Jamie on the shoulder in an attempt to end the conversation.

Jamie stroked the nose of John's mount for several moments before asking, "Why do you ride this old sorrel mare, John? We've got a hundred better horses."

John shrugged and again reached for the reins. "You go on. Take the hands up to the house and eat."

"It's her, isn't it? This horse has some sentimental attachment for you and I bet you anything it has to do with Jill."

John's head snapped up at the mention of her name. He forcefully took the reins and mounted the sorrel mare. "Leave it alone, Jamie."

Jamie patted the mare's flank as John turned to leave. An hour later he had readied the next group of calves and was in the barn trying to mend a saddle, waiting for Jamie and the rest of the hands to return. He noticed Jamie had stopped right outside the barn and was studying something intently.

"John, you expecting company?" Jamie called from the front of the barn.

"Nope." John never looked up from his work.

"Well, we've got company."

"Probably some of the hands from the Flying K. I told them we could use some help if they needed work."

"No, I don't think so." Jamie turned to walk away from the barn.

John set his mind back to the task at hand. He heard the gravel crunch in front of the barn and the opening and closing of a car door. He waited for their surprise guest to come in the barn. After several long moments he could hear the murmur of voices outside. He stepped out of the tack room and strode purposefully down the long corridor. A small car sat in front of the barn; the driver was blocked from his view by Jamie as he leaned against the car.

"Jamie," he called as he reached the barn door. Jamie stepped aside and John felt as if the earth shifted under his feet. There, standing in front of his barn, on his land, talking to his brother, was the one women who haunted him day and night. "Jill?" His voice was no more than a whisper.

"John," she answered, her voice thick with emotion.

He felt the world tilt and reached out for the barn door to steady himself. He briefly got his bearings and searched her face. She was scared, he could tell by the look in her eyes. She had also been crying, her red-rimmed eyes couldn't deny that.

"Jill?" he repeated, unable to form any other words. Jamie said something, but for the life of him John couldn't respond or take his eyes off of her. He vaguely noticed Jamie turn and walk back toward the house. He wasn't sure how long they stood there staring at each other. Finally she took a step toward him and spoke.

"It's good to see you." She nervously twisted her fingers as she stepped closer to him.

He opened his mouth trying to form words but couldn't. He gripped the barn door until his knuckles turned white. All of the pain from the last three months came rushing back; all of the emotions he had buried suddenly surfaced. He looked down at the ground and kicked the gravel around him to avoid looking at her. Tears rimmed his eyes and for the life of him, he didn't want her to see that. After several minutes he composed himself enough to look at her.

"What are you doing here, Jill?" He stood there with his hands on his hips but the emotions playing in his eyes were more than Jill could bear. His moisture-ridden eyes tore the last bit of her composure. She took another step closer and then another until she was mere inches from him.

"I was hoping you meant what you said." She had to stop herself reaching out to touch his face.

"What did I say?" he whispered.

"That you would always be here waiting for me. That you would always be here…" Her voice trailed off as she lost her nerve to bring up the word *love*.

"I thought you were determined to go home." He clenched his jaw to keep his emotions in check.

She searched his face, trying to determine what he was thinking. She had traveled this far and she wasn't going to walk away without letting him know exactly how she felt. "Tennessee isn't home. Where my parents are…that isn't home to me. I've never felt more alone in my life than I have in the past three months. Wherever you are…that's home to me. I love you—"

Before she could say anything else he quickly reached out and grabbed her, crushing her body hard against his and pressing his lips to hers. He broke the kiss and leaned his forehead against hers as he whispered,

"Welcome home, baby. Welcome home."

Made in the USA
San Bernardino, CA
19 April 2020